Praise for
Wound

"Both an elegy to the dead and a homecoming . . . Raw, hypnotic."
—Fernanda Eberstadt, *The New York Times Book Review*

"Only an author of great skill could hold such disparate material together while also questioning her own method throughout the process . . . Vasyakina successfully folds the untidy past into the unsettled present, demonstrating how inseparable they are to the person she is."
—*The Irish Times*

"[An] affecting début novel." —*The New Yorker*

"Bruisingly honest reflections on gender and trauma, brilliantly mediated by Elina Alter's translation." —*The Times Literary Supplement*

"An auto-fictional exploration of processing grief through language, and also a meditation on the Russian lesbian lyric—a polyphonic conversation with feminist thinkers across time and space." —*Asymptote*

"Ambitious in scope . . . Vasyakina powerfully encompasses the absurd and expansive universe of what Gogol described as the 'unbridled incomprehensible Rus,' the land with its terrors, its poetry and loftiness and its magic, to the skin and bones of the tender and violent people who inhabit it."
—*The Rumpus*

CATAPULT
NEW YORK

Wound

A NOVEL

Oksana Vasyakina

Translated from the Russian by Elina Alter

WOUND

This is a work of fiction. All of the characters, organizations, and events portrayed in this novel are either products of the author's imagination or are used fictitiously.

First Catapult edition: 2023
First paperback edition: 2024

Hardcover ISBN: 978-1-64622-144-8
Paperback ISBN: 978-1-64622-234-6

Library of Congress Control Number: 2023931473

The passage from Hélène Cixous's "The Laugh of the Medusa" on pages 167–68 was translated from French by Keith Cohen and Paula Cohen. The passage from Maurice Blanchot's *The Space of Literature* on page 211 was translated from French by Ann Smock. The excerpt on page 214 is from *Metamorphoses* by Ovid, translated by Charles Martin. Copyright © 2004 by Charles Martin. Used by permission of W. W. Norton & Company, Inc. The passage from Luce Irigaray's "And the One Doesn't Stir Without the Other" on page 225 was translated from French by Hélène Vivienne Wenzel.

Cover design by Nicole Caputo
Cover art © Jenny Barron / Bridgeman Images
Book design by Laura Berry

Catapult
New York, NY
books.catapult.co

Printed in the United States of America

10 9 8 7 6 5 4 3 2 1

For Alina Bakhmutskaya

One who doesn't remember death will die all the sooner.

—INNA LISNYANSKAYA

The beginning is an absence from which everything follows, including lyric experience.

—SHAMSHAD ABDULLAEV,
"Poetry and Death"

With your milk, Mother, I swallowed ice.

—LUCE IRIGARAY,
TR. HÉLÈNE VIVIENNE WENZEL,
"And the One Doesn't Stir Without the Other"

. . . so that a woman might try to face the void within the
meaning that is produced and destroyed
in all its connections and all its objects . . .

—JULIA KRISTEVA, TR. LEON S. ROUDIEZ,
Black Sun: Depression and Melancholia

Wound

I

Lyubov Mikhailovna said that Mama's breathing had been bad, heavy. She found that out from the priest. That's the way dying people breathe. The light was good, and there was no wind. The light was golden, like it is in August.

Lyubov Mikhailovna's arm lay across the back of the couch, a little swollen, grayish. How strange, I thought, looking at that arm, as if without a priest's say-so you can't understand that a person is dying, when it's plain to see that she is.

Lyubov Mikhailovna's face looked calm. She believed in God, and her own cancer was in remission. She probably thought her cancer was in remission because she believed in God. There was also superiority written across her face. As though in her lap laid life's invisible trophy, which she'd won from my mother.

Andrei said that at ten o'clock tomorrow morning I'd get a call from Mikhail Sergeyevich. Andrei had already given some cousin of Mikhail Sergeyevich money for gas, so that he'd drive me to pick up the ashes. I could have done it myself, but concern is important here. Care and concern. The light was very good, very warm. And the noodle soup turned out fine. Everything turned out fine, just as I promised. Concern is important.

The husband of Mama's old neighbor, as he was leaving the wake, said that Andrei shouldn't let himself get down. He said Andrei should call him if he wanted to go fishing. Andrei said he would call. But I knew he wouldn't, it's just that it's important to accept people's care and concern in these situations.

Lyubov Mikhailovna asked me to accept her condolences. I accepted them. For a month, she had dosed Mama with holy water: three tablespoons and a prayer in the morning, three tablespoons and a prayer at night. She said that after the priest's visit my mother had brightened and got to her feet. Lyubov Mikhailovna said that Mama had laughed and made some soup.

Mama had said that the priest laid some kind of bauble on her head and asked her to repent, while he himself read a prayer. Mama said she didn't understand a thing. But she never admitted to Lyubov Mikhailovna that Orthodox Christianity doesn't help much when you're sick. Particularly if you don't believe in God.

When I was a child, I was told that it's a good thing if it rains during a funeral. On the one hand, rain at the start of a journey is a good sign, and on the other, it's nature mourning. Nature doing its part, commiserating. There was a light drizzle when my father was buried. But it doesn't rain in February; instead of rain there's this good light. Everything looks very rosy and complete in this light, like an apple.

Everyone sat there on the couch where Mama had lain dying. And then they all left, all at once. Andrei and I cleared the table and washed the dishes. Andrei said that you aren't supposed to throw out any food from a wake, and that it can only be eaten with spoons. He said he'd wash everything, turned on the TV in the kitchen, and started doing the dishes. I brought him the empty plates. It was a long way to evening.

Andrei asked if the crematorium kept working at night. I don't know, I replied, but I know that our turn was at 4:30 p.m., which means they've already burned the body. Andrei said it was a disgrace, burning up living people. I didn't say anything, just thought that she wasn't living, she was dead. I sat on the couch and watched TV. And then lay down on the couch and fell asleep with a feeling of bitter relief. At night I dreamed of darkness.

Andrei told me that Mikhail Sergeyevich's cousin was a peculiar guy. He said I shouldn't pay him any mind. Andrei said he had given the cousin three hundred rubles for gas, to drive me to the crematorium at the central cemetery.

This is tough country. The steppe is all around, and in places where water flows there's greenery and moisture; locals call a spot like that *poima*, water meadow. My father lived five hundred kilometers from here, in Astrakhan, where ferries wait at the mouth of the Volga to be launched into rivers when the winter ice melts. In the towns, ferrymen are well respected—you can't get by without them. In the old days, the ferrymen had someone walk around collecting payment from the passengers for the crossing. But now, my father would tell me, there was an electronic payment system, and a camera had been installed on every ferry. And they brought in ticket collectors. There was one ferryman who said that he never took payment for transporting the dead. After all, it's already a loss if you're taking a body across, and it's not like the dead can pay for themselves. That's concern for people's grief.

But since the cameras were installed, there have been no fare dodgers on the crossings. Not even the dead can dodge the fare. A ferryman who didn't charge a car with a corpse in it got fined three thousand rubles.

Mikhail Sergeyevich called at 9:50 a.m. and told me to come out. I picked up a pink vinyl bag for groceries and went down. Everything around was gray. The light was gray, like fur, and the wind was savage, like a starving animal. Everything was the way it usually is in February. And it was February, in fact.

Mikhail Sergeyevich met me by the entryway. Without speaking to each other, we walked through the courtyards.

The cousin didn't say anything, just nodded at my greeting. They put me in the back. Then we waited. We sat silently waiting until a woman in a red down jacket showed up, carrying a shiny structured purse. She said hello and sat next to me. The cousin started the car and we drove out.

The woman said that the weather was nasty today. The cousin and Mikhail Sergeyevich agreed. We passed a Pyaterochka supermarket and some garages and entered a gray industrial district. We let the woman out there.

Nobody spoke to me. The cousin was complaining about the gas man, saying it was already expensive to replace the pipes, and now the fitter was asking for three thousand rubles on top of that. The cousin said that he told the gas fitter to go to hell and called the management office to complain about him. Mama had waited for the gas fitter for two weeks; a month before her death she bought a new gas stove, but she kept making soup on the old one because the fitter was never available. Mama had asked me to call the office again, and they told me that the fitter could only come in a week. In a week Mama was taken to hospice. And five days after that she died, and nobody was bothering about the gas. The sparkling new stove stood in the corner of the kitchen, all veiled in plastic, like a bride.

The cousin said that Western propaganda had gotten really shameless. What are they even doing over there in the West, he asked. Prancing around in sparkly underwear, those queers, and what if there's a war? What happens if there's a war? Sexual education is a travesty, said the cousin. Children should be taught how to hold a Kalashnikov in kindergarten. He would personally teach his grandson to assemble and disassemble an automatic rifle, so he'd know how it's done. That's how you do it, while all those American whores know how to do is pick up condoms by the time they're three years old. Our Russian kids can handle a rifle in diapers. If there's a war, everyone will go to defend the motherland. Young and old, everyone will defend the motherland. Anyone can fuck around, you don't need any brains for that. But loving your motherland, that's real work.

The cousin said that he had been talking to his friend, a German, over Skype. The friend made threats about World War Three. He said Germany had nuclear weapons, and the cousin told him, fine, come on over, but don't forget the lard, I'm going to shove your nukes up your ass. I said nothing. The cousin said that all of them were queers and their women were all whores, hopping from dick to dick like a carnival ride. I began to feel like I was suffocating.

I was running out of air. The steppe showed gray through the window. Mama's hair had been that color. When I stroked her hair, I saw that half of it had gone gray. And her hair was curly. Mama said that after chemo, the first hair she'd grown was all curly, as though she were Black. Mama said that after the first round of chemo, when some of her hair grew back, her own mother had mocked her for being Black now.

Queers and whores, said the cousin. I said, excuse me, could you be quiet for a little while. He stopped talking.

People talk a lot. I'm used to it. But we were going to pick up my mother's ashes, and the ride had to proceed in respectful silence. I was supposed to be weeping quietly in the back seat, and the cousin wasn't supposed to be saying anything. There could be hushed conversation, the radio could play, really anything was allowed except these political ramblings about queers and whores.

The cousin didn't know that I was a lesbian. But I wanted to say to him that he knew nothing about gay people. Why do you have this fixation on anal penetration? Why do you want to insert a rifle lubed with lard into the German's anus? I wanted to ask. But I didn't bother.

And after all, condoms don't hurt anyone, rather they help save lives. While what's a rifle for? A rifle exists to kill people.

It was stuffy from the heat and the stink of the little pine tree air freshener. What misery, I thought. And said nothing.

I asked them to wait for me in the parking lot by the cemetery. Then I walked behind the cemetery fence and lit a cigarette. The cemetery was strewn with bright artificial flowers. I turned my head to look at the cemetery office, which resembled a glass-walled provincial market. Beyond the roof of the glass building the crematorium chimney poured smoke. I went in through the first door I came across. Somebody said to me that documents were processed in the next department over. The door to that department had a line in front of it, and I sat down to wait. An older woman was speaking with a young man. They were discussing which plot would be better to buy for Granddad. Plots at the central cemetery were expensive, but he had to be buried next to his mother, like he'd asked. But they were so expensive at the central cemetery. Maybe he could be buried at the district cemetery with his son-in-law. But then Granddad would be angry and come at night and yell. All his life he'd yelled at everybody and he wasn't going to stop now. The woman said that just a few days ago he'd come around and yelled at her. What an irrepressible old man.

I went through the neighboring door. There was a glass display case in a small room, and on its shelves stood a couple of urns, among which I recognized my mother's. It was gray with a little beaded black flower on its lid. What a vulgar flower, I thought, like something you see on cheap underwear. Andrei had suggested this urn, while I wanted a bright red, hand-painted one. The flowers on it were like the flowers painted on decorative plates. But Andrei chose the gray one, since Mama didn't like flashy things. The urn was gray like the side of a freshwater fish, or the hood of a nineties Lada sedan, like my father drove in '97. The gray urn was half the price of the red, but I had wanted to get the more expensive one. I bought the most expensive version of everything—a pretty silk coverlet with embroidered flowers and the most expensive coffin for the cremation. The color of the coffin was like that of a mother-of-pearl perfume bottle. Mama had loved everything beautiful, and so she got a beautiful coffin.

Mama's urn stood next to a red urn, the kind I had originally wanted to buy for her. And they could have gotten mixed up, in which case I'd be leaving here with a stranger's ashes. But who could prove that Mama's urn contained Mama's ashes? Nobody, that's who. After all, the cremation had happened without us present. They could've just filled up the urn with regular ash and thrown Mama's body into a mass grave to save their energy. That would be illegal, but who worries about carrying out the law these days? Nobody, that's who. The only option was to have faith in the integrity of the funeral workers.

Also, I couldn't just take the urn and go. Without documentation of the ashes I wouldn't be able to have the urn buried or bring it on a plane. But the display case was unlocked, anyone could steal any of the urns. Though why would you want a stranger's ashes?

I returned to the place where the woman and her son wanted to buy a plot for the angry granddad. The waiting room was empty, so I knocked on the door. A woman told me to enter. She sat behind a desk, bundled in a dog-wool shawl. She said that she'd caught a chill and had a stiff back, and now she couldn't reach the shelf that held the papers she needed. I suggested she pick up some Nimesil. She asked where I would take the ashes, since the papers said I needed a certificate confirming no illegal substances were present in the urn. I said that I'd be taking the ashes to our homeland, Siberia. The woman asked how I would inter the ashes. They'll be interred in Ust-Ilimsk, I said. Then she said that I should send documentation to Volgograd, confirming that I'd interred the ashes. I promised that I would, although I didn't plan on sending anything. It seemed like the woman didn't really think I would, either, but she couldn't just tell me not to bother with mailing the papers. In this way she was transferring to me a certain responsibility, and I appeared to accept that responsibility. The woman looked at my passport and at me and said I didn't look like my picture. Then she gave me all of the documents and asked me to come along with her. I went.

She didn't put on her coat to go out. I told her that she should wear a coat, or she'd feel even worse, and I had nowhere to be, I could wait. The woman waved her hand at this and went out into the wind in her synthetic blouse and dog-wool shawl. We walked through the adjacent door. She opened the display case and invited me to take the urn containing Mama's ashes. I picked it up, smiling at her as though she were giving me bread or a slice of berry pie. In parting, I told her to feel better. The woman said she definitely would, and told me not to visit them again.

The urn was like a large, cold egg. Inside it lay a sealed capsule of ashes. I ran my hand over the capsule, and gray dust clung to my palm. Whose ashes were those? Mama's or a stranger's? I licked my finger. The ash didn't taste like dust, it was larger and harder. Like slate powder, like gunpowder. At the bottom of the urn I found a torn slip with my mother's initials and last name. The paper was also covered in ash. Whose ashes were these? Mama's or a stranger's?

I closed the urn and lowered it into my pink vinyl bag. On the internet it said that an urn containing ashes weighs no more than five kilos. This one weighed less. But it contained the ashes of a body, the ashes of clothes and coverlets, the ashes of an expensive cream-colored coffin, ashes of flowers, ashes of bandages that had been used to bind her arms and legs, ashes of chrysanthemums and roses. And maybe also the ashes of a plastic flower crown, though I had asked the funeral workers to remove it before the cremation. They had said that they would, but could I trust them? What if those terrible white plastic flowers were in there too? Were Mama's ashes even in there? Where were her ashes? Were these her ashes or a stranger's?

I smoked a cigarette, then got back in the car.

The cousin said nothing. Mikhail Sergeyevich didn't turn around but asked me if I had them. I said that I had them and now I needed to go to the morgue.

The cousin started the car and we drove out. We drove back through the gray steppe. The radio played, the pine tree air freshener swung to and fro.

I love the road best of all. I love to look through the window, and it's as if through looking I become the road. Once, in Kazakhstan, I saw camels in the steppe. They were grazing quietly, eating the short grass that grew out of the sand.

When Mama and I were traveling from Siberia to Astrakhan, she said that we would be approaching Astrakhan soon, and I would see some camels. I saw the steppe, but there were no camels in it. We'd been riding in a brown sleeper car for almost a week. We had some things to eat, probably doshirak noodles, hard-boiled eggs, and pies we would buy at the stations. I was ten. It was unbearably hot. Our neighbor in the sleeper car snored extremely loudly in the upper berth. We would choke with laughter, and the laughter was an ecstasy of closeness with Mama. There was no one else around, just us, laughing, because for us, in Siberia, it was already morning, but here in the south it was still night.

When the train approached cities in the south, there was always a fifteen-minute stop. Mama went to a kiosk to buy ice cream. And then the train began to move, rolling on very slowly, though Mama still wasn't back. The stuffiness of the car and a feeling of panic pressed in on my head. I was watching the station slip away, the blue-gray tents where pastries were sold, the posts, the white station building, and I was losing them all, they were no longer in the window, because the train was leaving the station. The woman on the neighboring berth was staring at me. She asked me where my mother was, and I replied that Mama had gone to get ice cream. The woman began sighing with concern. Mama ran out of time for ice cream, and she ran out of time for the train. There were another two days to go. I sat on my berth, unable to feel my body. I was afraid. It'll be fine, said the woman on the neighboring berth, after all, someone's meeting you there. We can feed you if it comes to that. Do you have a lot of things? she asked. I couldn't respond to her at all. My mama was back there somewhere, at the station, with her wallet and a pack of Winston Slims. The train was picking up speed. It was early morning. I was going to Astrakhan alone.

But Mama came back. She hadn't been able to find any ice cream at the station, so she ran to a more distant kiosk, and from there, already getting her change, she saw that the train was slowly beginning to pull away. She dove into the last car. The conductor didn't want to let her on, but Mama talked her into it. She said that there, in the third car, she had left her daughter.

I don't remember Mama's face at that moment, the moment when she ran into our car. I remember only her hysterically anxious voice. And the ice cream in a cone.

Why have I written that I don't remember her face? Probably to embellish my story. In truth, as I was writing this, I recalled her face at that moment. It was stony, jaw clenched tight, yellowish in the morning sunlight and because of the stuffiness of the car we'd been riding in for several days. The eyes in that face were shining and restless. There was horror and dread in her gaze. Her heavy face, with its slightly upraised lids and pursed lips, is the face I see even now. It's as if it were always coming closer to me, but always staying at a distance. It's ceaselessly coming closer to me. And the ice cream melts and drips down its rough beige wafer cone.

We were driving through the gray steppe. The pink bag with Mama's ashes was in my lap. I didn't really know if I could put the urn on the floor between my feet. You're supposed to treat a person's remains with respect. But it was uncomfortable holding it in my lap. So I parted my legs and squeezed the urn between them.

When the cousin parked by the district hospital on Zemlyachka Street, I asked Mikhail Sergeyevich to hold the urn. He took it from me carefully.

I have a dream, now, in which I'm walking and walking past the refrigerators at the morgue, and I know that inside one of them is Mama's body. A naked frozen body in a thick black bag.

When I passed those refrigerators on my way to pick up the pathologist's report, I didn't realize that this sectioned cabinet was the place where bodies were kept. I went up a staircase, and the pathologist met me at the top. She asked me what kind of education Mama had had, the year she was born, and what she'd died of: a specialized secondary education, 1970, cancer. The pathologist studied me attentively, like she was trying to understand if I really was my own mother's daughter. When she found the resemblance in my face, she took me into her office and gave me the report. Then she made a call, said my last name and Mama's, hung up, and ordered me to wait outside. She didn't say specifically what I was waiting for.

The wind was bitter. A very powerful wind. I stood on the

morgue's porch and opened the door a little, so I wouldn't freeze. Through the open door wafted the smell of formaldehyde and corpses. I didn't know what I was waiting for; I'd been ordered to wait, so I waited. A big man with a bald spot peered into the corridor and called out loudly that I was creating a draft. I asked if I could wait inside, and he replied that I was not authorized to be in the building. He said I had to wait outside. I shut the door.

I stood smoking and looking out at the morgue's half-ruined courtyard. In the high wind it appeared both dirty and frightening. A chipped concrete receptacle for cigarette butts, a damaged metal fence, crumbling stairs. I wasn't sure how much longer I had to wait. I got a text from Andrei asking me what was going on. I responded that I didn't know what was going on, I was just waiting. I had been told to wait. So I'd wait.

She had a terrible cough, and her breathing was hoarse. I was finally speaking with the forensic pathologist after picking up the ashes. She was a young woman of about twenty-five, a bottle blonde with fake eyelashes and tattooed eyebrows. She was very tiny. I asked what my mother had died of. The pathologist raised her fake-nailed thumb and forefinger up to her eyes, indicating the size of the metastatic tumors in Mama's lungs. Then she brought her fingers a little closer together, showing the size of the tumors on her spine, in the lumbar region. I asked about the state of her reproductive organs, and she said that Mama's uterus and ovaries were like a young woman's.

The pathologist said that Mama had died of a cerebral edema, a swelling of the brain. When the liver stops working, all the liquid first collects in the lungs, then travels to the heart, and then the brain stops working, too. And that's it. For a few days she was unconscious and connected to a ventilator machine. She wasn't in pain, the doctors had injected her with painkillers.

The previous year had been all about waiting. When a small

metastatic tumor was found in Mama's liver after chemo and radiation treatments, I began to wait. Everyone, quietly, began to wait. Except they were all waiting for a miracle, and I didn't expect one.

To spend a year waiting for death is not the same as a spending a year waiting for something else. To spend a year waiting for death is to await sorrow and relief simultaneously. To spend a year waiting for death is long, and it's somber. To spend a year waiting for death is not the same as waiting to move somewhere or waiting for a book to come out. It feels as though every moment now contains the possibility of a miracle and a happiness never before known. But it doesn't, really. It's a difficult time of premature grief. And then I waited for another two weeks, while Mama could no longer get up. Those two weeks were like a time of great catastrophe. An endless time of silence.

For precisely one week, while Mama was dying, I lived in her apartment. I went to the store and brought her flowers and gifts. Every time I went up the stairs of her building I thought that she had died while I was out. But she was still alive. She watched TV with unseeing eyes and didn't speak.

What was on her mind as she watched TV in the time before she died? I tried to figure it out myself, and I also asked her. She never told me. At night, we slept head-to-feet on the same couch. But I didn't sleep; I was listening to her breathe. I was listening to her dying.

The first time I came to the morgue, an ambulance had pulled up to the porch. Two sullen men opened the trunk and began pulling on blue rubber gloves, all without looking at me. Passing by, they asked for my last name. I asked if I should follow them, and they said they'd call me.

In the movies, people are only asked to identify the bodies of loved ones who've died under some horrific circumstances. They were murdered, or in a car accident, or dropped dead of a heart attack in the street. I never realized that you still have to identify the body if your loved one dies in the hospital or at home. Now I know that morticians require this procedure because they're afraid of laying out the wrong person in the coffin. They have to protect themselves.

A man wearing blue gloves looked out from behind the door and called me in. I tossed away my half-smoked cigarette and entered. In the foyer, by the sectioned cabinet, was a pile of thick black cellophane on a high gurney. I backed away. I did not want to and could not come closer. I was scared. I stood across from it and waited. The man in blue gloves uncovered Mama's body down to the waist. Her head was turned away, and I couldn't see her face. But I recognized her by her long forearm, thrown across her breastless chest. She was the color of an old overripe lemon. I recognized her ear and the sharp bend of her jawbone. My jaw is like that too, and my ear, and my nose. I recognized her hair, faded to the color of matted wool.

But the procedure required a more thorough identification. The man in blue gloves lifted Mama's head. He held it like a heavy, firm watermelon, and turned her face toward me. The cellophane bag rustled crudely. I saw Mama's face. It was peaceful.

I said yes, that's Mama. Then the man in blue gloves sealed her body back up, and another man in blue gloves asked me to come to a metal table to sign the death notice. The notice was printed on gray writing paper. The pen was simple, with a transparent body and a blue, gnawed-on cap—the kind of pen Mama would buy for me at the school fair for the first day of school. I signed the notice and went out into the wind.

On this visit, the pathologist was friendly. She led me into her office and shut the door carefully behind us. She described Mama's corpse as though she were a Young Pioneer asked to locate the capital cities of China and the Congo on a blank map. Thank you, I said. You're very welcome, she replied. I walked by the sectioned refrigerator-cabinet, by the row of gurneys, on one of which Mama's body had lain the day before yesterday. And now Mama's body was anonymous ash in a sealed capsule. Now there were no tumors in it, no brutal scar up to the armpit from the removal of her breast. No sharpish nose or beautiful hands. No jaw either.

I stepped out into the yard, toward the cement receptacle, and looked out at the hospital. There was no wind. Also there was no air. One of the men in blue gloves was standing by the porch and smoking. I didn't bother saying hello to him, he wouldn't have remembered me anyway. He stood there and smoked until a phone rang in his pocket. Then he threw away the butt, ended the call, went up the steps to the porch, and, passing me, entered the morgue.

I stayed for a while longer. I wanted to remember this place. I wanted to remember it the way you want to fit a beautiful landscape inside yourself, even though this place was hideous. But it was important. And like every other place of importance, it would not fit inside me.

I got into the car and picked up the urn again. Now I had to go to the pension fund. They drove me there through the steppe.

I wondered whether we had driven out the three hundred rubles already, or not yet.

When I think about the body, I see the steppe, the steppe or a wasteland. The kind of wasteland, I imagine, that we had in Siberia, where we once lived. A gray wasteland near the post office, with sun-bleached, dusty grass. Here and there, I see shards of concrete and metal framework sticking up out of the earth.

Why does this happen? When I remember Mama's body, I feel something tugging inside of me. The feeling resembles longing.

When I stroke my own belly before going to sleep, I remember Mama. Her half-profile and her voice. This memory conjures up a feeling of profound loss. As though Mama's presence in this world were connected somehow to a mistake or an absurdity. I feel my own self to be accidental. But I exist. And she existed in this world.

The steppe is the naked body of the earth.

But the steppe is not accidental, and I'm not accidental. And Mama is not, either.

When I lie in the dark, before going to sleep, I keep looking and looking into the darkness and replaying in my mind an image from the funeral reception hall. A dark hall with cheap heavy chairs, curtained windows, and stupid plastic music. In the very center there's a spot of soft-buttery color—the coffin in which Mama's body is laid. I look at her, I look as though something can still be altered. No, she won't come to life, her mouth will not move. But something must change. The image in my head must transform into something new or at least into nothingness. But the nothingness does not arrive, just as rest does not.

I saw the hem of the hospital-blue camisole beneath her funeral dress. The collar of the camisole lay on her raised-up rib cage. Someone else had dressed her body, washed her hair, put on her makeup, and laid her in the coffin. I could not make myself touch her.

I only stretched the back of my hand toward her, like I was feeling for her temperature. I touched her temple, the same temple I had kissed when saying goodbye. She was cold as a stone, but the outer layer of tissue was already giving way, and I felt that there was no living elasticity there, just the pliable icy tissue of her temple. Slowly, I withdrew my hand. And now I keep thinking: if I had kept touching her body for a while, her arm, her face, her leg, what would it be like for me now, how would my memory work? Maybe by touching her thoroughly, without fear, accepting with my hand her coldness and deadness, I could have hastened the process of turning her into nothingness in my own mind. But that's unlikely. My memory would have retained the bodily experience of the closeness of my mother's dead body.

Nothing can turn her to nothingness. She lies and lies inside me in her shining coffin. As though she were an integral and vital organ of mine. And so it seems she is. She's my integral wound.

The wound is there not because she didn't survive, but because she existed at all.

In the coffin, laid out on delicate, snow-white silk, she was the culmination of my pain. So beautiful and festive, like a doll. If I were going to pick a flower for my dress, I'd choose one with a rough black center and sparkling white and yellow petals, glowing in twilight.

I thanked the cousin and said that I would go on my own from here. He nodded, and I got out of the car.

At the pension fund, a woman told me I needed to go to a different window. I had simply told her that my mother died, and I was there to pick up her money. The clerk didn't look at me but handed me a torn stub with a number scrawled on it. She told me to wait until my number lit up on the board.

I sat by the board, holding the urn like a precious egg and stroking it. It was cold, and it contained a person's ashes.

A man in a leather jacket was sitting next to me. He had a rumpled kind of face, not from drinking or fatigue, it was just that kind of face. His jacket squeaked constantly against the plastic back of his chair. He kept glancing at his stub and his old Nokia phone. His number kept not appearing on the board, just like mine.

I gave up waiting and just knocked and went inside the office. Two women sat there chatting about their own affairs, as though they lived in a perpetual lunch break. They gave me another stub and told me to go to the post office to pick up five thousand, one hundred twenty-seven rubles and eighty-three kopeks. I thought about how strange it was that a person works and lives out a whole lifetime, and then at her death she gets peanuts; even the coffin had cost more than that. One of the women looked at me with concern and offered to search for my mother in their database, to find out if she had savings in other places. What savings, I said, she lived paycheck to paycheck her whole life. The woman said I was underestimating my mother, who had saved up one hundred seventy thousand rubles in a nongovernmental pension fund, money that I, as her legal heir, could now collect.

Andrei had always said that they never really had money, but once about every six months or so Mama would tell him to get ready to go shopping. They'd go buy a new TV or order a standing wardrobe set. And before her death Mama had bought the new gas stove.

How bizarre, I thought. She saved up and kept the money a secret from everyone.

I remembered that a week before her death, Mama had asked me to withdraw her pension using her card, and to put the money in the wardrobe, between the sheets and the blanket covers. That's where my grandmother, her mother, used to keep it. On birthdays and other holidays Grandma Valentina would take me into her bedroom, ask me to shut the door, and then open up the wardrobe. She would dig through and take out sometimes three hundred, sometimes five hundred rubles. The amount depended on the holiday. On birthdays I got five hundred, on New Year's three hundred. I was allowed to buy anything I wanted with the money. But then I had to bring what I'd bought to show my grandmother, proving that the money hadn't been spent in vain. For some reason I can't remember any of my purchases, though I distinctly recall Grandma's look of disappointment. Apparently whatever I bought was very different from what the older women in my family expected of me.

Mama kept her money in a stack of ironed linen. When I brought her the seventeen thousand, she could no longer get up to put the money away. She told me to put fourteen thousand rubles in there myself, and to take three thousand as a gift to remember her by. I pretended that I had taken it, but I didn't. Mama said that now I knew where the money was kept. Just in case.

"Just in case" is how we talk about death. Nobody calls death "death." Death is "a passing," "a loss," and various other words that don't mean death in everyday speech. Mama wasn't going to die, all of this was just in case.

Andrei had taken me to see their dog. A huge, hideous wolfhound that he and Mama kept on their rural plot. We drove there in his beige Niva, and I felt nauseated. He was saying things about the ruined Soviet state farms, about the cows his father used to keep, about the cats eating the dog's food but catching no mice.

I asked him if he understood that Mama was dying. Andrei said he wasn't a small child and he understood everything. I thought, then, if we weren't all small children, why did we keep saying "just in case" when we were talking about death? I asked what we would do when she died. Andrei said he didn't know. I said that I wanted to take her home, to Siberia. Andrei said, you two can decide on that.

There can only be one instance of "just in case" in a person's life. I peeled the potatoes for the herring and sat down on the floor by Mama's couch. I told her that it wouldn't make it easier for anyone if we didn't talk about it. She said, let's talk. I told her that I could take her to Siberia. Mama said that it would be very expensive. I said that no one would take a body, but I could cremate the body and take her to Siberia. Then bury me next to Grandma, she said. Not next to Sveta, we fought before she died. And bury me in the suit that's hanging in the wardrobe, the beige one. I said that I couldn't cremate her in that suit because it contained synthetic materials. Then in a black knee-length dress, she said. All right, I said. Enough talking, Mama said, go peel the potatoes, I'm going to watch TV. All right, I said.

It was all much easier with my aunt, Mama's cousin. She buries relatives every year, and not a few of them, either. I wrote her an email, saying that Mama was dying and wouldn't last two weeks, things were really bad. I asked her to go to the city administration and get permission to inter the ashes. My aunt wrote back that she'd do it.

I packed the urn into a box and covered it in black fabric. I wasn't particularly satisfied with my handiwork: the box came out uneven, and threads stuck out here and there from the cloth. As a little girl, I had been enrolled in an arts-and-crafts club, where strict Lyudmila Dmitrievna taught me to crochet, cross-stitch, and sew. She taught me to do everything neatly, the way women are supposed to do things. Mama also taught me to do everything that way. But I never could do anything neatly. Mama often reprimanded me for not thoroughly drying the forks and spoons after I washed the dishes. Once, Grandma Anna showed me how to dry the forks with a towel. She turned down the edge of a starched dishtowel to make a sharp corner, and demonstrated how to use the corner to wipe between the tines of a fork. I asked her if she really wiped each and every fork that way. Every one, said Grandma Anna. I felt sick with dread.

I sat staring at the lopsided container I'd made for the urn with Mama's ashes and reprimanded myself for rushing and not being careful. Mama would have told me that I had half-assed everything, as usual. But now there was no one. I got dressed and went outside. I had to buy a new box of dog food and a few new pairs of underwear.

Andrei had asked me not to show him the urn. I had gotten a

cardboard box at a kiosk that sold office supplies and bought a section of black fabric. On the airline's website it said that baggage containing human ashes had to be packed into a sturdy box covered in black cloth. The box from the kiosk didn't work, it was too narrow. I sliced it this way and that, but a suitable container for transporting human ashes did not transpire. I went to the kitchen and picked up the box the dog food was kept in. It was sturdier and wider, and I fashioned a box out of that, and sewed a cover from the black fabric. I put this container holding Mama into a purse and tucked the purse out of the way on the windowsill.

Andrei came home from work and glanced around the room. I hadn't had time to tidy away the fabric trimmings and cardboard bits. He stood there for a while, taking all of it in, then walked out. He turned on the TV in the kitchen and asked me from there if it was really all right to keep the ashes of the dead in the same apartment as living people. What if she comes here at night, he asked. I said that in Japan and in Europe lots of people kept ashes in their homes, there was nothing wrong with doing that. And that if Mama showed up, he could talk to her. At night she did not come.

II

Valya, my cousin, sent me a message on VKontakte. She wrote that she cries often, thinking that our whole family is cursed. First my father died, then Sveta—my mother's sister, Valya's mother—then our grandmother, and now my mother. We're all cursed along the female line, she wrote. She was glad that she'd had a son, the curse doesn't extend to men. She probably thinks that I'm trying to dodge the curse, I thought. I'm a lesbian, after all, meaning that I'm not a woman but a sort of half-man, or half-woman, or half-child. Or half-person. I don't really know what she thinks I am. But I know that the curse, if it exists, doesn't apply to me.

Who could have cursed us? A woman who thought that we were too happy and too beautiful. We were beautiful, yes, but no one in our family was happy.

My grandfather beat my grandmother half to death every day out of jealousy and rage. After he was sent packing, Grandma found herself Grandpa Tolya, who drank like a fish and played the harmonica and the accordion. He kept dogs and chickens and lived in a sloping house with raspberry bushes on a six-hundred-square-meter garden plot. He sat out on the raised foundation of his house and smoked, and when there were weddings or anniversaries in the village he'd go and play the accordion in exchange for vodka. Then she had Grandpa Kolya. Grandpa Kolya didn't work and stole Grandma's money to buy cheap Prima cigarettes. My grandmother was good-looking, and once a doctor named Lev fell in love with her. He'd operated on her after she'd broken a bone. Grandma went sledding on New Year's Eve and broke her leg, broke it so badly that she spent half a year in bed in a cast. He operated on her and tended to her, changed her bedpan. And fell deeply in love. He used to call her "Valentina, my heart." But Lev had a wife, another doctor. And Grandma was a proud woman. So Lev didn't leave his wife, but when times were hard he brought kolbasa and apples to Grandma's house. They went on seeing each other even in the days of Grandpa Kolya and Grandpa Tolya. Everyone said, what a good man, so impressive, doesn't drink. He outlived Grandma by several years. They say he wept bitterly at her funeral. Maybe it was his poor wife who cursed our entire family?

Sveta, my mother's sister, was a strong-willed woman. She had a lot of men. One even stuck around for a while. His name was Petya, but Petya's mother didn't like Sveta, she thought that Sveta was too loose and stubborn. Petya left when Sveta was three months pregnant. After she had the baby, they ran into each other on the street. She was pushing a stroller and he refused even to glance inside. Afraid to look at his own daughter. Maybe his mother cursed all of us? But no, Sveta had plenty of men after Petya, in particular she had Yegor, who was the brother of my mother's lover. Yegor had tuberculosis and a real magic touch, so he gave it to her, too. He beat her viciously. Beat her so hard her whole face turned blue, but they'd still make up after the bruises faded. Maybe Yegor had a secret admirer who cursed all of us? Sveta died of tuberculosis; she was only thirty-eight, but by the time she died she looked like a shriveled eighty-year-old lady.

My mother was the most beautiful of them all. And it seemed like she had the best of everything. But my father went to prison right after their wedding. The chief of police tried to court my mother, but she turned him down, said she didn't want a husband like him. Maybe we were cursed by his wife, whom he had wanted to leave for my mother? And later my father had a lot of women. Mama was always finding hair on his clothes, lipstick traces on his body, and the whole city buzzed about the fact that he cheated on her with every woman he met. Maybe we were cursed by one of these girlfriends of my father's, or by all of them together? But after my father my mother had Yermolaev. He was a monster in human guise. He got my mother to drink and he beat her. He was constantly going to the house next door to sleep with an older woman who lived there. This woman tried to steal him from my mother. And I would have been happy for him to go, but he wouldn't leave. Maybe it was this woman who cursed all of us?

Curses and God are convenient explanations for death, pain, and misfortune. But when my mother got sick, her sister, my aunt, took a photo of Mama to our distant relative, a folk healer in a village in the middle of nowhere. This woman looked at the photo and grimaced. She said that my mother had been "done," and not just once. Her arms and legs were all bound up with black thread, like smoke, she was black all over and would die soon. The folk healer said that if she'd been brought my mother's photo earlier, she could have stopped the curse, but now it was too late. And you can either believe in miracles, or you can believe in nothing and just go on living.

My mother knew there was a curse on her, and not just one. She knew that she had gone black all over, from head to toe. She was miserable. She was in pain and she was scared.

No, I wrote to Valya, there's no curse. There's poverty, environmental issues, alcohol, and poor patterns of behavior. But there's no curse. Just relax and go on living with your husband and son. And I'm going to relax and go on living, too. Because we haven't died yet.

But in reality I'm very scared, too. I can feel that I also bear this heavy dark stain.

The store was filled with glass display cases. Some of them looked exactly like the one from which I'd taken Mama's ashes. The display cases held gold-plated watches, plastic toys, souvenirs, nail files, stuffed animals. I felt sorry for all these things, because nobody needed them and they were just languishing here with their stuck-on bright orange price tags. And I felt even worse for the people who made and sold this junk. In the far corner, in a nook filled with gaudy bathrobes and padded bras, I found the underwear.

The woman behind the counter said that I could pay only in cash. I had a couple of thousands—I'd gotten them as change at the funeral home. I started to pick out underwear. The woman said, proudly, that the underwear was made in Moscow. I selected a few high-waisted black pairs; some even had lace insets. This was the first lace underwear I'd ever owned in my life. Mourning wear, I thought.

Who had put the evil eye on me, my mother asked, when I told her that I lived with Katya not as her friend, but as her lover. Nobody, I answered. I couldn't admit to her that lesbianism wasn't a forced condition, so I explained that I lived with a woman because I couldn't make it work with men. I'm still ashamed of this. I lost my nerve.

Now, in retrospect, I think I was afraid to acknowledge to myself that I'm a lesbian. That's common internalized homophobia, which devours many from the inside. I don't blame myself, but I do regret that Mama died without ever having learned that I'm a lesbian not because men didn't love me, but because I love women. And probably have always loved them. None of my women friends were my friends in the direct meaning of the word, I felt tenderness and attraction to all of them. When I was a kid it was innocent attraction and curiosity, and later it became suppressed desire. In changing rooms and public showers I secretly studied women's bodies. I thought everyone did that, but later found out this wasn't the case. And I was hurt when my friends found admirers and boyfriends, but it was a dull pain and there were no words to describe it. I burned with jealousy. I was tormented by a sense of unfairness. I honestly could not understand why my friends didn't want to be close to me. Just close to me. I had meaningless relationships with boys and men, but I felt nothing for them. Sleeping with men was a breeze for me, because they weren't women. Their bodies irritated me, their bodies were hard, dumb, misshapen. They weren't like the bodies of my girl friends, whom I silently adored. Adored while being unable to admit it to myself. It hurt me all the more that these girls seemed truly to want to be friends with me. But their friendship wasn't equal to my desire. The abyss of my dissatisfaction grew.

Until it burst into a brutal revelation. At twenty-three I admitted to myself and others that I was in love with my friend and classmate Polina. Polina was a pretty young woman who was into Silver Age poetry. But Polina rejected me. She said as much: I don't love you, and if one day I do fall in love with a woman, it's definitely not going to be you. Our closeness ended there. I had no way to reach her; she began to avoid me. I wrote a couple of poems about her. Later I found out that our mutual friend had told Polina about how the two of us got drunk and kissed in a passageway.

That woman's name was Masha. If Polina was someone I wanted to take care of and protect, Masha was someone with whom I wanted to constantly fuck, fight, and argue. But Masha was married: soon she and her husband went to Germany and stayed there. I still remember how her ass felt through the denim of her jeans.

Long before Masha and Polina there was Liza, the artist. Liza was beatific; she would sit drawing in her studio for hours, copying the paintings of Jenny Saville, who in turn had been copying pictures of dead women taken by crime scene photographers. My relationship with Liza was not healthy. I was afraid of myself and my own desire, so I left her. I went from Novosibirsk to Astrakhan, where my father lived. But Liza wasn't afraid of anything back then, she packed up her sketchbook and hitchhiked after me, from Novosibirsk to Astrakhan. We lived together in the apartment my father was renting for himself and his wife. It was a one-room apartment, and we slept in the kitchen, on a little children's blanket covered with a thin sheet; in the morning we folded it away onto a chair in the room. Liza was the first woman I had sex with. The sex caused me pain, it brought me agonizing pleasure and an enormous feeling of guilt. I was twenty years old. I wanted to forget about how this bald bright head worked her tongue between my legs. The orgasms made my whole body seize. Then I'd cry for a long time and hate Liza.

Our breakup was very simple. My father drove us to Moscow in his truck. In Moscow I proceeded to the Literature Institute dorm, while Liza went to her friend and lover's studio near Botanic Garden. We met again a few months later. Liza smelled like garbage, and I learned that in the studio there was neither a shower nor a washing machine, so I took her to stay with me in the dorm. She lived there illegally for a couple of months. She sat drawing in the common room, and the residential assistant didn't realize that she wasn't one of our students, not even when he approached to see what she was drawing. When she moved out, she left me a pack of cornmeal, a dried wood sprig, and a drawing, in which a few animals stood in a pyramid on a large planet that vaguely resembled Earth. Liza had drawn a little arrow pointing to the planet and labeled it with my name: Oksana. We never saw each other again. And the drawing disappeared—probably in some move it ended up in a pile of papers to throw away.

Before Liza there was Zhanna, my first love. I was eighteen and had a job at a clothing store. Zhanna was the senior salesperson. These days we would call it harassment, but at the time I thought of her gesture as just a strange kind of come-on. We were standing by the dressing rooms and waiting for shoppers to return the clothes that didn't fit. Zhanna grabbed my ass, and then moved her hand deeper and felt my crotch. What I felt at that moment made me ecstatic. She made me fall in love with her and delighted in my passion. But actually she lived with her wife, Yulya, and had no intention of leaving her. She just got bored at work. Meanwhile I, being obsessed with her, scheduled my shifts on the days when she was working. When the store was empty, she took advantage of the fact that no one was paying attention to us and stroked my thighs. At night I wrote her teary texts about how much I missed her. When we went out to clubs, I followed her into bathroom stalls, where, drunk and dumb, we made out. I begged her to leave Yulya so we could live together. But she couldn't, she couldn't leave Yulya, she and Yulya had a whole toxic life together. And I wanted to destroy that life. This went on for about half a year. Then I got tired of it; desire had burned me up completely, and I no longer felt any love, or jealousy, or pain. I felt nothing. I didn't even send in my resignation, because I worked at the store unofficially. I simply told the manager I wasn't going to work anymore, and stopped showing up.

Mama knew that Zhanna and I had a murky and painful office romance. This troubled and disappointed her. After all, it wasn't the kind of life she'd wanted for herself or for me. A few years later I looked back at all of them—at Olya, Zhanna, Masha, Polina, and others whom I'd loved and desired without quite knowing it. I looked back and I reflected. And then one morning, when I was about twenty-four, on a rare occasion when I woke up without a hangover, I asked myself a question: who were all of these women, young women, and girls? And I said to myself: they were the women I loved. And then I thought that if I didn't admit to myself that I was a lesbian, I would be miserable for the rest of my days. I was a lesbian before that, too, I'd just gotten a little lost, thinking that I could fool everyone, myself first and foremost.

My friend Vika once told me about a saying they have in Sweden: "Behind the mountain is another mountain." I think of this saying each time when, having dealt with some difficult decision or situation, and without a chance to breathe, I am faced with some new difficulty. When I understood that I was a lesbian I saw the mountain that was disproportionately larger than the mountain I had already climbed. Somewhere in the depths of my soul I knew that this mountain was Elbrus, Everest . . . a very high mountain. I had known that this mountain existed, but a fog had hidden it from me. And this great mountain was something that couldn't be summed up by a single word. I would have preferred to call it something short and laconic, but here my ability to fit the maximum amount of meaning into the minimum amount of words failed me. In short, I understood that to love and desire women was one thing, to admit it to myself was another, and that there was yet a different, third thing—having to learn to live alongside and communicate with women in everyday life. Anyone can fuck. But I had no idea how to have relationships with women. With men everything was simple: there were movies, conversations, and a model (almost always a bad one) of family life. Though in my case even those things didn't work. Men bored me, although the fact that heterosexuality was legal sometimes soothed me. But with women I ran headfirst into the fact that there wasn't anywhere to see a model of lesbian life. The paltry number of movies about lesbians had been made somewhere abroad, and these movies had little to say about me. My lesbian friends were reluctant to answer the question of "how to live," maybe they didn't understand what I was asking. For them, life with a woman was the natural arrangement of things from the very start, and they'd had time to learn how to build relationships and live together. Whereas I was just acquiring this experience and almost immediately started making stupid mistakes.

At twenty-five I began learning to live all over again. Practically in a new body, with new habits, new jokes, and a new way of life. And I also learned to constantly consider the best way to communicate something to my partner and how to behave in public places. It wasn't that I was embarrassed of myself—I could lose my nerve but I didn't try to hide my relationships—just that my then-girlfriend, Katya, was extremely lesbophobic. Almost none of her friends knew that we were together. At parties she pretended not to know me; after sex she cried on my shoulder and told me how sad she was that I couldn't give her a child. Now this seems unbearable to me, but my greatest mistake, as I see it, wasn't even that I started dating her. It was clear from the beginning that we weren't going to work, that she was egotistic, capricious, and unreliable. My actual mistake was that I moved in with her right away. The life we began to lead together was, simply put, awful. Neither one of us knew how to live with another person; possibly we didn't know how to love. We couldn't even share the cost of groceries. She'd get angry at me because I sometimes ate her cheese or kasha. The thought of a future with Katya filled me with dread. I couldn't understand how or why I should spend my time building this miserable life with her. Our sex life was also somehow absurd. I was always following her around and could have swept her up in my arms, kissed every inch of her, and taken care of her constantly. But Katya turned up her nose at me. Then everything would reverse and become some kind of sadistic game. Once I shoved Katya onto the couch, sat on top of her, and started screaming because she couldn't remember some lines from a Fet poem. I was drunk. And I couldn't stand what was happening, but for some reason I couldn't stop it. And I couldn't fix it, either.

It was also distressing when she accused me of rape. This was long before sex scandals. No one had even heard of the culture of consent, which of course doesn't absolve me of any responsibility. It happened the first time we slept together. Both of us were very drunk. First we danced some kind of infernal dance on wooden pallets laid out on the riverbank. As I was dancing, I felt transformed into earth, woods, lava, fire, and death. And then, having downed another few shots of moonshine, we went swimming. Here I have to admit that I barely knew how to swim, and we were carried off by a very quick current. We could have drowned. I didn't have the strength to resist the current, and the shore was very far away quite quickly. But Katya realized this just in time and began pulling us out. Then the others put us to bed together, as the rowdiest and drunkest of the group. When we had hung between life and death, I felt her warm body, which I was embracing in an attempt to climb out of the water, and I thought her body was responding to me. I liked her so much. We'd worked together at a children's summer camp for two weeks, and I tried to spend every break with Katya. She was a good dancer, and she had a very limber, tan body. When they put us in the tent, I embraced her immediately. I started stroking her, and for a while she didn't respond, then she did, and we started having drunken sex. This sex kept us together for twenty months. For a long time, Katya accused me of having raped her. I don't know what she felt at the time. Now I understand that I should have asked her if she wanted to kiss me and sleep with me. I hadn't done that, and now I think that over the course of those twenty torturous months she was getting her revenge on me for the night we spent in the tent. Maybe she'd just wanted to be my friend, but instead I'd dragged her into a relationship. I lived with her in a little one-room apartment by the Shchelkovskaya station and for almost all of that time I slept on a separate mattress on the floor. Katya could go for days without speaking to me. But for some reason I couldn't leave, something bound me to her. I tried to leave a couple of times, but I couldn't do it. I asked myself why the relationship continued, and I had no answer. These were pointless days and months. Today we'd call this a codependent relationship. But at the time I just felt a sharp need to be with Katya. I felt a perhaps dubious sense of safety, and I was terribly jealous of anyone who hung around her. Or maybe I was afraid of being alone. Though I was already alone, anyway. Finally, I packed my things and moved into the Literature Institute dorm. Katya later tried to get me back. But I no longer wanted her. And I'd started something with Lera, which also very quickly deteriorated and turned into a dismal routine that lasted for three years.

I was always thinking of Mama's question about who had put the evil eye on me. To her mind, my lesbianism was a consequence of being jinxed. But I thought differently. I thought that I was damaged somehow, broken, lacking the organ for feeling or experiencing life. And because of this I had no idea how to build and sustain relationships with women, and this was a serious problem.

Mama was a real woman. A woman squared. A woman-woman. A WOMAN. She often told me I'd become a woman one day, too. What becoming a woman meant was not clear to me, and it remains unclear to this day. When my wife, Alina, asked me what that meant—a woman-woman?—I replied that a woman-woman, even as she waits for a doctor while she is on the brink of death, asks for help putting on her three-kilo prosthetic silicone breast, so that the doctor won't see that she isn't whole. Even though the doctor knows full well that she's missing a breast. The surgeons cut all of it off, and they took out half of the tissue under her arm, because the first tumor had grown from her breast into her armpit.

She had tried to get the prosthesis for nearly a year. First, she'd had to prove that she needed it, then travel in the heat to some organization to file a request. But Mama couldn't live without the appearance of a breast. Anxious and downright indignant, she told me about the other women in her cancer ward, who weren't ashamed of their missing body part. She said: how can you show yourself in public with one breast. I'm a woman after all, she said, I'm supposed to have two breasts. These old women in the ward, they had had enormous breasts. And the absence of one was very noticeable.

Once I saw a woman who made no attempt to hide her missing breast. She spotted me on Tverskaya Street and approached me. She said that she was hungry, and she was sick, and she could show me that one of her breasts was gone. I asked her not to do that, not to show me the scar. I gave her money and asked when they'd removed her breast. Fifteen years ago, said the woman, adjusting the robe that served as her streetwear. How strange, I thought, they removed my mother's breast and three years later she was gone. I guess she was unlucky, I thought.

Until she received her prosthesis, my mother stuffed her bra with a colorful kerchief. She would meet me at the train station wearing this homemade prosthesis, and from a distance its shape and volume made it obvious that this wasn't a breast, but a fake. Mama couldn't wear a wig, it was too hot in Volzhsky, so she covered her bald head with a kerchief. Wearing it, she looked like a fortune-teller, a piratess, or an elephant herder. I soothed myself with the thought that the Amazons cut off their breasts voluntarily, so it'd be easier to strap a weapon over their shoulders. But Mama wasn't an Amazon, she was a woman's woman. She was ashamed of her illness, ashamed of the fact that she'd lost the chief attributes of a woman's woman—her hair and her breast.

Sometimes, when it was cooler outside, she wore a wig. On one of these occasions, a man started following her, insulting her because of the wig, calling her a skank and a whore, and when she snapped at him in response, he threw a rock at her. He didn't know she was sick. How could he have known? But he saw her lack. He insulted her. She told me this story a few days before she died. It hurt her to talk about it. She was wounded in her womanhood. She understood that she'd lost herself as a woman. But she wouldn't acknowledge this until the very end, the point at which she lost consciousness and had no control over her appearance.

When Andrei visited her in hospice, he saw that she wasn't looking after herself any longer. She lay in bed with her eyes open and her nightgown undone at the chest. The scar over half of her chest was visible to everyone. Everyone except her. When Andrei told me this I finally understood that she was already dead then. How strange, I thought, that her womanhood died first and that only then did her body follow.

I brought three things home from her apartment: a pair of leather gloves for myself; a knitted nylon openwork vest from the nineties, which was the manifestation of my mother's beauty for me when I was a child; her prosthetic breast. I assumed I'd donate the breast to some charitable organization, but I couldn't do it. Now it sits in the wardrobe of my Moscow apartment.

While she was alive, I struggled to understand how the breast that fed me when I was an infant could now be a lifeless body part. I sucked milk from it, and now there was nothing there. My breasts look like my mother's: large, rounded, with small pink nipples. She told me that she had to rub her nipples with a waffle towel so they'd swell up and I could have milk. Sometimes I look at my breasts and imagine rubbing them down with some rough fabric, and I feel pain, my nipples burn. I used to study her breasts when I was a child, and when she saw me looking, she'd say that her chest began to sag after breastfeeding. Then I'd look at my own flat chest and feel unable to believe that one day I'd have breasts, too. I felt fear and revulsion; I didn't want to have breasts. I didn't want to have anything my mother had.

At the wake after the farewell, Andrei said that in my mother's version of events, the tumor had formed from a congealed drop of breast milk. The drop had been there inside her nipple for many years, ever since I was born. What a stupid theory, I thought. In general, all of Mama's theories about what had caused her cancer were mystical. She said someone gave her cancer. She tried to treat herself with soda and with herbs of some kind that a friend sent her from Siberia. She even wanted to visit a shaman, but the shaman refused to see her, explaining that he wouldn't treat her after she'd gone under the knife. This meant he only treated people who turned down medical help and surgical intervention.

The congealed drop of breast milk that had developed into a cancerous tumor sounded to me like an accusation. But I didn't feel guilt. I didn't feel anything at all.

While she was alive, I thought about how a body part that had once fed something that was still living could die. I tried to summon the animal feeling of my infant lips touching my mother's breast. I couldn't manage it. Mama's breasts were a stranger's breasts. I can't even remember the smell of her body. I remember the smell of the uniform that she brought home from the factory to wash. Her canvas jacket smelled like damp wood—a stuffy and dizzying smell, mixed with the smell of cigarettes. But the warm aroma of wood was stronger than the dry scent of singed tobacco. It was more capacious, the entire apartment filled with it when Mama dunked her jacket and work mittens into the scratched red washbasin. Then a thin film of wood dust formed on the surface of the water. It had a milky yellowish color.

It's also likely that I don't remember my mother's smell because whenever I came close to her I held my breath.

The penetrating smell of cigarettes woke me every morning as she was getting ready for her shift. She smoked in the kitchen at six, right after she woke up. She'd light up and I would wake. The smell wouldn't let me sleep. I'd bury my head in the pillow and, smelling only the scent of my own head, would fall asleep for another two hours, to wake again at eight for school.

Once I was coming home from work on the subway. I was sitting there with a book, but looking somewhere past the pages, at a point on the ground. I was too tired to read; I wanted to sleep, but sleep was impossible because my head ached and in my throat stood the usual lump of anxiety. I'd been suffering in this complicated state for quite a while. Work and school exhausted me, so simply sitting there and staring at the scuffed floor of the subway car felt a little like rest. When I started seeing spots because of the constant back-and-forth motion of rushing legs, I closed my eyes and felt how much they hurt; my temples throbbed, my eyelids burned. With my eyes shut, noises seemed even louder and more unbearable, so I opened them again, and saw, standing in front of me, a pair of sturdy white legs and feet clad in leather sandals. The knees were halfway covered by a patterned skirt, and down by the legs hung a plastic bag from Perekrestok, through which I could see a red Yalta onion shining pinkly in its netting, a hunk of soft cheese, and a few large tomatoes. I sat studying those feet with their little pink toes and flattish arches, the skin of the ankles and calves marked almost imperceptibly by dimples of shaven hair, and the onion net visible in relief through the plastic bag. I didn't raise my head. Because I recognized those feet. I had known those legs for a long time, and I had loved them for a long time. I remember that I could have spent hours looking at them, while Polina bathed in the dacha banya or lay on a blanket in the grass while reading a book. I knew them, but I didn't know what it was like to touch them. I hadn't touched them even once.

The bag rustled quietly as Polina stood across from me, apparently without noticing I was there. I was afraid to raise my head, afraid that she'd see my face and become embarrassed, unnerved. Carefully, I lifted my head and looked at her surreptitiously. Polina was standing there engrossed in a small white iPhone. Her fingers, shaped similarly to her toes, were carefully positioned on the smooth plastic. The sleeve of her blue denim jacket had fallen back and revealed her soft forearm; it was a little darker than her legs. I didn't dare to raise my head higher and look her in the face.

I lowered my head again and stared at her pinkish toes.

We passed seven stations that way, one across from the other. We hadn't spoken in a long time. After my declaration of love, we barely saw each other at the Institute, because I was always skipping class. Occasionally we'd run into each other at a seminar, but she always sat some ways away from me, and I couldn't look at her. Now she was standing across from me. The paleness of her skin, her rounded calves, the delicate skin of her feet—all of it crashed into me. As though she were an extended flash, blinding and painful.

Just before the Izmaylovskaya station was announced, her skirt jerked, her feet turned sharply, and I raised my head. Polina was walking toward the door of the subway car. I could finally see all of her—she'd cut her long, thick hair, and now a neat bob revealed the curve of her head. On her shoulder hung a worn, familiar tote bag; she'd brought me back the same one, only with a different print, from Belgium, where at the start of our second year she'd gone with another girl from our program. I recognized everything about her. It was Polina. I knew everything about her, but she didn't want to know anything about that.

Mama had stopped getting up. I made borscht and went out to the store. I didn't have anything to buy, I was just going in order to go somewhere. I didn't have the strength to go wandering aimlessly over the emptied-out, rutted Volzhsky pavements. And I didn't have the strength to be out in the January wind, in which everything somehow seemed even darker. So I went to Lenta, which was a half-hour walk away from the apartment: I calculated that in this way I could spend not just half an hour but a full hour and a half on the errand. I also went to the store because it was a simple thing to do, with a beginning, an ending, an aim. It was that easy: in an hour you could start something and finish it, and produce an outcome. When you live in a time of waiting, minor, meaningless errands become extremely important.

When I reached Lenta, I stopped to light a cigarette. The setting sun hung above the horizon in a haze of cold, pinkish light. The color of the sky was like the heart of an unripe watermelon. I could have stood there for a long time, until the sun had completely set, but a nagging feeling of either obligation or sadness let me know that soon I would have to return home. I didn't even have a reason to be standing there, so I had to hurry.

I had to hurry in order to return to a tiny apartment where somebody lay dying. I had the persistent thought that every moment spent with her was precious, that every moment contained the possibility of saying something to her, of being told something by her, even just being with her in an emotionally honest way. Every moment that lay before us seemed deeply precious and important. But every moment was one of frustration, in which nothing happened except for dying.

I had gone to Lenta in the hope of buying Mama some books. I thought that a book was the kind of thing that can help people live through certain experiences. It appears I had totally failed to understand that it was taking all the strength my mother had left to just go on existing, even a little. Blinking, looking, asking someone to bring her water or take her to the toilet. Her gaze, directed at the TV, required no effort from her. Her eyes, watching TV shows about cops, resembled the eyes of a woman who'd been traveling somewhere for a long time. The image changes from a forest to a plain to a swamp, to cities, trees, a woman with a bucket slowly walking along the tracks, workers sitting by the roadside, birds disturbed by something rising as a flock to the skies: all of this is only reflected in her eyes, her eyes see everything but they do not feel it, they don't take it in. That's what her gaze was like. There was no pain in it, only the quiet void of indifference.

I had gone to buy books hoping that my almost totally annihilated mother would pick one up and begin reading. I looked for a long time at the shelves labeled Russian Prose. Anxiety about my ignorance of contemporary Russian prose was making me sick to my stomach; I didn't recognize a single title or name. I wanted to buy my mother books. I was hoping that she would read them, but I knew they would remain unopened. Buying books was a symbolic gesture to show that I cared, or it was passive mockery of the fact that she had grown so weak she could no longer read. Looking at the books, I felt conscious of my own superiority. I was still able to spend money and to buy books I would go on to read. But she couldn't do that anymore. This dumb, disgusting superiority twinged inside me as feelings of guilt, fear, anxiety, and pain.

I picked up one book after another, paged through them, then put them back on the shelf. A Chitai-Gorod bookshop clerk asked if I needed help, but I said no. What was I supposed to say to him? "You know, my mother's dying, I want to pick up some books for her." I could have said that, I could have made myself sound detached and even tried to force a friendly smile. But I didn't bother. For my dying mother I had to choose the books myself.

I picked out Yevgenia Ginzburg's *Journey into the Whirlwind* and Aleksandr Solzhenitsyn's *Cancer Ward*. Should pre-death reading be light and inspire hope? Does anyone even need to read before dying? What's the point of books, in this case? I began to imagine that it wasn't Mama who was dying, but me—what would I want to read, then? Would I be able to read on my own or would I ask someone close to me to read aloud? Why these pointless questions?

I was on my way home, I was bringing her a blooming rosebush from the Perekrestok supermarket, roses that were white and had an overpowering scent. As I ascended the narrow stinking staircase to the fourth floor, I knew I could find her dead. And what would I do then? But Mama was breathing in the silence. She'd turned off the TV and was just lying there with her eyes shut. I went up to her, called her name, showed her the rosebush, waited for her approval and her gratitude. But she simply asked me to put it on the shelf so she could see the flowers.

Mama said she'd read *Cancer Ward*, it was just another sad book.

I put the books down by her couch and said that I could read aloud to her. I said that *Journey into the Whirlwind* was one of my favorite books. I waited for her response, but she said nothing.

I used to prefer the images of Saint Agatha that showed her holding her own breasts on a tray. The breasts sit there neatly, like porcelain souvenirs. Agatha's expression contains neither embarrassment nor suffering; aloof, she looks somewhere above her, or playfully right into the eyes of the viewer. These images are sterile, as though Agatha, along with her body, were a doll that had had its plump breasts painlessly removed.

But there are other images: scenes of torture, in which several men torment Agatha. They grasp her torn breasts with pincers, while Agatha, tied to a tree or post, half-deliriously offers up a prayer. Once I came across an engraving depicting Agatha right after her breasts have been severed. She has a fleshy, classical body that seems to be merging with the tree to which she's bound, and her hair, waving in the wind, is becoming the tree's branches and leaves. In this engraving her breasts have been cut off. Both of them have been cut off, and the bases of her breasts look like chipped seashells. The rough, mutilated flesh is repellent in its darkness.

Then there are paintings in which Agatha covers her mutilated chest shamefully with the bloodied hem of her garment. These are the images that best depict the state of a tormented woman. They're grim canvases that evoke repulsion and pity. As though I had come across a bloody rag in a pile of trash. The images are awful to the same extent as they are attractive. When you see something frightening, you can hardly look away. You want to look on, feeling and experiencing the horror of the flesh with greater and greater intensity.

In the chaste Orthodox tradition, Agatha—that is, Agafia—is depicted without the anatomical particulars of her torments. She's just another martyr and miracle worker. In a children's cartoon about Saint Agafia, she's tortured with her back to the viewers, but in the dungeon Agafia faces forward, and brownish bloodstains are visible on her dress.

Mama died on the eighteenth of February, Saint Agafia's day. Sicilians venerate Agatha for her ability to rescue people from fires. They brought out Agatha's relics during volcanic eruptions and were saved. I cremated Mama two days after her death. In the capsule of her ashes there were bone fragments that hadn't been completely incinerated, and I could hear them knocking against the hard plastic when I shifted the capsule in my hands. The oven of the Volgograd crematorium was not so good as the video had promised: it couldn't transform my mother's medium-sized body into homogenous ash. I think that this little piece was her hip bone, or a fragment of her skull. I even considered unsealing the capsule to see which hard little bone had withstood the fire. But that would have been indecent, you're not supposed to disturb someone's remains. I settled for occasionally taking out the capsule and maneuvering it like a large black maraca. The sound calmed me.

My aunt said that I ought to go to a notary to put the apartment in my name. I decided to do it the day after the farewell and went to an office with leather couches. The secretary said that the office was open until four, and I'd shown up fifteen minutes before closing time, but she could still let me in to see the notary so I could ask all my questions.

The notary asked me when my mother had died, whether half a year had passed. I replied that my mother died two days ago. The office grew quiet; the secretaries, the notary, and a few visitors who were waiting to receive their documents went silent and stared at me. I was a horrible daughter who had skipped to a notary immediately after her mother's death to formalize an inheritance.

I didn't feel awkward. The notary told me that I had to go to a municipal document-processing center to remove Mama from the deed to the apartment. There turned out to be no copy machine at the center, but an employee asked me to provide a copy of the death notice, which I could make in a kiosk by the bus stop.

But the kiosk, plastered with flyers advertising apartment sales and jobs, was closed. One job notice promised sixty thousand a week. Who's ever seen such a thing, I thought, in a little southern city they're paying sixty thousand a week for unskilled labor. Bullshit. Or it's something illegal, I thought, drugs probably. The lunch break at the kiosk went on, though on the piece of cardboard stuck to the inside of the glass door it said that lunch would last fifteen minutes. I stood out in the wind for half an hour, bought some cigarettes, smoked two from the new pack and one from an old one. The cigarettes from the new pack tasted worse. Singed, I thought. Though I don't know what unsinged cigarettes would be, maybe they're all like that. Some cigarettes are simply worse, some are better. An old woman holding a folder came up to the door of the kiosk and yanked at it several times. Then she looked up and saw that they were on their lunch break. She asked how long I'd been there. I said I'd been standing there for about twenty-five minutes; the woman shook clean the sleeve she'd smudged against the door and stayed to wait with me. I had nowhere to be, I would wait for as long as it took for someone who worked at the kiosk. My flight was in the afternoon of the following day, and I wasn't going to make it back to the notary in time anyway.

I could have stood there in the wind for as long as I wanted, smoking and looking at the gray street. In addition to the old woman, there were now a few other women and men standing by the kiosk with the copy machine, all of them holding folders of documents. I felt cramped among them. Although I was first in line, I didn't want to stand there with other people. I walked down the road to try my luck and find some other establishment with a copy machine.

I walked and peered into the glass displays. I looked into a clothing store, a shawarma shop, even a pharmacy. At the end of the street I found a post office. A postal clerk glanced out from behind a plastic display of cheap colorful postcards and said that copies cost fifteen rubles. She accepted Mama's death notice as though she couldn't see what it said. She made a few copies, took the money, and gave me a receipt.

I thanked her, went out, and walked back toward the document-processing center.

Mama taught me that everything we bought had to be put to use. If we bought shoes, we had to wear them out. If we bought a sketchbook, it had to be filled with drawing exercises.

Her salary at the factory was paid on the twenty-fifth of every month. But Mama also managed to forge some train tickets in order to be reimbursed for travel, though we didn't go anywhere. Mama wasn't a scammer, just an ordinary woman in a difficult situation. A single mother with functional alcoholism and a lover leeching off her. All the things we bought had to be used; all the food we made had to be eaten. I still feel ashamed when I don't finish a meal and the leftovers sit in the fridge for a few days while I move on to some other, fresher food.

When I was ten years old, Zemfira released a new album, called *Forgive Me, My Love*. We'd been waiting for the album because they were always playing the single from it on the radio, and the video on

TV. Every day, I went to a kiosk to find out if the new Zemfira cassette had arrived. It was finally in stock five days before my mother's paycheck. I came home and said that the tape was at the kiosk already, but I didn't have enough lunch money saved up to buy it. The tape cost twenty-five rubles. Of course it was a pirated version, but nobody cared about that. Mama said she didn't have the money. I said that was all right, we'd wait until she got paid and then we'd buy Zemfira's new album. No, Mama said, that wans't going to work, what if while we waited for her paycheck the album sold out? She took out her large leather wallet and shook out all of her change. Then she extracted a few coins from beneath the doily on the nightstand and a couple more from a makeup case on the vanity. She gave me twenty-eight rubles to buy some bread and the tape.

April was ending, but it was still winter in Siberia. Snowbanks and blizzards. I walked through falling snow to get the tape. I came home without the bread; the Zemfira album was more expensive than other tapes because everyone wanted it. I brought back only the tape, but Mama said, that's all right. We put it on and started listening. It was Sunday, Mama didn't have work, I didn't have school. There were only twelve songs on the tape, six per side. I studied the faded insert with its picture of a misty city. I felt ashamed that I'd spent the money on twelve short songs and hadn't bought any bread.

In 1954, between her second and third exiles, the poetess Anna Barkova wrote a very short essay called "Time Regained." She uses the title of the final book, which she hadn't read, of Proust's *In Search of Lost Time* cycle. In Russian, Barkova changes the grammatical form of the participle from perfective to imperfective, and insists that states of being that are conjured by memory are lived anew each time they're remembered, and that it's neither possible nor required to lose them forever.

As an example, she cites her first love for her teacher, and a late love for another gulag inmate. Barkova writes that encounters with these women in the dark camp barracks light up everything around her, and she experiences again and again the nearness of the women she loves. Memory alters the light, color, and scent of space. Memory is a time machine and a body machine. It doesn't accord with the classical idea of narrative . . . On occasion, memory deals in its own way with composition and with facts. I think that memory and work with personal memory are important tools for the project of women's writing. What do I remember here and now, at the very height of golden autumn, sitting in my dark, book-strewn apartment? And how do I remember it? To remember, Barkova writes, is to gain time again and again. To return it to yourself. To regain your body and to construct yourself over and over. Memory is what the eternal prisoner Anna Barkova always had to hand. She spent more than twenty years in the camps, and when she was dying in the hospital, she suffered an episode of madness, convinced that she'd been taken back to the camp barracks. She was wretched, she suffered, she moaned, she was dying. A long, silent memory hidden in her body rose up in her death throes and remade everything around her. It turned the whole world into a barracks.

Time regained, on the one hand, is a very important thing, of which you should under no circumstances deprive yourself. But it's also a dangerous toy. It can go on indefinitely, transforming the entire world into itself. This is what I'm afraid of, and what I'm living through. I keep walking and walking down the streets of Ust-Ilimsk, I keep approaching my mother's body, first living, then dead. I look into the bright brown eyes of my grandmother Valentina, I smell my own sweat and their bodies. And I constantly feel a sense of my presence there. It's as though I were always there, and I experience this like an endless loop. This is my interior time. A dark, difficult time, without which there is no me, and which tires me immensely. It torments me, as though there were an additional organ within my body, like an extra interior skin, a skin beneath the skin. It keeps trying to tear its way out and turn the entire world into my wound. And it's probably to save myself from this that I'm writing this book. For me, to write is to tame the time that regains me.

I got up on my own, walked to the bathroom on my own, undressed, first swung over one leg, then the other, and when I was already standing in the tub realized I had no strength left, so, holding on to the tiled wall, I lowered myself and sat down. I sat there for a long time until I finally understood that I couldn't manage by myself. Then I called Andrei. He didn't hear me at first—the TV was loud in the kitchen. I sat for a little while longer, and then, mustering all the strength I had left, with difficulty, forced out his name. It came out not as a shout but a long moan. Then he came, and I asked him to wash me. That day, for the first time in two years, he saw my entire body. After my breast was removed, I hid the swollen red suture from him, and then I hid the scar in the place where the breast had been. When we did it, I didn't take off the T-shirt I wore under my robe, and I wouldn't let him touch me there. Now he could see me. He came in, but I didn't see the expression on his face, I didn't see his eyes, I don't know what he felt when he saw me completely naked and aged, hideous. I sat with my back to the door and I couldn't raise my head to look at him. I felt awful and ashamed.

He ran the water without saying anything, adjusted the temperature, and turned on the shower. Andrei washed me, he washed my hair, and I closed my eyes so that water wouldn't get in them. He neatly shampooed my short, gray hair, rinsed it, then raised my arms one after the other and washed my armpits. My legs, my stomach, between my legs. He touched that spot as though he'd always touched it, just passed the washcloth matter-of-factly over my chest. Then he turned off the water and dried me with a towel.

I said that I couldn't get up and started to cry. I was ashamed of my powerlessness and hideousness, they made me angry. Through my teeth I said to him that I didn't have the strength to stand. I cried and groaned with rage at myself and at him. I hated him for seeing me like that.

He picked me up in his arms like a dead body and carried me to the couch. Then he dressed me in clean clothes and turned on the TV.

*

I see a lot of different things during the day when I'm not asleep, and at night when I'm woken by the sound of my own coughing. I see a bright green light, I see a path that runs down a hill into a green wood. I smell wet earth mixed with fallen needles and rotting leaves, and the fresh smell of a meadow of mushrooms. And there's the smell of gasoline, which makes me nauseated and dizzy. But I don't tell anyone about what I see. I see a lot of things. Sometimes, when I'm watching TV, the loud chirping of birds drowns out the dialogue of the characters in the film. That frightens me. It's like I've been lying in a forest for a long time, but I'm warm. It's usually cold in the woods, particularly at night, and smells like a bonfire, but in this forest it's as warm as it is at home, and also dry. Sometimes giant grasshoppers, the size of fists, flit through the air above me, glowing in the dark like beautiful birds, but I'm afraid of them.

I feel pain. It hurts everywhere.

I feel rocked all the time, as though I were in a large cradle or a boat on the waves. I can't see who it is that's rocking me, but I catch the scent of that person's breath. It's a little bitter, sort of nutty, and sometimes I see a blood-tinged light. There are no borders in the space where I am, and I'm floating.

I would like this text to be polyphonic. Aided by my imagination, I'm trying to enter the mind of my dying mother and to feel what she felt then. It's extremely difficult work, it isn't even work, but rather an attempt to draw an excruciating breath in a place where breathing isn't possible. How do you gain entry into the mind and body of a dying person? You don't, and what I'm imagining is one continuous, unwieldy, viscous time that goes on forever—but when does it end? With the coming of death, that's when it ends. Every limit is a death; waiting in line for the register at the supermarket, waiting for a package, waiting for a friend who's running late.

About four months after my mother's death, I was supposed to be awarded a poetry prize. I remember waiting for the day of the ceremony. The time of waiting is a time that bowls you over, eats away at you, opens up a space of scrambling and anxiety inside. But what about waiting for death? What is the internal monologue of someone who's dying? Was she afraid or just very sad? Did she feel a dull rage at the injustice of impending death?

I have so many questions, but not a single answer. And when you don't know the answer, you shouldn't try to speak for others. Or does the question itself give rise to the possibility of speaking for those who can no longer speak? That's the approach the writer Polina Barskova takes when she writes about Siege-era Leningrad and its inhabitants. That's what the Korean writer Han Kang does; she's even managed to write from the perspective of a dead teenager. But may I speak for my own mother? The ethical dilemma has tormented me for a long time. To speak for her is to assume complete control over her. Essentially, Mama became mine alone only after her death. I gained the right to dispose of her body and even here, in this text, to speak for her. To construct her speech however I want.

After her death I felt overjoyed. Mama was mine. I picked out everything for her on my own, I had her burned in the crematorium, and for two months I lived in the same room as her ashes. She had been closer to me, I think, only when I was an infant. It felt like the gray urn now contained my entire world. If you conceive of the world as a stretched canvas, then in the center of the canvas stood the urn with her ashes. It formed a crater, and all the things of this world rolled along the canvas toward it, toward this four-kilogram capsule.

We waited for her death together. I'd wanted to rent a separate place because that would have been less hard on me. A few years before, my mother sold our apartment in Ust-Ilimsk and bought a tiny apartment in a small-family dormitory on the outskirts of the city of Volzhsky. That's where she and Andrei lived. They had two TVs, one in the kitchen and another in the main room. Both TVs roared constantly and interrupted each other. On one of them my mother watched cop shows, on the other Andrei watched the Russia-24 channel all day long. I didn't end up renting a place of my own because I was afraid to admit to her and to myself that I found it extremely painful to look at her. That's why all three of us lived together in a twenty-square-meter apartment. Andrei slept in the kitchen, feet against the washing machine and head against the door of the cupboard. His snoring sometimes interrupted the screaming TV, which stayed on through the night. Mama and I slept on the same couch, head-to-feet, because I was afraid of her breath.

Something medieval had woken in me, and with my entire body I anticipated the contamination of my own body with some disease-causing miasma. But I couldn't sleep on the floor; that would have indicated that I was disgusted by or afraid of my dying mother.

I actually was afraid, but for five nights I slept next to her on the twin-size fold-out couch. Mama did not sleep, lying there in a partial delirium that she carefully concealed behind a solemn expression. In reality, by this point she could barely speak. At night she was tormented by coughing that turned to vomiting. After she threw up I'd take the basin that stood by the couch and carry it into the bathroom to scrub it clean. Mama pissed and vomited into it, and spat into it, and sometimes poured in water she hadn't drunk. I rinsed out the basin each time so that it wouldn't smell in the apartment. Since childhood, I'd been sure that in any place where there was suffering and sorrow there would also be a standing odor. When first I walked into Mama's apartment, I felt that it didn't have any particular smell. An ordinary apartment, not terribly neat, because for the past month Andrei had been running the household and he wasn't very good at dusting or washing the floors. Mama's very presence had made the apartment an ordinary little place. A few months after her death I came back to pick up some documents, and the apartment smelled like a man. It was like the light in it had changed, as though the chemical makeup of everything had been altered, and an apartment containing all the same furniture and dishes as before had become the awful burrow of a widower.

I came and brought flowers. They were lush white chrysanthemums; Mama loved chrysanthemums. And so it smelled like flowers in the apartment, not like dying and sorrow. Only now does it occur to me that the scent of flowers holds not only the sweetness of their fragrance but a trace of death.

*

We slept head-to-feet, and she was dying.

I knew that she was dying, and Andrei knew that she was dying, and Mama knew that she was dying.

We all understood that she was dying.

The only smell I remember very vividly is the smell of her urine on the day I left. Mama could no longer get up, and she pissed while hanging off the couch and then called for me; I'd pick up the basin and rinse it with solution. Her urine smelled like urine that had been standing in the sun for several days. But she had just gone, which meant that her insides were no longer working; they were old and poisonous, it was killing her from the inside. The urine was like poison. It made my stomach turn, and I tried to pour it into the toilet as quickly as possible and fill the red, scratched basin with Domestos bleach.

*

We slept head-to-feet, and she was dying.

I return to those nights in my mind, I'm trying to write about what it's like, sleeping on the same couch as your dying mother, but I keep writing about the apartment, its smell, the TV. Maybe all this dodging is tied to the fact that it's impossible in this small, shadowed space to shed light on writing. You could say that there was a heavy feeling of muteness. Yes, precisely that, muteness. I would lie down by the wall and tense my entire body so that I wouldn't brush against her body if I could help it. I would lie down and fall into a stupor. What clouded nights there are in February. I never liked February because of its sky, cloudy, swathed in a light shroud.

I would lie down and try to think. I would say to myself: think about the fact that she's dying. Come to terms with it, experience it now. But I couldn't do it, and I felt dumb, meaningless time as it dragged on, crawling. I thought I understood this kind of time. I thought that I could feel it, but in reality, I was only guessing.

*

We slept head-to-feet, and she was dying.

It wasn't easy for me, but it wasn't difficult, either. It wasn't anything for me. I didn't feel anything, like an anesthetized gum; in my thoughts I touched myself and responded to myself as if through thick glass painted with milk paint.

*

We slept head-to-feet, and she was dying.

I kept thinking and thinking about myself, forcing myself to come to terms with what was happening. I wanted to feel what she was feeling. But Mama didn't talk to me about anything except everyday things—she asked me to help her get up, she spoke about food, she asked for tea.

And she kept watching those shows. She lay on her right side, practically without blinking, and watched one cop show after another. Her eyes were still and the TV was reflected in them, her yellow face lit up by alternating pink and blue light.

I asked if she was following the plot, because I could see that her eyes didn't move and her expression didn't change. She responded that she was getting some of it.

*

The time before death is an exceptional time. I was ashamed of Mama and of myself, that we were spending this time on cop shows. But was another kind of time possible? No, I think this was the best possible version of time spent.

On one of those evenings, I was sitting on the floor by her couch. We were watching some show. The room was illuminated by the cold gray-blue glare of the screen. I was following the plot—the cops were trying to find the person responsible for the death of a businessman's son—and at the same time scrolling through Facebook. Mama and I were speaking quietly about something. There were moments when I thought she'd drifted off, and I would reach for the remote to turn off the TV. But as soon as the image faded she would open her eyes and say that she wasn't asleep.

She was lying quietly, but then she shuddered and started suddenly gasping for air. I turned around and asked what was the matter. Mama exhaled and admitted that she thought a large salad-green locust had been flying over her. Flying and chirring. She pointed at the corner of the room from which the insect had sprung and the corner into which it had vanished. But she immediately added that there was no locust, of course. It was a waking dream or a hallucination.

Those were likely her first hallucinations—or perhaps not the first, but she just couldn't hide the locust, that's how abrupt the movement of the giant insect had been. For several days by then she had been unable to get up and had been receiving injections of Tramadol, which brought on the hallucinations. Now I think that she was embarrassed by them, that she experienced the things she saw as unreal, something born out of a consciousness occluded by drugs and illness.

It seems to me that if you're dying from cancer in a tiny apartment in a gray winter, seeing a bright, chattering locust isn't so bad. There's something joyful in the flight of an insect. Maybe in her hallucination she rested in tall, warm grass.

My aunt told me to find all the documents pertaining to the apartment and to formalize my status as a beneficiary right away. A week before her death Mama asked me to take out all the photo albums and sort through the photographs. She asked me to throw out the ones of people whose faces I didn't recognize. And she asked me to collect all the bad pictures of her and burn them. What for, I asked, and she said, so that they don't turn up at the dump where someone could mock them.

I took out three bulging Soviet-era photo albums with imitation-leather burgundy covers and sorted through the photographs. There were none for me to throw away. I knew all the faces and occasions they depicted. And I found a photo from the nineties: a very slender Mama at about thirty, in a denim sundress over a striped knitted T-shirt. She's standing there in white leather sandals on a long piece of driftwood on the shore of the Ust-Ilimsk Reservoir. Mama looks at ease in the photo. Not like the woman I knew. I took this photo to keep as a reminder of the fact that my mother had once led an easy, happy life.

After her death I was looking for the apartment documents in a pile of papers and found some porn magazines. I was surprised by their tattered state. Could Mama really have looked at porn? If I had found them while she was alive, what would her reaction have been? Would she have been embarrassed or looked at me sternly? And why, knowing that she was dying, didn't she throw them away? She'd had plenty of time to hide all traces of her private life from me. But she hadn't done it. Was that in order for me to find them? Did she want to poke fun at me after her death? Or did she want to show me that she had been an ordinary woman? Most likely she just forgot about them, and there wasn't anything that she was trying to tell me at all.

I know that there wasn't anything she wanted to tell me. The little unlined notepad that I bought and put under her pillow, so she could leave me her unofficial will, remained blank.

When I was going back to Moscow, a few days before her death, she casually asked me to hug her. I walked into the room in my street shoes, and she raised herself up and hugged me. I kissed her on her ear. She said, "All right, go," the same way she'd said it to me many times before when I was leaving. And then I left. A few days later her heart stopped in a Volgograd hospice. Her final words to me, spoken over the phone, were "I feel terrible."

Mama didn't want to tell me anything, while my entire being was a message to her about myself. When, as a teenager, I started writing poems and keeping a diary, I would leave them around the apartment so she could read them. I wanted to be reflected in my mother's eyes, which never noticed me.

She read my diary and my poems, but she never said anything about them. It was many years later, in passing, that she mentioned having read my earliest poems and having been unable to understand them. Those poems rhymed; I had written about time and unrequited love. Sorting through her papers, in the pile with the porn magazines I also discovered a selection of my poems from the period when I started studying at the Literature Institute. They were stupid poems, in which I was imitating, all at once, Fyodor Svarovsky and Elena Fanailova. I have no memory of how these poems could have found their way into my mother's hands. The sheets had grayed, the corners of some pages were bent. Mama had moved them from place to place. Maybe she'd reread them many times. Maybe she reread them to understand and to imagine me. But I don't know anything about that.

Mama liked to relax by the water. After work, she'd take a beer or a cocktail and head to the reservoir or the river. On summer weekends, she'd pack a bottle of water, sandwiches, a rough, faded blanket, and go sunbathing. She lay beneath the blazing Siberian sun for hours, tracking its movement and slowly rotating so that her legs pointed sunwise. Mama was obsessed with making sure her legs got the best tan. The color faded fastest from your legs and it was difficult to get them to tan in the first place.

Usually she went sunbathing with friends, and sometimes she'd bring me along, but I was only an inconvenience: I'd either block the light or sprawl next to her heated body and annoy her with my wet, ice-cold feet. Little me always had to be supervised—the amount of time I spent in the water, the bucket hat on my head, which had to be worn at all times. I was always hungry and constantly begging for food. I devoured the day's supply of sandwiches within the first half hour, then whined that I wanted ice cream or cotton candy. I was always a nuisance. I wanted attention, but Mama wanted some peace and quiet, or a leisurely conversation with her friends, gossip or recommendations for cucumber eye masks.

To deflect my attention, she brought along friends who had

children. The women lay silently with T-shirts over their faces; perhaps they were dozing. I played in the water and on the stony beach, piled with snags and driftwood, with my friends of the day. Friendship is so simple in childhood, it's enough to just be a child. On one of those days, my mother brought along an acquaintance whose name and face I don't remember at all. I don't remember the color of her bathing suit, but I assume that the selection at the Ust-Ilimsk market was not very wide, which means that it was a two-piece suit with foam cups. This woman tucked away the straps so that she wouldn't have an ugly gradient on her shoulders, going from white to golden skin. The bathing suit could have been blue-black or red-purple. But it wasn't this woman who was so important, it was her daughter. I don't remember the girl's face, and her chest hadn't yet started to develop, so she ran around in faded pink bathing suit bottoms. My mother's blanket wasn't big enough for all four of us, so the women lay on my mother's gray one, and gave us a small, worn, blue-and-white checkered children's blanket.

We splashed around in the water collecting pebbles, and when the games went on too long, Mama would insist that we come out into the sun to warm up. We sat side by side with lips blue from cold, and the hot Siberian sun baked our backs. We chatted about something. The girl was a year older than me.

The girl was different. She was entirely different and separate from me, as though we were two creatures of a different order. My skin was marble-white, while she was breaking out here and there in spots of raspberry-colored sunburn. The girl's skin was taut, firm, and golden. Her bones were long and neat, her movements flowed, while I was angular, uncomfortable, and very ashamed of my body, awkward in my mother's uncompromising view.

The women pulled us out of the water and insisted that we lie down and spend at least ten minutes resting quietly; it was time for us to dry off and warm up. I was first to throw myself down onto the blanket. It was all covered in pebbles and sand, and little chips of driftwood dug into my sun-chafed back. Mama insisted that I lie on my back, since my stomach persisted in being white while my back was aflame. I lay on the blanket and the girl knelt in front of me. Her mother also shouted at her to settle down and lie there. Then the girl lowered her arms, bending them at the elbows, adjusting her torso on the warm blanket. Her narrow jutting pelvis remained in the air. Having found a spot for her chest on the blanket, she lowered it, too.

Once I'd seen a show on TV about the fawns of roe deer or some other kind of deer; they were small and graceless, and their skeletons seemed to be made of the most delicate spokes. The fawns were coming to rest on the grass. First they lowered the front parts of their bodies, then the rear. I thought then that this girl was like a fawn. And I said to her that her movements looked like a baby deer's. I marveled at her like my own love. I liked her body so much. It was all like a tender lozenge that I wanted to put in my mouth.

The glitter of her skin in the sun and the dimples at the small of her back still hover before my eyes. Was I aware in that moment that what I felt about this girl was erotic excitement? Did I know such a thing existed? I don't remember, but I remember that the feeling didn't scare me at all. It elevated me, made me something very expansive. I wanted to die for her.

What does it mean to write a poem? For me, poetry was always the way I conceptualized the world and myself in it. These were dark, difficult poems; they were like sodden, filthy, bloody scraps of loose fabric. That was the way I saw and felt the world to be. And I wanted to show it to other people; I wanted everything, or no, not everything, *everyone* to hear what I had to say. In reality, *everyone* turned out to be my mother's cool eyes. I wanted to show myself to my mother. I was waiting for her approval, or no, not approval, but rather her pity and sympathy, and also her repentance. After she died, writing poems became, for me, a totally useless task. There was no longer anyone to show or want to show them to. Mama didn't read my poems, and I both wanted her to read them and felt ashamed of the fact that she would see them, would understand that they were only ever addressed to her. After her death, my poems slammed shut like a door in a crosswind, and I had no poems left at all. Could I call myself a poetess after that? And what is poetry, anyway? Can poetry exist without the hope of a gaze directed its way?

I think of this potential gaze as a space of possibility: the possibility of writing and of the development of an interpretation of the world. The gaze, my mother's gaze, is a place. My mother's place was the tiny apartment on the outskirts of the city of Volzhsky. My place was her gaze, extending beyond the borders of the world visible to me. That gaze was the guarantee of my presence here and at the same time it tried in every possible way not to take any note of me, to turn me into a place of emptiness, a stone, a beige river pebble, damp but losing its intricate pattern in the sun.

When I stood by her coffin I looked at her calm expression and at the mysterious smile on her lips. Andrei called it her Mona Lisa smile. I didn't understand why, since my mother didn't smile with just the corners of her lips, but with her whole mouth, showing her teeth. Probably Andrei knew another smile that I wouldn't have seen—though now I saw it. I wanted to calm him and say that this smile was not the work of her deceased muscles but the deft efforts of the funeral home workers, who inject special substances into dead muscle tissue. I decided not to do that. Andrei needed that natural smile. And he got it.

I had only the closed eyes. While the head of the funeral brigade showed me her unbound arms and legs, I looked at her face. I studied the half-moon of her eyelid, fringed with short, dense lashes, painted by the makeup artists. I was waiting for them to open, for her gaze to go on just a little longer. I even thought that I could open her eyes myself. It would have been quite simple—just press a finger into the lid and pull it up. But I knew that the gaze there was dead.

I felt my mother as a space. A matrix. A place. After her death this place disappeared. The world itself didn't disappear, but the complex symbolic network that had allowed me to orient myself using my surroundings was gone. A matrix is the continuous interpretation of lived experience. After her death I had to become accustomed to a space rendered meaningless and become my own matrix. But I became suspended in an empty world without meanings or names.

A world without meanings or names is uncomplicated and transparent. There is no place in it for metaphors, and poetry has no function here.

A world without meanings or names is very straightforward. I'm looking at a rounded vase of delicate glass, which holds wilting, open, poisonous-pink peonies. Their interior isn't complicated, it's solid and simple.

Did my mother know how to love? Loving is not a matter of skill or even of habit, but of possibility. It's difficult to become skilled at something if you're not predisposed to it: love, labor, fishing, it doesn't matter which. Say you just don't want to do it, you have no interest—but love is a daily practice, requiring both predisposition and desire.

But that isn't the issue. The issue is me. She didn't love me, specifically. Meanwhile I adored her, adored her convulsively. Yet with time my adoration became quiet, deep-rooted resentment and hurt. This was also because she both wanted to and knew how to love men, but didn't want to or know how to love me.

We talked a few days before her death. She was looking through me, but it was like her gaze remained unfocused, taking in only the general outlines of things, as though I were part of the household furniture, a stool or the TV console. I told her that I'd do everything she told me to do, that she shouldn't worry. And she did tell me. She told me how and in which clothes to bury her. She also told me that Andrei would live in my apartment for a decade following her death. I could have kept what she said a secret from everyone, it wasn't written down, but I passed on her message to Andrei and to everyone else. I carried out her oral will. Such a silly and at the same time serious thing—a twenty-square-meter apartment on the outskirts of a provincial town, left not to me but to him, to inhabit over the next ten years.

It was obvious to her that I, like a weed, would survive anywhere. But her helpless boyfriend wouldn't make it without her posthumous help. That was my mother entirely. She chose men, and not me. I observed her selections with fascination, and was bitterly, passionately, furiously jealous. She was mine, but she didn't belong to me, just as I didn't possess her quiet, mysterious smile. What was left for me was only a cold gaze, slipping through space, looking through me.

The constant narcissistic orbiting of my attention around myself is nothing other than an attempt to find and establish myself here, in this cold, empty matrix. To point from one empty place to another, so that something can coalesce here, just a bit. So that I can see myself and move my finger. Move my finger and acknowledge that I did it myself.

Today I was riding the tram and I saw a woman who looked a little like Mama a few years before her death. I spun around and tried get a better look at her through the window. The woman was half turned away; she had the same hairstyle as Mama did before she got sick. But she was a full head shorter than my mother. I was drawn by what I recognized as my mother's stately posture and her proudly raised chin. She could stand anywhere with her head tilted up, looking at everyone from a slight height: at a bus stop in Ust-Ilimsk, in line at the store, waiting for a friend at the intersection of Mechtatel Street and Mir Avenue. She was a queen, a tsaritsa. It didn't matter to her who she was or where she lived, what her job was or how heavy her lot in life. She was a proud woman, extremely strong and equally unhappy. Like this woman standing by the tram tracks. Suddenly everything inside me seized. And then abruptly relaxed. I felt the warmth of grief and unrealized love.

The box containing my mother's ashes lay in a plain denim bag. I packed the things I had brought on the three-day trip in the same bag—they were all I needed to take care of the funeral affairs.

I went down to the bus stop and boarded a minibus going to Volgograd. Mama was embarking on a long return voyage. The final stop of the journey would be our Siberia, the city of Ust-Ilimsk. I sat in the back seat with the bag of ashes and clothes beside me. I was trying to process what was going on. I saw the Motherland statue emerging slowly from behind the hill, her stone breasts soaring above it. I saw the sparse city, sprawling over a few dozen kilometers; it was sickly and gray. I stroked the bag as though it were a carrier holding a quiet animal. I wanted to convey a sense of warmth to my mother's ashes, communion, love, the significance of the moment. But it was a pointless exercise.

I knew that the S7 airline used a special transportation company to move remains, so I came to the airport early to check the ashes.

It's hard to imagine how to check baggage that consists of your mother, but I was ready to part with the urn for a few hours in order to pick it up again and bring it to my apartment in Moscow. Ahead of me lay two difficult months of work in a state art gallery. And after that there would be several flights and a fourteen-hour bus trip through the taiga. Hourly, I reviewed this trajectory in my mind. I imagined not an ordinary journey but a ceremonial one. A road into the depths of the taiga. I thought trumpets would sound above me as I went. I imagined myself as Charon, as Persephone, as a funeral crier. I was going to enter hell.

But it was an ordinary journey.

I arrived at the airport and found an airline worker, who told me that all the baggage had already been loaded and I was out of time to check mine. I became anxious. Would I really not be able to get on the flight? What about my job? I'd been prepared to fly to the din of ceremonial music, but now I wouldn't fly at all. Would I sit tediously in the waiting area until I could board the next Moscow flight? I addressed the S7 worker again, explaining the situation. He looked at me indifferently, tugging on a salad-green tie. Silently, he picked up a landline receiver and spoke to someone about something I couldn't quite hear because of the plastic partition. Probably he was saying something along the lines of "This woman is carrying an urn with ashes, she didn't make it in time for cargo, can we let her in the cabin with that?" He put down the receiver and said that I could board.

I was celebrating internally. I didn't have to deposit my mother in the cargo hold; she would fly with me. The woman at baggage inspection was rattled and glanced up at me. I explained that I had an urn containing ashes in my bag, and I had all the necessary documents, digging into my leather backpack to get the folder with the papers. The woman came out from behind her computer and told me that I wasn't allowed to bring ashes into the cabin. To which I responded that I knew that, but a man who worked for the airline had given me the green light. The woman returned to her work station behind the metal detector. A line of people waited nervously by the full-body scanner. The woman asked me to open my bag, and gingerly, apologizing for her every move, began to use the detector wand to scan the box that contained my mother. Then she looked over our documents: first mine, then Mama's. She nodded at me and wished me a safe flight.

In the cabin I tried to stuff the bag into the overhead compartment.

It was as though I weren't carrying my own mother's ashes but a large, awkward, hollow object containing neither power, nor meaning, nor purpose.

In a small interior pocket of the bag with the ashes I'd also brought a handful of my mother's gold jewelry. Mama loved her gold. She treasured it and kept it in a small silk pouch, which held her chains, rings, and the ruby rings she'd gotten from my grandmother and her aunt on her father's side. In a little bag lay a formless, blackened, two-gram bar that once had been a crown of hers, and other little bits of gold scrap that she'd planned to have recast into rings and earrings. In the aughts Mama often pawned her gold to make it to her next paycheck, and for every holiday she expected gifts in the form of money. She used this money to buy pieces she'd long since picked out at the jeweler's. She had a special relationship to gold. When she saw a lot of it, her hands shook. She always wore several gold chains and rings at the same time. She'd joke that she looked like a trimmed New Year's tree in all that jewelry, all shining and glowing, except a tree glows only once a year, whereas she, a real woman, had to be beautiful every day.

When she was being taken to hospice, Andrei took off the gold jewelry that she never removed—a delicate chain with a little cross, the relic of her baptism at thirty-five, and a tiny gold ring from her ear. The other ring, in her left ear, wouldn't yield to his large unskilled hands. Neither the morgue nor the hospice returned it to us. Such was Charon's fee.

I didn't know what I would do with my mother's gold. But it was my inheritance. She worried about it even as she lay dying. When she learned that her downstairs neighbor would be visiting, she asked us to hide the jewelry well away. Andrei stashed the pouch in a box of spare silverware.

The day after her death he gave me the packet of gold, saying that it now belonged to me.

Later I sorted out the jewelry. I tried on the earrings, the chains. All of them felt heavy and cold. I picked through her gold and left myself only the things that distinctly reminded me of her. A pair of earrings, a chain, and the "family" rings. I gave the rest to a jeweler to make wedding bands for me and my wife. This symbolic loop seemed to me the most just and correct.

I couldn't read or listen to music. The man in the next seat kept falling asleep, and his slackened neck allowed his head to fall on my shoulder. The head was heavy and smelled of sweetish eau de cologne. I attempted to wake him a few times. He would look around sheepishly, try to get a hold of himself, but then fall asleep again and lean his entire body against me.

I was flying to Moscow. Above me, in the compartment for hand luggage, lay the urn that contained Mama's ashes. On the back of the seat in front of me was a sticker depicting the emergency exits and instructions in case of an accident. I read the instructions as we flew. What would happen if we fell? What if something was wrong with the plane? What would I do? In the commotion, would I reach for the bag with Mama's ashes, to save her? Or would I save myself? I felt the sting of guilt inside myself. Flying at a solemn time and thinking about such nonsense.

Suddenly I was overcome with fear. What if someone had stolen the bag with Mama's ashes? What if it wasn't there, above me, anymore? What would I tell my family? What if someone had stolen my mother while I was going to the restroom or asking the flight attendant for water? The feeling that Mama was slipping away from me persisted even after she had been transformed into a small object. I had the feeling that the bag with the urn had dissolved. It was gone. By some kind of magic, or some other force that had now finally taken my mother away from me.

My anxiety was getting the best of me. Have I really, I thought, been sitting for half an hour beneath an empty overhead compartment and staring into the void while my mother's ashes move farther away from me? But where would they be going? How could you hide them on a plane? Where could you put a metallic urn the size of a prehistoric dinosaur egg, packed into a cardboard box, several layers of clear tape, and thick black fabric? I was certain that it had vanished into thin air.

I broke out in a sweat. I was prepared to tear apart the cabin. I intended to find the urn. I was convinced that it had disappeared.

My heart began beating hard. I shook the shoulder of the man sleeping on top of me. He came to again—he had a sleepy look on his face—and for the fifth time apologized for nodding off on my shoulder. I apologized for bothering him and asked him to let me out.

First, I went to the bathroom. I wanted to postpone the moment for as long as I could. I was afraid that I'd open the compartment and discover the emptiness I didn't want to see.

There was a line for the bathroom.

Once inside, I immediately rinsed my hands and face. I decided that since I had gone there I may as well pee: I positioned myself above the toilet, squeezed out a thin stream of urine, and then stayed suspended, wondering what I would do if the urn was really gone. I don't know how much time I spent in that uncomfortable position with my pants down, but voices sounded on the other side of the door and somebody knocked. The knocking shook me from my thoughts; I used a tissue, quickly pulled on my jeans, and looked at myself in the mirror. The light made me appear older, heavier. I looked haggard and swollen, like a drowned woman or someone seriously ill. On my way out, I felt that my legs were sore from hovering in a half-crouch, and the parts of my thighs where I'd dug my elbows in were burning.

I left the bathroom and apologized to a woman holding the hand of a little boy who was crossing his legs. I floated along the aisle to my seat. I floated to my seat, where my mother's ashes weren't. My neighbor wasn't sleeping anymore, he was looking at the in-flight magazine, a page with an ad for a new BMW.

I had to decide to do it, and having decided, I jerked open the door of the compartment.

My bag stood where I had put it. It was an ordinary, totally unremarkable, swamp-green bag. Its right corner bulged because the corner of the box with the urn was pressed against it. To reassure myself that it wasn't an illusion, I felt along the entire bag. My things were there, everything was there. I felt, folded into a pocket and packed into a plastic bag, the handful of Mama's gold.

Nobody needed Mama but me.

Nobody even knew that she was in my bag. Why would she disappear?

I was flying to Moscow, where I had a job I didn't love and a girlfriend I also didn't love. All things that I didn't love. When Mama was alive, she would call me to talk about herself. She talked about the hospital and her painful medical procedures. She talked about the dog she and Andrei were training, about their vegetable garden, which was becoming harder for her to tend each year. The heat of the Volgograd region intensified her illness; she was getting worse and worse. After her long stories she curtly asked me about my life, and I responded just as curtly that everything was fine. I wanted to and just as strongly did not want to tell her about how I spent my days. I didn't know what language to use to describe my life to her.

I had poetry, which I treasured, but my poetry was a heavy black stone that was impossible to unlock-unstitch and casually put before her, like a simple story about going to the store or buying winter boots. When I started working at the gallery, we put together a large exhibition about literary magazines. In the exhibition space, we built a huge rectangular crib. It was beautiful, it looked like it was soaring above the floor beneath heavy white tulle. I took a picture of the installation and sent it to my mother via the Odnoklassniki website. For a long time she didn't say anything, and then she asked me, "What is that?" I explained it to her as best as I could, and she replied, "I see."

Now I was carrying her inside a cold little capsule and talking to her about myself in my mind, telling her that I would show her my Moscow life. And I did show it to her, as though she were alive. I put the urn on my writing desk next to a pile of books, so that it couldn't be seen through the window. I was afraid that somebody would come and take her from me. Just climb through the ground-floor window and take her.

I love being on the road. The road seems like the only sure way of being here, in this world. It's a space in which there are no concerns about place, but instead a slow mastering of places, an absorption of places into yourself, into your memory. Later, memory doesn't offer up places in their entirety; it lives on within you, like a complex, tangled ribbon. The road is a register of being, in which your traveling companion is your only reflection. If there is no companion, there is no you, either. I loved traveling with my mother, loved riding trains with her or going to the beach or to the store.

I love being on the road. On the road there is no emptiness, the road is filled with spaces and with time. You move like Mandelstam’s Odysseus. It’s when the road ends that silence and emptiness begin. On maps, trajectories are plotted as red and blue lines, while cities and other places are indicated by dots. Travelers mark the locations of their stops with pins. A paper map tears in the place where a stop is marked, becoming a round, rough-edged little hole, an emptiness.

Back in my Moscow apartment, without taking off my shoes, I walked to my room. Everything inside it had been turned upside down, my girlfriend had been living there while I was gone. I asked her why she stayed in my room, and she said she felt calmer that way. I was annoyed; my space and my things had been disturbed by her presence. There were mugs of half-drunk tea everywhere, socks lying around, and in the course of three days the cat had managed to dig up all of my flowers and seedlings—on the varnished wood floor lay clumps of grayish dried earth.

I cleared a place for myself on the floor, sat down still wearing my jacket and shoes, and started unpacking Mama’s ashes. Agitatedly, I worked a pair of scissors, but the fabric into which the cardboard box had been sewn refused to cooperate. My hands began to sweat. When I finally removed the fabric I saw the shining, scotch-taped box. I couldn’t believe that there, beneath several layers of tape and cardboard, laid the ashes. I was certain that someone had swapped them out for a bottle of sand or a bundle of damp cloth. The intrusive thought that I’d lost the urn had tormented me throughout the entire trip. There was not a single reason to think this, but I had been frantically imagining that it was true.

A stop on a journey is an emptiness. The time of emptiness was beginning. A stop turns even the most radical activities into boredom and routine. There was no rational reason to delay the rest of my journey with Mama. I could have bought new tickets to Siberia and requested personal time off. I could have gone back on the road as soon as the next day. But I did nothing. I sat and stared at the urn, which glinted in the darkness between my books. I was hostage to my own plans, which I had made several months earlier.

I had bought the tickets to Siberia without any ulterior motive. I'd been given a New Year's bonus at work, and I decided to use the money nostalgically. I signed off on a schedule according to which my allotted vacation would take place in April, and I planned my route: from Moscow to Novosibirsk, from Novosibirsk a flight to Irkutsk, then a bus to Ust-Ilimsk; from Ust-Ilimsk back to Irkutsk, and from Irkutsk straight to Moscow. Back at the end of December I had unfolded an A2-sized calendar-style planner on the floor of my room and slotted in everything I would do, day by day. The itinerary included two poetry readings in Novosibirsk (in a bar called Open Your Mouth and at the district library), a visit to the legendarily kitsch Museum of Death, a walk around the city, and a trip to Akademgorodok, to the Ob Reservoir. The Irkutsk section of the trip was more complicated. That's where Mama's friends lived; they'd helped raise me, and my plans depended on theirs. As for Ust-Ilimsk, I intended to travel there incognito, stay at a hotel, and wander around the city, get a good look at it.

Folding up the planner, I felt very proud of myself: I'd planned the trip entirely on my own, I was going to Siberia, where I hadn't been in almost a decade. I imagined a return that would be glorious, triumphant. I'd left Siberia at nineteen as a browbeaten young woman without a clear idea of who I could, or wanted to, become. Now I would return and introduce the new me to myself. I was terribly upset that my book of poems wouldn't be published by AST, the largest of the Moscow publishing houses, in time for my trip. I couldn't launch the book in Siberia; it wouldn't be printed by April. The book was my pride and joy, and it would have been very apropos to bring it to Novosibirsk. But we'd spent a long while putting it together, and then it was stuck in the printing queue for a very long time. Daily, in March and April, I had received new versions of the layout and read through them. Here and there I found typos and incorrect line breaks; in some places several words had merged into one long incomprehensible word, elsewhere entire sections of the text had just gotten lost. I nervously read and reread the PDFs and sent round after round of corrections.

In January, when Mama began to decline, it became clear to me that my triumphant return to Siberia was not going to be so triumphant. Of course, the return kept its ritual character, but the logic behind my movements and my feelings had changed. Everything shifted into the mode of mourning. My journey became my mother's journey.

Now I was sitting in my Moscow apartment on Mir Avenue and staring at a point in space. The world had shrunk. Everything I had been building and imagining had come down to one gray metal urn. We were at the outset of a two-month stop. A hole stabbed in the map. I had to occupy myself somehow. I imagined myself as an Indigenous person in Australia, sitting in a tiny tent in the desert of the world, stroking a ritual object and afraid to move, because any movement would bring pain and shift space in the wrong direction. Any movement would be meaningless, anyway—time was the main object of observation here.

Mama's decision to move from Ust-Ilimsk to Volzhsky hadn't surprised me at all. She was about forty-three then. She left her job at the factory, gave away her houseplants, sold the dacha plot, and put our two-room apartment on the market. She packed up everything she owned and had accumulated over twenty-five years. The washing machine, the upholstered furniture, chairs, tables, kitchen towels, all of it went in a large container that she sent to Volzhsky. And a month later Mama went there herself. In Volzhsky Andrei waited for her, Andrei who had been waiting for her for her entire life. He'd wanted to be with her since before I was born. They worked together at the factory then, Mama as a sorter, Andrei as a driver. Mama turned him down, he got married and had children, and then he left the factory altogether. Sometimes he drove a taxi near our house, and when he spotted Mama walking to the market or to the bus stop, he offered her a ride. I was nearly twenty by the time Mama just barely, with the help of G. and Andrei, threw Yermolaev out of our apartment.

I had been trying to throw him out since I was fourteen. But after every fight I was racked with guilt because of all the things I'd said to his face. And Mama, used to being beaten and humiliated and not knowing how to get out of this hell, only cried when I asked why we couldn't make him leave. She answered honestly: she was afraid to be alone. There are photos of her from those days: swollen, overweight, with red splotches on her face and neck, she smiles a dull, pitiful smile, dressed in a shapeless purple bathrobe. I found these photographs when Mama asked me to go through the photo albums. They tumbled in a little stack out of a plastic sleeve in the old album, and unnerved me. For a long time I didn't want to remember those days, when my magnificent mother, who before that had always dazzled at family gatherings in a little black dress, was rendered soft, corpulent, depressing, unbearable, pathetic. I quickly gathered the photographs and slid them back into the album. But the suffocating, boggy feeling that arises when you remember something you actively wish to forget had taken hold of me. I lifted my head toward my dying mother, looked at her, her face distorted by pain, her gray hands. And I felt a sharp pity thinking of the years she'd wasted on that bastard. She had lived as though time would never run out, but when her life changed, time began to run out very fast. Faster than fast, like water from a cracked glass.

Incidentally, Yermolaev was already gone by the time of Mama's death. His going was long and painful; he rotted to death. When I found out what had happened to him, I burst into genuine, ringing laughter, because I'd wished death upon him many times. Sometimes I want to believe that I was the one who killed him, through the sheer force of my hatred. But it was all much simpler and more prosaic than that. During a big bash for his fortieth birthday he bear-hugged his brother, who somehow, accidentally, out of fraternal love and tenderness, broke his neck. Provincial medicine took care of the rest: first the doctors promised him a wheelchair, then they didn't promise anything at all, and then they forgot about him entirely. When his wife, following a great deal of effort and hysterics, finally broke into his hospital room, she found him covered in bedsores up to his forehead. His heart couldn't take it, liquid pooled in his lungs, his weak liver gave up, and, not even forty-one, he died.

But while he was still alive and living with Mama in our apartment, someone else, some other man, had to enter the picture. That person turned out to be Andrei. Andrei, as usual, was driving a taxi and waiting by the Druzhba stop when he saw Mama. Mama was standing there waiting for the bus and smoking. Andrei pulled up to her in his silvery Lada Priora, lowered his window, lifted his cap, and gallantly offered her a ride. Then he asked her to become his lover. They were hardly young by then; they were nearly forty. He had loved her for a long time, and she said yes.

It sounds nice, like a fairy tale. But it wasn't a fairy tale at all, because Andrei was married and had two daughters, the daughters started hating him for cheating on their mother, and his wife decided that if she and the children moved from Ust-Ilimsk to Volzhsky, Andrei's hometown, everything would right itself and she'd be able to drag him along too. She wasn't wrong. They sold their apartment, packed their things, and left.

Mama found herself alone for the first time in many years. But Andrei called six months later and said that it was warm in Volzhsky and that he was waiting for her. She called and told me she was selling the apartment and going to Volzhsky to be with the man she loved. When Mama told me she was moving, I pretended to be surprised, but really I wasn't. I could understand her desire to flee Ust-Ilimsk, and I also understood that flight is possible only if you feel homeless even when you're at home. You just leave behind everything you've acquired, abandon it all and move to a strange, unfamiliar city, because everything that surrounds you and belongs to you isn't actually yours. I felt this homelessness in myself as well—it felt like it predated me. Thinking of the geography of my family on my mother's side, I see that the twentieth century was, for us, an era of journeys and homeless wandering. Why did my great-grandmother move from Kamchatka to Winter Station? How did my great-aunt Minnegel Muzafarova, who in Russian was simply called Masha, wind up in Siberia, responsible for her little brother, my grandfather Rafik? And moreover, how did all of us end up in Ust-Ilimsk, and what was the price of my mother's birth, and then of mine? It wasn't our way to talk about the reasons, instead we talked about the present—food, warmth, the basic requirements of life. That was my way, too. And I, too, as soon as I had the chance, did everything I could to flee Ust-Ilimsk. Mama's decision seemed natural to me—nothing more ordinary than rising from your warm comfortable spot and going somewhere else. Going for a better life, going to save yourself. Mama was going for love, like a real woman.

In Volzhsky she rented a little room in a communal apartment and waited for someone to buy our place in Ust-Ilimsk. Having worked all her life at a wood-processing factory, she discovered that she didn't know how to do anything else. By forty she hadn't learned to use a computer, simply because we didn't have one, and the machine she used at work had only four buttons, each designating a particular type of wood. In Volzhsky there was no forest and no wood-processing factory, and the sawmills and furniture manufacturers received shipments of wood that had already been processed. Mama's training and her skills were no use in the steppe. She couldn't get hired as a salesclerk because of her age. The flower shop in which she tried to work was a terrible fit for her: it was cold and damp, her joints hurt, and in the event it became clear that she had no idea how to sell things. Then she responded to an ad and got hired at a warehouse. She packed tea, coffee, grains, candy. She worked nights and came home to a noisy communal apartment each morning. Mama admitted to me that she didn't steal from the warehouse, even though her colleagues helped themselves to everything they needed for their own kitchens. Mama regularly bought everything for herself with her employee discount. But occasionally she allowed herself to take some candy to bring to Andrei. Sleepily, Andrei would greet her from the couch and ask if she'd brought any candy this time. In the pocket of her jacket she'd sometimes have a Levushka, or a Lastochka, or a Vesna.

And then Andrei went back to his wife and Mama was left alone. She knew how to make connections, and by the time he left she had already befriended the women in her communal apartment and at work. Today, thinking about her, I realize that in many ways her life resembled the plot of a three-hour made-for-TV movie on Russia-1. This is also because when Andrei left, my father reappeared on the scene. They had divorced when I was nine, and my father immediately moved to Astrakhan. He was in a great hurry to leave; Mama said that some of his buddies had framed him. In her version of events, he'd fallen asleep at some party, and when he woke up he was already at a police station being questioned. It turned out that while he was asleep, his friends had stolen half of the apartment's electronics, gold jewelry, and cash. This was in 1999, anything could happen in those days. My father fled from the investigation to his native Astrakhan. A year later, in August, we went to visit him. I still have photographs of us swimming in the Volga. The river is murky yellow with silt and sand. I'm ten, childishly skinny, laughing, up to my knees in the water, but you can tell from my tense shoulders that I'm uncomfortable. My father, after meeting us at the train station, took us right away to stay with my great-grandparents in the village of Trudfront, but rarely came there himself. From the adults' conversations and Mama's tears when Grandma Anya told her fortune with beans, I understood that something wasn't working. Later Mama told me that in Astrakhan my father spent a long time addicted to heroin. We had no return tickets. No one was able to get return tickets in the summer of 2000. Mama wanted to leave right away, as soon as she saw my father, but we were essentially hostages of the situation. One of my father's relatives was able to get us tickets to Yekaterinburg. My father didn't come to see us off. In Yekaterinburg, Mama and I lived at the train station for over a week. When the money ran out, Mama called Ust-Ilimsk on a pay phone, and Grandma wired us a thousand rubles. Mama's beauty attracted men. There was a traveling fruit seller who talked to her all night, while I stealthily, with unwashed hands, ate cherries out of his large wheeled bag. When I'd had enough, Mama tactfully said goodbye, and I got terrible diarrhea. It was the seventh day that we had spent at the station; we were worn out, filthy, broke, and now also had diarrhea to deal with. With the last of the money Mama paid for station showers for both of us. While we washed, other people in similar circumstances watched our things, people without money or train tickets. We took turns doing it for one another. While we kept an eye on the corner these people had taken up, they went to smoke, use the restroom, and get food. While we washed and ate, they didn't let anyone sit in our spot. We had been at the train station for a long time, and our spot was the most comfortable and safe—we were on the floor by the far wall, next to the pay phone. After showering, Mama left me to watch our things while she went to smoke on the station's spiral marble staircase. A man passing by inquired obnoxiously whether she lived at the station. She replied that she did, and turned to look him in the eye. The man was taken aback by her response, and stopped, asking if she was alone there; Mama said she was there with her child. Then an everyday miracle occurred. Like it does in the movies. The man turned out to work for the station management, and just then he was going through a divorce, and his wife was taking away their kid. After hearing that my mother had spent a week broke, hanging around the train station with her ten-year-old daughter in thirty-degree heat, he procured tickets for us. The tickets had three transfers; one of the transfers, in Tayshet, would last a day and some hours. In the meantime, as we sat at the station, and then at a hotel paid for by this man while we waited for the tickets and the train to Tayshet, autumn came to Siberia. The windows at the Tayshet station were broken, and we spent all night freezing in the September draft while a homeless man snored loudly next to us. We were coming from the south, we hadn't counted on Tayshet or a September night spent being buffeted by wind. We sat there in shorts and light shirts, both of us covered with Mama's sweater. Mama didn't tell me anything about this man. I don't know if he truly pitied us, if this was why he took care of us and bought us the tickets, or if Mama had hidden something from me.

After our trip to Astrakhan my father disappeared for another six years. Later, when everyone started getting cell phones, he called home to Ust-Ilimsk. For a few years we exchanged text messages and called each other once a month. He worked as a long-distance truck driver, and Volgograd was one his regular delivery points. Sometimes he loaded up in Volzhsky, thirty kilometers from Volgograd. I was living in Moscow, and never answered my phone, so he and Mama occasionally called each other to find out who had been the last to talk to me. Just after Andrei left Mama, my father called her to find out why I had dropped off this time. The two of them moved back in together for another two years. You couldn't say that Mama was happy with him. I thought they decided to live together out of inertia, sheer helplessness. And that was true. When I went to Volzhsky to see them both, we bought beer and dried fish, and went for a walk. We stood by the concrete railing above the water of a poima, put down a small newspaper, poured the beer into little plastic cups, and pulled apart the fish. The beer was warm and flat, the day was stuffy, still. We didn't speak, my father only huffed a little, looking out over the poima. Mama tried to smile. I felt uneasy; we were strangers to one another. And I was even more of a stranger to them than they were to each other. Then my father died of AIDS. When he died, Mama ran into Andrei in the street. He consoled her and stayed with her until her death, five more years. Our Ust-Ilimsk apartment was finally sold, and Mama used the money to buy a one-room apartment on the outskirts of Volzhsky. That was where she died.

As a child I always waited for Mama's payday. In the morning we would wake up and go to the bank, and then set out on a long journey around Ust-Ilimsk. Our next stop was the housing administration office at the very edge of the city, by the stadium. The housing office took up the first floor of what had been a dormitory for athletes. The office was always damp, people's faces tinted greenish by the light of the lamps. We walked there silently; in winter we passed snowbanks piled on the iced-over black concrete staircase, steam coming from our mouths. You could breathe in such a way that the steam reached your lashes, and they became covered in delicate white rime, like the Snow Maiden's. My feet got cold, but I didn't tell my mother that. We walked side by side, and I knew that later we would go to the market and buy food. The best was boiled kolbasa. Only on paydays did Mama allow herself to slice a piece of kolbasa and eat it plain, without any bread. It was a kind of a minor holiday when we came out of the cold and lay all of our bought bounty on the table. Pork fat, ripe apples, eggs, grains, salty orange soft Russian cheese, and kolbasa. We would come home before sunset, Mama would stand with her back to the window and slice the kolbasa without a cutting board, right on the tabletop. That was usually against the rules, but on payday you were allowed to cut without a cutting board. With her pretty long fingernail she'd scoop up a round of pink sausage, raise it high, and somehow especially, triumphantly, feed it to herself. I've written "feed it to herself" specifically because in those moments it was like she split into two, hands and head. The hand was the feeder; it deftly held the kolbasa slice at eye level. While the head with its heavy square chin, like an animal, adjusted itself, snatched the slice with its teeth. Mama would smile; she liked kolbasa without bread.

She stood with her back to the white Siberian sun, framed by the light of the winter sunset and the lace of the kitchen curtains. In a silk, eggplant-colored wraparound robe, with thin penciled eyebrows and glinting golden chains around her white neck, speckled with birthmarks. I loved her, adored her, wanted to draw out these thirty-minute feasts. Mama was like light and was made out of light, entirely. She laughed and fed herself boiled kolbasa. And I ate the kolbasa, too. It was sweetish, and I liked the way my teeth cut into its springy flesh. In these moments I wanted to both cry and laugh out of sheer joy.

We were together, we walked for a long time in the cold, we wandered through the nooks and crannies of the market together, together we picked out our groceries. I watched as my mother, squinting, examined sacks of rice and buckwheat, as though she wanted to see straight through them, spot any hidden rotten grains or tiny stones. I watched as she asked for slabs of thick-skinned pork fat, which she would salt and serve with garlic, to be lifted one by one and shown to her. A woman in a frilly blue polyester apron stained with greasy brown spots reluctantly lifted pieces of pork fat, and my mother examined them very carefully, and then sweetly asked for that one over there to be wrapped up for her, the one without so much fat and more crimson meat. My mother looked at food appraisingly, bargained with the men, calmly paid the women the prices displayed on dirty calculators. While I watched her towering, stately, over piles of food in her brown sheepskin coat.

My mother knew how to choose, she knew how to pay attention to food. She had a special bag with plastic handles into which she neatly packed her large rectangular leather wallet.

All of this fascinated me. She took me through the city and the market, and I could have walked and walked forever. She could have led me anywhere. Into the woods, into a blazing furnace. And I would have perished there without complaint. Even now, I think her ability to wield power over me hasn't slackened a bit. I am still following her and gazing into her death. I am bewitched by her. By my mother.

Mama liked fish: herring, grayling, sprats. We often ate herring, we had sprat pie, and on holidays there was redfish. Usually Mama would buy a few fresh herring and gut them herself. I remember the smell of gutted fish, it was stuffy and reeked of tender blood. I remember the dark fish blood beneath Mama's fingernails. She always had beautiful hands and well-tended nails. Dressed in a yellow bathrobe she gutted the fish, and when a bone dug into her finger she would yelp with annoyance. Then the herring had to be cut up. Nobody in our household would dare to throw away the heads; Mama salted pieces of herring with their heads still on. After a few hours she poured oil over the fish and mixed the pieces of herring with rings of fresh onion. Mama ate the fish meticulously, sucking out the brains and the other juices.

Once she salted down a two-liter jar of herring. Other than porous white bread there was nothing else to eat in the house, so we ate the jar in a single evening, and then we were terribly nauseated. I was a kid, I didn't like herring. But I loved Mama and copied everything she did. So, in front of the TV, we finished the entire jar. I remember the warm yellow lamplight, the cold light of *Field of Wonders*, and the oppressive nausea brought on by the greasy herring. We laughed at ourselves and said that we'd stuffed ourselves with herring.

I remember Mama's hands, her beautiful hands. They were always stingy and offered no affection. When the head of the funeral brigade untied Mama's hands in the coffin I saw that they were still beautiful, only now they were stiff. Even colder and stingier. In the coffin she looked small. Two months before her death she'd stopped eating. She wasn't able to eat because of the metastatic tumors on her liver. I saw online what a liver with cancerous tumors looks like, like a chunk of shared modeling clay in kindergarten. Violet-black-green with beige veins.

Mama got up for the last time in her life to salt some herring. Then she lay down, and the potatoes I had to make myself. I like the starchy crumbs of boiled potatoes. They're dry and smell like paper. I brought Mama a couple of pieces of herring and a few clumps of boiled potatoes. She didn't eat the potatoes but ate the herring eagerly and asked for more. I said that the herring was extremely salty, with her liver it was very bad to eat so much salt. But she asked for more, so I brought her more. And then she stopped eating completely and stopped getting up.

I lived in a large two-room apartment in an old manor house on Mir Avenue. The landlord had shown Lera and me into a half-ruined apartment that didn't even have electricity. Beneath the windows hung heavy, black cast-iron heaters, and by the entrance of the smaller room stood a rickety toilet. The landlord advised us against standing on it, or it would break. I joked that I wouldn't do at home what I do on a train. Three days before we moved in, the landlord installed a light bulb in each room, put in a used shower cubicle, and from the remnants of several kitchen sets cobbled together a new one. There was another room in the apartment, which had once been the bathroom, but it was dangerous to go in there—the ceiling had started coming down because of the damp, and through the holes in the plaster the supports were visible; in one spot a part of the ceiling hung down like a stalactite. We used this room as a storage space. Later the cat took a liking to it—it could lounge in peace there on the extra mattress and observe any activity from a safe distance, through a crack in the door. In the old kitchen the landlord installed a shower room, and in the third small room with curved corners he put the kitchen.

There were two rooms left for us to live in. For a fifty-square-meter apartment we were paying almost nothing. I had found the apartment through the landlord of our previous place. On the second floor of the house lived the landlord's first family and his mother, a descendant of the Soviet architect Ivan Fomin. His ex-wife was a publisher of children's and young adult literature. His second, current family lived in the apartment next door—his French wife, a literary translator, and two kids a year apart in age. The rest of the house was being renovated. The family was always short of money, so the renovations were never finished.

We moved into the apartment with one mattress and ten boxes of books; the second mattress was lent to me by a philosopher friend who lived in the next house over. That was all we owned. But the really terrible thing was that we weren't in love. So the old Russian saying about finding heaven in a hut sounded, in this instance, like mockery.

I had insisted on moving to a two-room apartment so that I could have some personal space. Until then we'd lived in a communal apartment along with a few friends: the crowding, constant noise, and other people's mess drove me insane. Although crowding and other people's messes were two of the few topics Mama and I could bond over. She hated both. She, a forty-five-year-old woman who'd always lived in her own apartment, was once forced to live in a communal setting. When she moved from Ust-Ilimsk to Volzhsky, until the apartment in Ust-Ilimsk sold, she rented a ten-square-meter room in a six-room communal apartment. Her gold jewelry and her phone got stolen, her washing machine was scratched, and she could never get to sleep after her night shift.

The two-room apartment on the first floor of the 1960s-era building where we'd lived before moving to Mir Avenue wasn't full of criminals, no one was stealing our jewelry, and anyway I didn't own anything that could really be ruined. At various times the residents were artists, gender studies scholars, political activists, and poets. But this didn't make the apartment any more orderly. In this environment, my depression gradually began to worsen, my bursts of anxiety became more frequent, and at night I started suffering from panic attacks. Insisting that we move to a different apartment was petty on my part. I was exploiting Lera's attachment to me. And she couldn't tell me no, because I handled our finances. No, I didn't take her money or live off her, I just knew that living with a group was cheaper, but I also knew that Lera would do as I said. And I took advantage of that.

I paid for my pettiness by having to listen to complaints all day. Lera was completely hopeless at the requirements of daily life, and I had to deal with all routine matters—paying the bills, buying a mattress, washing the windows. In the new apartment, I had to strip and paint Lera's room myself, just so that I wouldn't have to hear her whining and claiming that I had taken the bigger and cleaner room. This monstrous symbiosis more or less suited me. We had stopped having sex a long time ago, two months into living together.

These days I studied her body in secret. It was flabby and white; she walked smoothly, as though all of her joints had been oiled. Her hands made me feel even worse; they were pink and limp. I studied her and kept asking myself why we were living together. I wondered at myself and my own indecisiveness. Mama had taught me always to tell the truth, and I always did tell the truth—in poetry and in personal conversations. But I couldn't admit to Lera that I didn't love her. I quietly poisoned myself with my loathing of her and bore it; the worst was that I stayed with her. I put up with her shrill voice and barking laughter. I felt physically repulsed by her. But I bore it and bore it and bore it. I looked at pictures of our mutual friend Alina on social media, but I wasn't sure she liked me. What a simple, common lesbian story. Only half a year after Mama's death, when Alina came to visit us in Moscow, was I able to admit my feelings to her.

Lera walked into my room and glanced indifferently at the urn with Mama's ashes. Mama's dying had conclusively taken me away from Lera. Now she had no right to whine and complain, to demand my attention and my love. I had a lawful reason to tune her out emotionally. And this seemed to make her mad.

The day was coming to an end. The following morning I was supposed to be at work. A white Moscow day, it darkened to gray quickly in the garden by the house and grew into a dim twilight. There was hardly any snow, and the trees in the garden looked filthy against the background of murky sky and black earth.

Lera asked if she could lie down next to me. For the first time, I said no. I had to be alone and sleep alone. I stroked the warm bluish cat, and the cat kept circling Mama's urn and sniffing at it, rubbing its face against the steel, purring lightly. For the cat, it was just a new object in the house, a new smell.

I was about sixteen when I first visited Novosibirsk. My school friend Olesya, who was a few years older than me, had been living and studying there for around a year. She had invited me to visit her on vacation. Ust-Ilimsk is a white city of low, rounded hills and the taiga; in winter it's blinding and calm, like a cave where you can dwell in silence and safety. It's surrounded by the immense, remote taiga. Novosibirsk is different—a dull steppe city, where there's always a lot of wind.

I adored Olesya and did whatever she said. She had long, thin hair with highlights and angled bangs and a narrow hooked nose, and she was always making faces and joking around. Olesya liked touching other people; she could sit there with an arm around me, chattering away, for hours at a time. This kind of closeness tormented me. Mama was cold: she kissed me until I was about thirteen, but only to say good night and on holidays. The kisses were anxious, oblique. They communicated no emotion, they were empty, ritual kisses. Olesya could put her soft warm lips to my cheek and spend a long time breathing in my smell. She found pleasure in touching. Her touches turned me into a post. I smiled with embarrassment and watched her bold movements with fascination—how perfectly the collar of her T-shirt lay against her throat.

I had seen her breasts many times because we often traded clothes, and when I came to get her to go out, she would change in front of me. She lived with her mother in a small-family dormitory, there was nowhere to hide: one room was the bedroom and living room, the other served as office and kitchen. Olesya had large, pear-shaped breasts, and I looked at them often. I looked at the narrow and broad violet veins showing through the thin skin.

She thought of me as a friend. We hung out by the Naymushin House of Culture with a bunch of rockers and punks. She taught me to smoke weed. I didn't like weed, it made me drowsy, but I would have done anything Olesya did. She was my friend, and I was certain that all women felt this way about their women friends—they watched their friends with fascination, they wanted to listen, to obey, to give their friends anything they asked. Fifteen years passed before I realized that friendship isn't like that at all. But at that time my friendship amounted to this feeling, and my friend was Olesya.

There were guys in my life, but our relationships turned out to be empty and pointless. I was doing everything expected of a teenage girl: I dated and kissed boys, had sex with them, went through breakups. One night, lying in my room, I cried because I couldn't understand why I needed to play this dumb game of loving boys. But I kept at it, because it was the normal thing to do.

I had taken a train to visit Olesya. A thirty-six-hour trip in a sleeper car. I brought my best clothes, hoping to impress Olesya and Novosibirsk generally. The train from Ust-Ilimsk arrived at about five in the morning. Olesya stood on the platform, enveloped in white winter morning mist, smoking a slim cigarette. She started chatting with me right away, the cigarette smoldering between her fingers. I asked for another cigarette for myself, and she took from her pocket a crumpled pack of apple-flavored Kiss cigarettes. It was unpleasant to smoke in the freezing wind, so we went down into the subway.

Olesya took me to a small two-room apartment hung with carpets. She lived there with her older sister. The sister was out, and Olesya, reclining on a love seat, loudly told me all about the music she'd discovered in Novosibirsk. She put discs into the CD player one after the other, and let me listen through her large AKG headphones. It was drum and bass. We had been listening to drum and bass for a while, but there was no internet in Ust-Ilimsk, so new music had to come to us from other cities, and then we spread it through local networks. This was in 2006. The music that Olesya was listening to and sharing with me now frightened me. It was gloomy. In Ust-Ilimsk we listened to regular, light, poppy liquid funk, whereas Olesya was making me listen to dramatic, dense neurofunk. She pelted me with the names of tracks and artists.

The music felt oppressive. And I felt oppressed because I'd been tossed in a smelly train car all night and hadn't been able to sleep. I felt afraid.

I was also afraid because I could see Olesya's belly beneath her short, stretched-out tank top. Her belly looked bluish in the pre-dawn light, a few birthmarks on her skin. And her large round breasts, and the pink stripe imprinted by the fabric on her hip bone. The air was thick, it trembled around my head like a stifling gelatinous mass. I felt drops of sweat break out on my forehead, and the crotch of my underwear was suddenly damp, then the dampness immediately cooled. I felt afraid. I was afraid of myself.

I could have said to her that I wanted to kiss her right then. To take off her T-shirt with the cartoon lion, pull off the washed-out gray fabric and be inside. First inside her large thin-lipped mouth, and then inside her. I had never done that, but I understood then what I had to do. I wanted to be between her legs. To touch her skin, her sides, her belly, her breasts, to kiss the delicate skin on the inside of her thigh. I knew how to do it, and that made me even more afraid. I couldn't breathe.

Olesya chattered. She was telling me about her cool boyfriend, who worked as a dancer at techno parties. The guy's name was Leo, and he was tall, good-looking, strange. They were having sex, she was saying, and she really liked it.

She had put both hands behind her head, and her breasts jerked and pulled upward. My vision grew dark. I wanted her and at the same time was waiting impatiently for this spasm to be over. I couldn't do anything with myself.

I asked Olesya to make up a bed for me. I was very tired from the trip, and she had to leave for the university in an hour. We agreed that I would meet her there and we'd go to meet Leo. Olesya explained how to get to Novosibirsk State.

In the bathroom I undressed. On the gusset of the underwear I'd bought specifically for travel shone a large clear spot. I felt hurt by myself.

What could I have known then about myself? My desire was very strong, but it also scared me. I didn't know anything about lesbians. In little Ust-Ilimsk lesbians did not exist. When in eighth grade my girl friends kissed in the entryway of a building and said they were lesbians nobody believed them, it was a joke. But for some reason I didn't think it was funny. I liked the band Night Snipers, I had their live acoustic CD *Trigonometry*, which I listened to several times a day. The voice I heard in my headphones made sense to me on a physiological level, I felt drawn to it. The meaning of some of the songs was unclear, but I could feel everything that the songs were about; I identified with their lyric heroine. They were teaching me how to feel.

I found out that Night Snipers were and remain lesbian icons much later, when I started working at the clothing store where I met Zhanna.

My year of working at Depot, as the store was called, was a real immersion in lesbian culture at the end of the aughts. We went to clubs, watched *The L Word*, listened to Zemfira and Night Snipers, and the store manager gave me a disc of movies about lesbians, so I could download the files to my computer. I kept watching and rewatching both parts of *If These Walls Could Talk* and *Imagine Me & You*. I didn't like *The L Word* because all the women were too glamorous and their world was alien to me. I did think that one of the characters, Shane, was very cool, but watching her was intolerable because Zhanna tried to look like her, and everything that had to do with Zhanna caused me pain and heartache. Zhanna was a seductive, silent type like Shane; she wore low-rise pants and had dark hair that fell into her eyes. I wanted Zhanna very badly. But she, sensing the power she had over me, quickly cooled to me.

At clubs we got drunk, danced, and discussed other lesbians. From these conversations I found out that lesbians could be separated into types: women who looked like Zhanna were called dykes and were the most popular, since their androgyny and meticulous attention to their appearance were highly valued in lesbian society. Feminine women were called femmes, and were treated dismissively because they exemplified all the attributes of femininity. But held in the deepest disdain were butches—masculine women. It was thought that they imitated men, had sex without taking off their clothes, and got into drunken fights at parties. You fell in love with butches only if you were a femme or insane.

I seemed to be both. Because I really liked masculine, short-haired women. I thought they were perfect. At the club, Zhanna noticed how carefully I was watching a woman in a blue denim shirt; she poked me in the side and burst out laughing. She was laughing at me because I liked this large woman, I liked how she moved, how she spoke, reached for her glass of beer, held that glass. But most importantly I liked her gaze. It was a gaze that gathered things into itself, a gaze in which I wanted to go limp and open, as though I were something hard that wanted to be something soft and agape. Her gaze was a key.

But Zhanna was laughing at me. I saw her eyes grow damp from laughing, smearing the greasy black mascara on her lashes. She was laughing at me, at my sexuality. When she'd had enough, she leaned toward the ear of her wife, Yulya, and told her about me. Yulya's mouth dropped open in shock and she stared at me as though I'd come out to party in a tutu.

That night I danced with the woman in the blue shirt, and in the morning at work everyone made jokes about it. I tolerated their teasing and felt unable to defend my desire, because it was directed at "a guy with a cunt."

Shame about being a lesbian who liked masculine women lived within me. It devoured me from the inside, and I forbade myself from looking in their direction. When I found myself among feminists, I encountered an even greater condemnation of butches. Though I was already familiar with it from the second part of *If These Walls Could Talk*, in which the young red-haired feminist Linda meets the silent biker Amy at a lesbian bar. Amy is a rebel in a leather jacket, Linda is a redheaded coed. Amy infuriates Linda's friends; she's far from the essential femininity that second-wave feminists are fighting for, she imitates men, thus she is an agent of the patriarchy. Moscow feminists of the mid-2010s thought similarly, and it seems that many people think this way even now, though it's precisely this essentialist view that chains women to femininity and doesn't give them the right to behave variously. Masculinity and femininity are not properties of either men or women, and masculine women are direct evidence of this. In lesbian and feminist circles, a "golden mean" was considered acceptable, but anything that had to do with a radical move toward one end of the gender spectrum was frightening and frowned upon. Coming down from the heights of gender theory, I can say that masculine women scared the feminists even more than men did. And since I had for several years been influenced by the lesbians around me, I couldn't even allow myself to look at butches. And this tormented me. I could have sex with and date feminine women, but that never lasted long; usually I quickly became disappointed and put the brakes on. Such was the nature of my relationships with Katya and Lera. At first we had nonstop sex, and then I discovered that being with them in daily life was difficult for me. Difficult and boring, and also uncomfortable, because everything I had in spades, they had, too. But neither they nor I contained the qualities that had always attracted me in women.

And then I met Alina. She came to visit us when Lera and I lived in Kuzminki, and I knew right away that she was there for me. First I realized that her thoughtful gaze was directed at me, following my every move. Then I noticed how attentively she was listening to me. Then I heard her speak. Alina was younger than me by several years, but I felt that she possessed everything that I'd always liked and always lacked. She had autonomy, she always had her own opinion and kept it. But it wasn't about how she acted—what I noticed was her gaze, which transformed space into a warm, safe place.

I could stay in that space for a long time and not think about anything. Sometimes I secretly pulled up her profile and felt bitterly jealous of the woman who would end up with her. I hated that woman because I wanted to be her.

Alina's large, warm dark eyes were always looking at me, and I felt calm when she was with me. I had forbidden myself from looking at all of her for so long that I didn't immediately notice her hands. But two years after we met I finally got a good look at them. She was sitting in an armchair in my little kitchen, holding a bottle of Hoegaarden; we were celebrating her return from Israel. Alina was saying something about Lebanon and Georgia while I watched her surreptitiously. I first noted her large, tan, sculpted feet with their protruding ankles, and was taken aback by their beauty. I thought that if she had such beautiful feet, her hands must be beautiful too. I looked up to her hands. Her broad palm was wrapped around the sweating bottle of beer, and there was a thread tied around her broad wrist. I was most surprised by the contrast created by her long nut-colored fingers on the light-gray label of the bottle. Alina saw me looking at her hand, and I looked down at the ashtray, embarrassed. I wanted to touch her. To touch the brown skin with the black tattoos on her shoulder. To touch her curly dark hair. To stroke her feet. But most of all I wanted to put both of her hands in my mouth. I really wanted to lick her fingers.

As I listened to her story I imagined those hands stroking me. I couldn't sleep that night: thoughts of her, of her hands touching me everywhere, gave me no rest. I wandered to the bathroom, to the kitchen for water, and back to bed, thinking that this woman could touch me. When I began to imagine her undressing me, grasping me with her hand, then touching my vulva, a cold spasm seized my lower belly. It was pleasurable and terrifying all at once. I wanted to be with her, I wanted her to take me to be with her forever. On an intuitive level I understood that this woman was my future wife and my support, but first I had to touch her, breathe her in, and kiss her.

This morning a large, curious crow landed on my balcony. I was woken by the scraping of its claws against the wooden window frame. The crow was pecking at seeds that had fallen from the trees. It was going about this very attentively and didn't notice as I slowly approached the window for a better look. The crow pecked through all the tender hulls and commenced looking around. First it noticed that on a stepladder in the depths of the balcony stood a plastic flowerpot of wilted parsley. The parsley started to come in, but lacked for something—light, or nutrients—and now hung down the sides of the flowerpot in thin little filaments, weighed down by yellow leaves. The crow moved along the windowsill toward the plant. On the way it examined everything with its wet pebble eyes and awkwardly rotated its head. Screeching, it made its way into the depths of the balcony. Past the windowsill, the crow examined the pathetic parsley, then looked over at the plastic bucket with the sleeping bag rolled up inside it, the terra-cotta pots holding bits of clay aggregate mixed with dry black earth. Nothing it saw was of interest, nothing qualified as spoils. The crow turned its swaying bottom and noticed a tiny porcelain coffee cup with painted flowers. I use the cup as an ashtray; it has a narrow base, you can stand it on a little wooden windowsill, it fills up quickly with cigarette butts, and it's easy to carry from the room to the kitchen. The crow, jerking its black head and shifting from leg to leg, proceeded toward my ashtray. It assessed the cup from every side and suddenly seized the round handle with its bony beak. The cup overturned, butts tumbled out. The crow pulled again; the cup was too heavy for it, so the bird lifted the cup above the sill, hurled it to the ground, turned, and flew from the window.

The crow's antics made me laugh, but I also thought that a crow's visit could be a sign. Birds are their own creatures with their own agency, and they've always held some significance for people. They brought news of misfortune and death; the ancient Greeks foretold the future using their innards. I also tell fortunes based on birds. Something very old and rural inside me arises with their approach.

In the apartment on Mir Avenue the windows looked out into the garden, which was full of little birds whose names I didn't know. In spring the cat dragged in baby birds that had fallen from their nests; those are called fledglings. A few months before Mama's death I sat in my room working. I almost never left the house; my depression was so bad that I could hardly walk to the kitchen and open up my old laptop. Doctors prescribed me one regimen after another but not one of them worked. The pills made me feel even worse. I did all my work remotely. I was sitting with my computer by an open window, sweating from the difficulty of sending work emails. Since the window was open, I heard an orderly knocking. I turned and saw a large robin on the windowsill, sitting and looking at me. When I noticed it, it chirped and fluttered from the sill. I felt a strange heaviness inside me, as though an unwieldy darkness had appeared in my belly. I knew something was going to happen. That day Mama called me and told me she had new tumors. Two, each one the size of a bean, Mama said, and the liver was an inoperable organ.

At the beginning of January the following year, I was coming home from work. I don't remember why I was going home so early, but it was still light out. I stopped by Perekrestok to buy sausages, eggs, and some other groceries for the night. Our courtyard was private property, so in winter the landlord was responsible for clearing the snow. Snowbanks surrounded the paths and the parking lot, no one shoveled, and over the course of the season, high, dense mounds of snow piled up. The landlord's kids would slide down them like slides and scoop out little dugouts. I saw a red spot on one of those snowbanks and came closer—on the gray slope of the snow lay a neat, tiny bullfinch. Its breast was crimson, not like blood but like a ripe southern tomato. It was as though the dead bullfinch were sleeping. I was amazed by this bird. Until then I had seen bullfinches only in book illustrations and on Soviet-era New Year's cards. Now the bird lay before my eyes, and it was hard for me to believe in its materiality. I touched the fuzzy red breast with my index finger. The bullfinch felt hard, and its chest feathers had clumped together in places. I understood that the dead crimson bird was a sign of impending death. I froze and looked at it as if awaiting its resurrection. The following day I received a text telling me that Mama could no longer get up.

The day before I left for Volzhsky, I saw another bird. Right by the entrance to the house, in the middle of the path, sat a gray sparrow. It was alive but breathing quite heavily. When I came near it didn't move but remained in its spot, and I even thought that I could hear its loud, laborious breathing. I took off my mittens, swept it up in both hands, and carried it from the path toward a corner of the house. I knew that the bird contained within it a sign that I should help my mother pass without pain. That's why, returning to Moscow after five days of living with her, I found a way to get her admitted to hospice, where in the absence of feelings or suffering she died after a few days. I thought a lot about the fact that birds were drawn to me and to this house because I would be leaving it to see my dying mother and bringing her back precisely there. They could feel death and were warning me about it, and about the path that lay before me, my silent experience of her death, life with my mother's ashes in the same room. I knew the language of the birds, and the birds knew that I could interpret their messages.

Now the funny crow didn't seem to me like an ill omen. Mama's death had nullified the significance of events; her world had shrunk and the magical properties of birds had melted away. A crow is just a curious bird. It visited just because. The crow didn't know me, and death was distant now. The bird had come for delicate seeds and the light flickering on the porcelain cup; it wanted to eat and mess around a little.

Recently I noticed that in addition to the sounds that carry from the road and the courtyard, there are also other sounds: thudding, screeching, and squeaking. I spent a long time walking around the apartment, trying to find the spot the noises were coming from, and then, out on the balcony for the fifth time, I went down on my knees and listened. Below, in a crack in the balcony cladding, some small birds had built a nest and hatched chicks. The chicks' cries harmonized, and sometimes the chirping of the adult birds was audible, too. They live alongside us, in a world that's separate and extremely fragile. I don't think the birds need us to go on existing or to pass life along from one generation of birds to the next.

When fine hairs began to appear on my pubis, I didn't notice. It was Mama who saw them, when I was sitting naked on the wooden bar in the bathroom and warming my feet in a red plastic tub. Mama approached me to help me get out, she came to me with a towel and bent down to reach my steaming feet. Suddenly she froze and touched my plump pubis with her long-nailed fingers. She felt the few thin curly hairs, hemmed, and distantly said that I was becoming a woman.

I did not want to become a woman. I wanted to remain the body that I was. Becoming a woman meant becoming my mother. I loved her passionately, but my love was a love that wanted to possess. To *be* meant to be equivalent to yourself, but to *possess* implied that you possessed something that existed outside yourself. It meant not being equivalent to just yourself. Something you possessed lost its autonomy.

The next day I brought myself to touch the hair on my soft pubis. They were the hairs of disappointment, mourning hairs. They were golden and glistening. They were coarse beneath my fingers.

I didn't become a woman for a long time. I resisted being a woman and failed to notice my developing breasts, my first period; I didn't notice that my body was becoming a woman's.

Standing by my mother's coffin, I looked at myself: I was wearing wide black jeans and a black shirt, beneath which I had hidden my own body from myself and from the world.

My mother died leaving nothing behind her: on her worn flip phone there were only texts about paying for light and gas. After her death I felt that inside me there was a new emptiness, and slowly, feeling my way, I began to enter into it. I entered it, and my language and my gaze gradually became my mother's, just like my daily habits. When I look at the world, I feel that she is looking at the world through me. I feel her inside me all the time.

After her death the mechanism of my poetry broke down, pulled like a muscle. When you do many squats, your calf muscles begin to burn, they tighten and no longer obey. That's exactly what happened to my poetic speech, it stopped obeying me. My language broke: the organ that produces the stuff of poetry.

My writing now is quick and rough but I did manage to do some things after her death, which became the focus of all of my attention. I went into death after her, and I looked at how the world of dying was arranged; I remembered the way her body broke down. Lying there in the dark before sleeping, I pored over my mother's image, and in my imagination I observed her dying. I was afraid of looking there, but I couldn't look away. Because after death there was nothing. Because death was the only place into which I could look and see.

And also love. Though love is more complex than death. In death a single person is involved, but love is a space of cooperation. I tried to weld love and death together inside myself. I didn't want vulgarity; I wanted life, a daily practice, labor. And then I wrote a poem. Love brought me pain, and death brought me pain. But love brought the pain of being, while death brought the pain of nonbeing. And that was where they met, through pain.

women young women
are becoming sand
beautiful slim in nylon glitter
are becoming sand

I'm reading you Inna Lisnyanskaya's poems from her book *In the Suburbs of Sodom*
and in one poem she compares her stomach
her old worn-out stomach
to waves of sand
they are such flawless poems about old age and regret
(but what do I know about old age and regret except that
women young women are becoming sand
and that death exists and it's coming)

little girls becoming
inconsolably becoming ashes
little girls' heels turning to unconquerable cliffs

little girls' hands becoming heavy stone bones
and little girls become little bones

I show you poems like small fragile objects
feeling as though I keep them in a velvet bag with golden ties
here I have Mandelstam, Glazova, Grimberg, Fanailova, Shvarts
I display them and you
touch them with your sensitive gaze
as though your gaze were a tender little trunk with a thousand
tiny receptors
you look at them along with me
they're like treasures untainted
untainted because they never had a price
and won't today
they're like treasures untainted they're like air imperceptible
quick explosions inaccessible
and very rarely—thrown wide open

I put my foot on the edge of the bath
you bend and show me your back your large curly nape
and briskly one after the other
clip the grown nails
first on the right foot then on the left foot
and I watch your back like a sturdy delicate thing
I look at how neatly your ears are attached to your head
they're whorls of flesh and skin cartilage
so delicate
while you clip carefully and don't see my gaze
it's cloudy like water with love and an erotic hymn
here you're closer to me

in sweet service to my body
than when you're looking at me from the distance of parted
fingers
here I see you
here you carefully wield the clippers
as though you were a large bird
with black mother-of-pearl plumage
swaying blinking and saying:
like that, and again like that, and click the steel
and saying again:
What funny little nails!
and then kissing and kissing again

and I see you big
big as a stone island
big as a dark breathing island
strewn with breeds grasses and the burrows of small animals
you're like the earth you're like a boundless stone body

and then I read you bits of this poem
and you smile
say that it's very beautiful
and I love beautiful objects and poems
poems are objects actually—complicated sparks
trimmed with glass lace
or living wounded flesh
poems are like little stones
when there are many of them rustling inside you as river
pebbles do
when the water breathes

---

it's so old-fashioned
thinking about poetry not as something that goes beyond borders
but the other way around—packages a feeling or event into one complex unbreakable thing
poems are sparks stones and small sensitive things
poems are interior things
they are micro-tears in the heart scabbed over
they breathe in the heart like sweet gentle insects
crackling and stabbing a little
they are the work of pain and time
they are light blindingly precise
they are the work of grief and joy

In 1995, every three months Mama left to take a course in the neighboring town. She worked at a factory, and in Bratsk there was a technical school where she went for advanced training. After her course ended, her sketches lay for a long time in the sideboard: notes on tracing paper and heavy black notebooks in oilcloth binding. The graph paper in the notebooks faded, but her thick blue handwriting remained. Sometimes I went through her notes, and I understood nothing in them—engineering formulas, tables with types of wood, graphs and sketches of woodworking machines. It felt like the sheets had retained moisture. They were heavyish, sodden, and yellow, like fresh wood. They smelled like something sour and dry. The sheets stuck to my fingers; they were still covered in a thin film of wood sap.

Mama would leave and I'd remain with my father. And everything would fall apart. Mama was a matrix, she structured time and space. My father fed me congealed spaghetti while his friends slunk around the apartment. He didn't take me to kindergarten. I was alone. There were only two channels I could watch on TV, but they didn't show anything that could have interested me. At five years old, I was left to my own devices. There was a VCR and only one videotape. On the first part of the tape there were Enigma music videos; I remember a horrifying howling voice and analog special effects used to make a person float against a fluorescent background, waving his arms. I was afraid of that video, there was something sinister about it. On the second half of the tape was Alan Parker's film *Pink Floyd: The Wall.* The movie was suffused with an anti-militaristic pathos; its realistic depiction of war didn't look like the war clips that ran on TV. I would shut my eyes at the very beginning, when, following an explosion, the camera panned along the bodies of the wounded and stopped at a man whose head was completely wrapped in bloody bandages. His face was invisible, he was entirely the body of war, terrifying, an experience of pain and horror. The bandaged head looked like the masks worn by adults and children in the film's crowd scenes. I didn't have the necessary words, but I could feel the film's message: we are scared, and we are all equal before totalitarianism and death.

The cartoon inserts—the march of the hammers and the genital-like judges—were off-putting. I rewound the film again and again, watching it several times a day. At five, I could press the button on the VCR but couldn't understand what exactly fascinated me in this realistic depiction of human suffering. Now I understand that what drew me was the boy, the protagonist of the film. He was very lonely. Together, the boy and I wandered onto the playground and asked some grown-up I didn't know to spin me on the merry-go-round. Together, we found a huge sick rat in an orange sunset field. Together, we buried our rat friend in the canal. The film abounded with images of dead bodies and dying, and I was fascinated by the fact that everything in it was touched by the theme of death; death was the beginning and the cause of everything that happened to the protagonist. I think this is the origin of my powerful attachment to meticulously thinking through the body: dead, living, dying. Here is the genesis of my fixed gaze in a direction where people don't usually look, where they would rather not look.

I should have become a medical pathologist or an attendant at a natural history museum, but I chose to write poetry. I think the reason for this was *The Wall*, *The Wall* was my first guide to understanding metaphor. The film taught me that the world is a complicated, interconnected thing, and that understanding it becomes possible only as you gain experience and transform it. Poetry is the work of experience and understanding. Poetry is always intertwined with memory and oblivion: from the time when Homer began to name the ships and Simonides called the names of those fallen at the feast.

Poetry is my method of forgetting in such a way that what I forget becomes known to others: those who will read and hear. In Pink Floyd's song "Mother," there's a line in which the singer wonders if people will like the song, and another in which he worries about getting his balls busted because of it. Poetry about memory and oblivion is a dangerous thing. It threatens those who are remembered, but even more so those who remember and wish to forget. It saves the ones who must be remembered.

I wanted to forget many things—violence, the feeling of alienation, poverty—and I wrote a whole book about them, after which I was condemned for writing it by those who remembered and knew me. And then I was forgiven. In this, too, is the power of poetry; it can help to forgive. It teaches to forgive and draw on another's experience.

I started writing the "Ode to Death" cycle when my mother was still alive.

III

Ode to Death

1

a few weeks before her death my mother confessed that when she
stopped getting up
she noticed the discharge on her daily liner had a strange odor

I asked her: what was the odor like?
and she replied: the odor was like an old ship that was never
launched into water
and then I joked that Mama had become a poet
and she smiled at me a little. I don't think she understood why I
called her a poet since it was really so simple—
the little boat of the vagina had rotted
had never made it to water and her life had stopped as though
there never was a life
but always an air of heavy mute helplessness and pain
and the work of enduring
and now she lies on the couch like a gray weathered hull
and life never did happen

we sleep head-to-feet on the same hinged flimsy couch and
together we wait for her death
watch TV shows about criminals and cops
before Mama's eyes tens of people die daily
and I want to believe that gets her used to the thought of her own
death

she watches glassy-eyed as the cops save our Russian unthinkable world
while I sit on the floor next to her and join in watching
and it's as though in this joint endless viewing of TV shows
I confess to her my wild unrequited love
and wordlessly she accepts it

while spring presses in with its beige brutal belly and any second the rivers and rills will swell with the murky water of thaw
any second the greenery will explode in dazzling bareness
while spring presses on with its beige brutal belly
and my mother curled into a ball after her injection
looks with a tranquil expression at the branches slicing the twilight southern sky
and there's no fatigue in her only a quiet weightlessness trembling

we sleep head-to-feet on the same couch
I look into her bright eyes browning in her gray childish head and say nothing
just look at her as half-asleep she moves her toes
listen as she squeals in her sleep and says "no no don't"
as she pukes
she tries to puke very quietly so as not to wake me
I play along with her pretending to sleep
so as not to bother her with my attention

I asked how she came up with this metaphor of the odor
but she wasn't able to tell me
I want to believe that the whole terrible deathbed world is a world of appearances and even the dark discharge seems like something imbued with meaning

as though the worn couch the color of sand is a quiet open shore
and the cry of the TV is a complex ensemble of the cries of gulls
   water and rustling grass
and that she isn't in pain but only
a gray boat
lying and waiting to disappear
or not even waiting
just lying
and thus she will remain forever

2

before my eyes night becomes a wild furious unsightly garden

*

I wanted to explain and reimagine it for myself

*

and to show others that there are no evil schemes in the night
   only a different known world
consisting of a thousand tongues and constructions
imagined by dead difficult evil minds
but there are no dead all of them
reside here among us
and have taken on our features and our desires they have
   become us
come back as our people
and more than us they have become our world

my mother died slowly and silently
she breathed for a long time on her little hard couch

before I left she raised herself up and sat
saying only "maybe you should kiss me goodbye"
and I went and kissed her
as though the tender gesture weren't a farewell
but a ceaseless soft gesture with an animal tinge of timelessness
kissed her on her gray delicate ear
and put my hand on her head with its tangled hair
she was all soft as though made of wool
as though warmth had for a moment returned to her body
and life had returned
and this final touch
resounded in her as a short animal tender jolt
of live unrealized life

she was dying
the way trees die
or large heavy organisms
silently but so
that the surrounding space rippled
from each of my mother's exhalations
silently but so
that each little drop of life she gave to the world of the living
illuminated space
with a bright condensed light like in the early evenings of august
and my mother died slowly

I see death but I don't see the rest
it is stitched like light through our furious world
flawless world like a light lucent chaos

the world is flawless as though it were the head
of a hideous yellow monster like a beast it is flawless
like the head of my now forever dead mother dead
or her turned-up yellowish nose

the world is flawless
like my dead mother who's lying
in a beautiful coffin carelessly draped by the funeral workers in
   delicate silk the see-through color of sand

it is flawless like the dead body of my mother
it is completed and flawless
like a bunch of grapes
shining through a brittle bag stilled in sunlight

and my mother is flawlessly complete
she lay there in a black kerchief
as though everything I had picked out for her in the end
the coverlet of snow-white pearly satin
and the fine slippers with trim
all that outlined her
was a grammar of light
and the light and her loosening skin like a mature tree stripped of
   its bark
were more honest and more beautiful

night comes but day is more frightening and more beautiful
at twilight all the clouds appear above the rooftops like
   remembrances

like a horrible pain and a threat
like the white body of terror and the undressed body of a threat
night comes like a complex liberation of the face and the organs of the spirit
night comes and I recognize nothing in it
except a black wall safety unbeing

my mother died on a stiff government-issue bed
without the music of a voice or a touch of warmth
her eyes were open as though
unseeing they sliced through space
and saw where burrowing its way precise death approached
her eyes were open
and her single-breasted chest bare to the air
as though she were already weightless like a ship sailing
and trailing behind light blue yellow pinkish sheets
all washed threadbare to a stupefied light
laid out by the strange government-issue hands of medical personnel
she didn't close her eyes
as though in moving toward death
she was gathering space into herself like a sail
like a fine worn by hard labor torn furious sail
stitched through all of its crossbar

my mother died and the horrifying world stopped
it became whole as though it were a severe flawless droplet
shining without end
and cleaving consciousness
with furious clarity

3

something obscure beats above the frenzied steppe
at night breathing becomes stifled
and a cough shatters space like a rock

and I see nothing except the ruined grim life of Andrei
who asked me with mute eyes to leave my mother's body on this earth
but I took her away in a smooth chrome-plated vessel to our Siberia
he sleeps on the floor in the tiny kitchen
between the washing machine my mother brought from Siberia and the windowsill
he shouts in his sleep he howls like a heavy wounded boar
like a one-eyed god
like the caverns of the earth
he howls in the streaming light
of the Russia-24 TV channel
and the TV voices shout disgorge a magical clichéd fanatical worn-out Russian world
now he speaks now he grows silent
now he roars like the blade of a coarse saw lodged in the damp tight body of brown wood
and he speaks to my mother
the way he always spoke to her while she was alive and even after
in his roaring he sings: Daughter! Daughter! Don't go!
so strange he always did
call her daughter his difficult cruel woman with a wooden face
and when she was single-breasted

he loved her pityingly
as though she really were his daughter
his frail daughter with frightening hair

when she no longer lived
but just sailed on the sheet
like a crumpled ghost
and all her feminine awkwardness because of the missing breast had fallen away leaving just the yellowish body
he saw her in a gaping gown
and in her deathbed floating she no longer knew that her breastless breast and her wild pathetic old age were out in the open for people to see
he tried to cover her woman's disgrace
and cried the way that dumb beasts cry
and wiped blood from her lips
and tried to spoon-feed her the last of the stale water

something obscure whirls above the frenzied steppe
the steppe enlightens you
studies you your body and your face
and rages rages in the wind
night in the steppe is flawless
horrible like the stomach of a sick crippled cow
wild like a bullfinch dead on a gray snowbank

something obscure speeds above the unbridled steppe
that's her the naked steppe
she beats against you
and you'll be no barrier for her
she looks at you as if she utterly didn't exist

the steppe sings
as a beautiful merciless canvas
beats beats tirelessly against the windows of the car

and now she looks into you like a poor hoarse daughter

and now she's looked into you and that feeling convinces you to
collapse into painlessness

something obscure crumples above the unrestrainable steppe
that's him getting up at five in the morning and quietly washing
the dishes
that's him going to work in the steppe wind and not seeing the
wind
that's him opening the miserly book of war and death
that's the collective gathering their poor alms
creased fifties and five hundreds
tender succinct alms
for the funeral
for the memorial
for life after life
that's him going
that's him sleeping
that's him wearing himself out

glorious enormous like a frenzied animal a sturdy man
with a puppy's little damp eyes

that's him going
that's him going
that's his heart dying

something obscure crumples above the mourning steppe
that's him closing his eyes
on the hard little couch
where my mother lay dying
a heavy orphaned man
that's him sleeping that's him sleeping
that's him sleeping and roaring in his sleep
that's him sleeping
see Andrei
that's Andrei

4

death squeezes and brief time beats like a rag like a canvas scrap
my mother in a black bag
as though we were just in a stupid movie
about the criminal workdays of shivering immortal cops

and they open the bag with a dry broken-off crunch
and my mother lies inside it
on a metal tray like a body
like a bodily mass
and in the hands of the orderly I notice her head
is heavy like a ripe watermelon
he lifts it with his hands and turns it to me for identification
as though I wouldn't have known her
by her dead turned-away profile
while now I can say with certainty: yes, this is my mama
as though by the folded over her chest
elongated thin lemon-colored

forearm as though by that I wouldn't have known her
and by the back of her head with its tangled graying hair

this is the process

time like rags time is sawn-up bread
wet and wafting cold toward you
reminding you of the body
the world will not hold you
the world is a very weak place to hold your gaze
and to keep you by its side inside it its soft mother-of-pearl self
the world is scorching and has such strange hollows
empty hollows and it's horrifying to peer inside them
as though they were the quiet modest pits of graves
of eviscerated burnt beings

My text is perpetually sidetracked by reminiscences and attempts to understand what exactly my mother was for me. I'm writing my poem in order to read it at the same time. The poet Vladimir Burich wrote:

The time of reading poems
Is the time of their writing

To which I say: no, it is the time of writing that is the time of reading. I think of this book, and of writing, as a path, a road I follow through myself toward others.

When I stopped writing poems, I fell into a panic. I thought that I'd never write poems again. But a different, new kind of thinking came to replace them. I began to write essays about poetry, writing, and language, and through these essays I was trying to speak to the world of the dead. If poetry for me was a way of presenting myself to the world of the living, then these essays became my way of speaking to my dead mother. I became drawn to the genre of notes, a liminal genre that contains many possibilities still not fully realized in Russophone literature. I'd like to think that notes, like fragments, are the most appropriate genre for women's writing. One's attention wanders, but it's very close attention—isn't that why the perceptive Elena Guro and the analytical Lidiya Ginzburg both chose this genre? Notes provide an opportunity to capture space and experience, to look at objects very closely and to feel the nearness of what's being described. The subject of notes is always sketched in, it isn't alienated through the positioning of the author and the storyteller. Notes are an honest genre, a genre in which the speaker isn't afraid of her relationship to things. She looks and isn't afraid to look. This is also because the status of notes isn't always totally clear. What are they, exactly? A diary? An intimate letter? Intimacy here isn't linked to the realm of the erotic but to the realm of nearness to the object of description. To the realm of nearness to the *subject* of description. For instance, in her notes Guro is equal to what she describes: she's the same as the earth and the pines, the same as speech, the same as space and also able to fit space inside herself. Notes make possible a wide-open gaze and honest inquiry.

Notes on Parchment and Flowers

There are so many things in the past that I seem to be looking at the world through tulle. These things have been thrown over my head like netting. Though the kitchen window, I see a sprawling yellow hill. In the wind, the grasses lie down this way and that. They look like coarse pile and, at the same time, like notches in soft nylon.

What is living like if there is no past? It would probably be endless light and a day that lasts. No, I didn't swim in the cool waters of the reservoir and I didn't carry a half-dead baby otter in my palms. No, I didn't drop it on the rocks. No, I haven't seen death. No, I didn't smoke like that, looking through the wind. Looking at the wind rippling the blooming water before the storm.

I saw nothing. Memory, like a veil, can be brushed out of your face, and then you can look directly through the balcony shutters at an anxious sparrow.

*

I write her letters every day. I write as though she lived on the other side of the river and a limping mailwoman would deliver the mail. The mailwoman has a lilac beret with a brooch pinned to it, beige woolen tights, and rubber boots splashed with gray spring mud. Heavyset and limping, she walks at first along the riverbank and then steps from the bank onto the water. And she walks and walks until her outline disappears from my sight. I write her letters every day. There are shards of rough amphorae, bits of skin, and everything else that seems to me to be signs of a naïve farewell or forgiveness. Or confession.

*

A woman's death destroys the world of the people around her. A shrinking occurs, as though in a single instant the walls of your house had collapsed while you remained standing there in your slippers, a book in one hand, a kitchen rag in the other. A woman's death, even the death of a bitter woman, is not a man's death. A woman is the envelope and the guarantee of your world. She extends you into the future and leaves room for you in the past. She is the condition of your experience and its interpretation.

When she died I was left naked in the road.

*

To take the coffeepot from the stove and understand that here it is—the edge of time. Feeling that edge is the privilege of the living.

*

Memory is a parchment. A fragile brown membrane. It's made out of the skin of a murdered animal. It's a very costly material, it can't fit much. You end up having to erase text after text, image after image, in order to create new ones. The old images don't die, they remain as smears on bull hide, and as the scratches left by the writing tool. A person is an analog creature, a very ancient one. Within a person there's still a place for memory and things that have been erased. See, I've pressed my nail against the springy stalk of the pungent tulip, and liquid wells up in the crescent wound. What an old-fashioned metaphor: parchment and flowers. Flowers and parchment—they're warm things, I'm going to save them.

*

You asked me to write a poem for you. It's very simple, writing poems. Everyone knows how to write a poem. But it turns out that I don't. Writing poems is like licking a stone's skin. Or like listening to the rustle of caution tape strung up on a playground. A poem is a very simple thing, it's made out of sound and body. Like any substance that doesn't have any use but for which there's a dire need. Why did Catullus write his love elegies? That was two thousand years ago. The passion for writing, for licking stones, lived in that long-ago person, too. It also lives in me. Especially when I see a white street cat with orange spots crossing an empty courtyard. Then I'm able to write something for you.

When I see the red tip of a new high-rise beyond the railroad tracks, I am able to write something.

I am able to write something when I hear far-off sounds.

*

So everyone writes and says: women’s writing is extremely physical. But then what can you say about the lesbian lyric? That’s physicality squared. An endless litany of liquids and component parts of vaginas and breasts. A confirmation of women’s mirror sexuality. If I look into a vagina, like a peephole, and see in it a crimson becoming universe, can I tear my gaze away and look above the belly, past the domes of breasts, into your eyes? Should all of my experience come down to the pleasures of digital penetration? Do I want to be a vagina on legs, without time or breath?

I don’t want to throw myself into the cauldron of sticky hot anonymity. I have a mind, a character, experiences, and I want to look above the belly.

I want to write about love not as a universe of fucking. But as the space of a room, where at dusk glances meet and give rise to warmth and a path. I want to look above the belly, into the eyes of the woman I love.

*

Writing is a slow approach. What did I want to say? I just wanted to write about the lesbian lyric I’d like to see. But I’ve asked too many questions. I brought stones here, and decaying parchment. What else? Synthetic black lace, a policeman’s anxious voice, carrying over from the patrol car. I just wanted to write about love. Writing is an approach to love. I think that’s true.

Writing is a path.

Sometimes a path loops.

*

A woman is inseparable from space. If a woman is fading, her apartment withers. On my visits to our Ust-Ilimsk apartment after my move to Novosibirsk, Mama was already unwell; she was drinking heavily, and she was utterly devoured by the man she lived with then. I remember my mother's house as a sterile, clean space. Mama cleaned every Sunday: scrubbed the wainscoting, cleaned the toilet and the kitchen cupboards. The apartment smelled like bleach and cleaning solution. Everything had its place, its purpose, and its point. There were no superfluous souvenirs or doilies, just a scrubbed uncluttered space.

I'd moved to Novosibirsk after school. Returning a year after my departure, I found a thick layer of dust on my framed photograph, and a reddish ring in the toilet bowl at the level of the water. My room, with its children's wallpaper printed with monkeys and islands, had become a storage space. In front of my teenage posters of Zemfira and various rappers there were shelves, and in one corner I spotted an electric stove onto which Mama had piled old clothes. The small room had grown even smaller. It was no longer my room, or my home.

But in the room stood the same old folding couch. On a similar couch, in Double Game, Anna Alchuk and her partner for the photo series lay in the poses of seductresses reading potboilers. It's the kind of couch that hurts your back, and I slept on it when I stayed at our Ust-Ilimsk apartment.

Mama's apartment in Volzhsky suffered as she grew weaker. I could see that Mama was no longer able to take care of it as she once had. I saw the yellow grime on the washable wallpaper in the kitchen and the accumulating postcards tucked into the wooden frame of a small amber landscape. Mama kept her pragmatic approach to space, but as she grew weak she became sentimental. On the walls hung a watercolor painted by Mama's childhood friend, a postcard from me, and a mass of pictures, calendars, and valentines that I would have considered trash.

Dying, a woman slams space shut, deadens it. Everything around becomes lifeless, the small apartment begins to smell of something sour.

I went there seven months after Mama's death and didn't recognize the place. I asked Andrei for permission to take the striped cotton kitchen towels from the wardrobe, towels Grandma had sewn for Mama. The towels were basically new. Grandma had made them from a single piece of fabric, and along their edges I saw neat machine stitching. She had a foot-pedal sewing machine, on which she and my mother sewed my New Year's outfits, covers for armchairs, and kitchen towels, and hemmed pants and skirts bought at the market. Mama had brought the towels from Siberia along with the rest of her household things, from the amber landscape to the washing machine she'd bought on credit in the early aughts. The tech store Eldorado had just arrived in Ust-Ilimsk, and she bought a washing machine and a CD player for me.

A woman is a space.

IV

Even before her death I struggled with the purchase of a black cotton dress for the cremation. On funeral home websites I browsed through clothes intended for old ladies: tasteless, lacy and ornate, the color of jasmine and unripe apricots. None of these dresses would work, since Mama had asked to be buried in black.

The colorful, flowery housecoat-dresses, which first my great-grandmother Olga wore, and then, nearing fifty, my grandmother Valentina started wearing too, had always repulsed my mother. I understood how she felt. What made them gaudy was that the women picked out red-blue, chintzy, belted housecoats, then called them dresses. They bought these housecoats for going out and for the house. The ones for going out were more expensive and busier; for home they chose smaller patterns and cheaper material. When the fabric wore out, they cut them into rags for household chores, and snipped off the buttons to keep in tin candy boxes. Later, these colorful buttons came in handy for me in home economics classes; they were blue, mother-of-pearl, and black, always the same size, and a little worn around the edges, like old plastic teeth.

Thanks to a lecture by the anthropologist Svetlana Adonyeva I discovered that the appeal of colorful housecoats inheres in their echo of village life and dress. In this way, women from the villages found an analogue for their village clothes in the new circumstances of urban life. These dresses didn't appear ridiculous to them, like they did to Mama and me, who'd lived our entire lives in the city. But as she approached forty, Mama began to change. I didn't notice it right away, only when I was going through her things after her death. I upended the entire wardrobe and among her clothes I found T-shirts with color schemes vaguely reminiscent of my grandmother's housecoats. Mama's scarves, which she'd used to cover her head during chemo, had a light blue floral pattern. How strange, I thought then. Why did my mother, who when she was young would only consider wearing little black dresses or marsh-colored chiffon slacks paired with black blouses, suddenly turn to blue forget-me-nots and violet stripes? By forty, will I also abandon all my normcore, Levi's, and plain T-shirts, trading them in for shirts with floral patterns and belted housecoats?

I knew that old people traditionally put together funeral bundles for themselves. Usually, a special place in a chest of drawers was designated for this purpose, a place to store the money for the funeral and the clothes in which to dress the future departed. Grandmother Anna kept cuttings of old wallpaper: she insisted that her coffin be covered in kitchen wallpaper, so she'd be at home in it. Mama hadn't been able to put together her bundle. She knew that death was inevitable; she said, "I know my disease," but lived as though death would never come. She lived as though her life would never end, and putting together her funeral bundle fell to me. Two weeks before her death I already knew that the dress I needed wouldn't be found at a funeral home, so I asked my friend Zhenya, a seamstress, to make a dress for my mother. A black dress, knee-length, height 170 cm., size 46. Zhenya brought the dress a few days later. She had made a plain black headscarf to go with it. She said that women's dress sets for funerals always come with headscarves. I opened the canvas bag that held Mama's dress: it was black, simple, with a deep opening in the back, to make it easy to pull onto a stiffened body. It looked a bit like a modest kimono, and I even wanted to try it on. But I knew you couldn't do that, try on a dead woman's dress—it's bad luck. Even if she's only a soon-to-be dead woman.

I offered to pay Zhenya for her work, but she refused, saying that in these situations everyone pitches in however they can.

I passed the dress on to the funeral agent. We hadn't taken into account the fact that they don't put people in a coffin bare-legged. How were we supposed to know that? And in any case why did we have to think about it, if in our society all the procedures of death aren't passed down from old women to young ones, but instead fall into the purview of funeral homes? Meanwhile, mentioning or discussing death and funeral rites is always inappropriate and sometimes even offensive.

At the funeral home, I was also forced to buy a pair of matronly ribbed brown tights, for which Mama would have never forgiven me. "And the shift," the funeral agent asked me, "did you bring a shift?" If I had known that she needed a shift, I would have bought a pretty one for her ahead of time. But there weren't many options at the home, and so beneath the prim black dress her body was dressed in a bluish cotton hospital gown. I also had to buy underwear from the home. It was probably the simplest jersey underwear they had.

I lived with Mama's ashes for two months. All around me was the empty time of waiting. I put her favorite white chrysanthemums by the urn and stroked the cold metal. She didn't visit me and I didn't dream of her. She was an empty object, a ritual object.

It seemed that everything around me was hollow, like a white eggshell. So that the world would not appear so empty and meaningless, and so that Mama's death would not seem unremarkable and quotidian, at the end of forty days I held a wake: I made a private event on Facebook and invited everyone with whom I wanted to share my emptiness.

They all came and brought flowers, food; they offered me their condolences, and I thought that the house, filling with women, was gathering bodily strength and life. And I was filling up too, with gratitude and people's concern. In some sense I had reimagined the format of the wake: it was a quiet party with wine, flowers, hummus, and conversations about death, dying, and grief. I read poems about Mama. I was filling up and finally felt sorrow. It was probably precisely then that I understood the point of funeral rituals. There's a need for other people to be involved in the business of burial. The community shows up when there's a death. I had activated the mechanism of care.

Grief is a complicated thing. It's impossible without the presence of others, and death is above all a communal event. Mama barely had a community. The people who came to bid farewell to her coffin were Andrei, Sergei Mikhailovich, a friend of hers, and the friend's daughter. A final farewell only has a point if a community participates. Having invited thirty-odd women to my home, I understood the use of other people's presence when one is living through an experience of death. In a sense, the emptiness I was living through in my Moscow apartment was the calm before another event—the real funeral. But I didn't know that. I was like a machine that does whatever is necessary.

I couldn't just slap together another cardboard box for Mama's ashes. I was taking her home, she had to travel in something that looked worthy of the journey. I asked my friend Sonya, a carpenter, to make a wooden box of 30 by 30 centimeters. She made a tidy box with a fastening lid and a movable metal handle. Simple and unostentatious. It was heavy and a bit overlarge. So I padded the urn with the clothes that I was bringing on the two-week trip, and clicked it shut.

Then I had to figure out a bag. The box didn't fit into any of the bags I owned. And Aeroflot, the airline I was flying to Novosibirsk, allowed the transport of ashes only as checked luggage. I needed a sturdy, spacious bag, so I went to wander around the shops.

I had no idea where people bought luggage, but I didn't have much time left. I had to find something quickly. I looked in a few familiar stores but didn't see a suitable bag in any of them. Despairing of finding anything, I went into the Benetton on Tverskaya Street.

At Benetton, I skipped the women's section out of habit and looked into the men's. As usual, there were cute woolen sweaters and beautiful light overcoats on display. It was April, and they had already put out the spring collection. Among everything else, I noticed a large, bright orange, nearly carrot-colored backpack with black-and-white stripes. I dove toward it madly, afraid someone would grab it out of my hands. The backpack was enormous; it could easily be worn as a shoulder bag, and it had width adjustors at the top. It occurred to me that when I had to take the urn as a carry-on, I could shrink the backpack down to the necessary size. I studied the backpack like a treasure and genuinely didn't understand what it was doing at Benetton. Were such enormous, unwieldy things really the style now?

At the register I handed the bag to a young salesclerk in a little gray blazer and blue tie. The clerk was very tall, but had a quiet voice—he said something to me that I couldn't make out. I asked him to repeat himself, and understanding that I hadn't heard, he said, a bit more loudly, "What sport do you play?" I didn't understand right away why he thought I did sports. I looked at him in confusion. The clerk lifted the bag and said, "You're buying this, right?" "Yes, I am," I said. Then the clerk said that the bag was a sports equipment bag, usually hockey players bought it. I felt totally lost. Why were athletes shopping at a clothing store when there were sports specialty stores everywhere? And in addition to everything else I understood that the bag wasn't as practical as it seemed. It just worked perfectly for me because of its size, nothing else about it really concerned me.

I replied that I didn't do any sports. I had huge shadows under my eyes from insomnia, and the color of my complexion gave me away as a heavy smoker. One quick glance at me should have been enough to realize that I was no kind of athlete, just another Muscovite with an eight-hour office workday and bad habits. Pausing and running through all this in my mind, I answered truthfully that I needed the bag to transport ashes on a plane. It seemed like the guy didn't understand what I meant, or didn't want to understand. He kept smiling and nodding at me in a friendly way. After my response he waited for the receipt, handed it to me, and thanked me for my purchase.

Ever since I was a very small child I slept in a room of my own. Constructing a nursery in a two-room apartment in a Khrushchev-era apartment block is a difficult and irrational undertaking. But as soon as I turned one, my parents removed the spindles from one side of my wooden crib so I could climb in and out by myself, got rid of their large bed, and began sleeping on the fold-out couch in the room that served as both living room and bedroom.

Mama bathed me every night, and after my bath she carried me to bed wrapped in a worn pink terry-cloth towel. The towel was covered in snags. It had a picture of a large tiger lily, which with time and frequent washing had become a large brown spot.

Evenings after my bath, Mama hung the towel on one of the sides of the crib to dry, put me to bed, kissed me, wished me good night, and went to the other room to watch television or smoke in the kitchen.

I lay sleepless in the dark and listened to the house. I heard the mysterious ticking of the clock in the next room and Mama's regular footsteps; she didn't wear slippers, and I could hear her feet sticking to the linoleum when she stepped on the floor. I knew that besides her and me there was something else in the house that only I could see. I lay there with my eyes open, and thought that the wooden crib on its wheels was a large drawer keeping me safe from whatever it was. With my eyes closed I listened and heard how someone walked around my crib, standing there silently and watching me in the dark. I fell asleep to the sounds of this presence and of Mama's footsteps.

The minute during which Mama carried me into my dark room was a minute of closeness and weightless warmth. I became part of my mother's body, because her arms held me close to her shoulders, breasts, stomach. I don't remember the smell, but I remember a meager little sorrow inside me because this nearness would soon end. The sorrow lasted through the sweltering bliss of the presence of my mother's body beside me. She carried me, and I couldn't feel my own weight, as though she were deep water, rocking me in her body.

I was unable to remember this feeling for a long time; I knew it was there somewhere, deep within me, but it didn't want to be with me, because it was difficult for me to believe in the very possibility of motherly closeness, in the very possibility of her acknowledging my presence here, in this world.

A year and a half after Mama's death, my wife and I were bathing in the sea, and jumping up, I grasped her tanned body with my legs and threw my arms around her neck. Alina picked me up easily and carried me. Closing my eyes, I encountered the water; it touched me as though I were part of it, the thinking part. Light pounded against my eyelids. Alina carried me in her arms, and I grew smaller and smaller, returning to a place where closeness was possible, where the body is wide open to being present. Alina held me in her arms, and I was there.

Then we competed to see who could stay underwater the longest. I floated in the fetal position, and Alina kept her hand on my back to hold me in the water for the longest possible time. I could feel her large, powerful hand, which covered half my back and was capable of pulling me from the water at any moment. I floated like a little bobber, and Alina held me. I feared neither the sea nor the possibility of suffocating. There was enough air for twenty or thirty seconds or longer. Surfacing, I was overjoyed by my endurance, but my head spun from a lack of oxygen.

It was August, the water bloomed, and we parted thin filaments of seaweed to wade into it. But weeds still got into the top and bottom of Alina's bathing suit, and my one-piece suit turned green inside and began to smell like fish. The sun lasted in the murky green water and in droplets caught in my lashes. Time lasted like the sun.

When I look at my wife's body, it enchants me. It's so strong and golden, it glows in space, it's like bread or a stone, I love it. I look at her like she is a complex, rich landscape. I'm stunned by the life in her. I stroke her arms and her asymmetrical eyes; the lid of her right eye is slightly lowered, which makes it seem like the right eye is calmer than the left, and sometimes it looks a little sly. I stroke her eyes and touch her closed eyelids with my lips. I tell her that I love her eyes. And she tells me that she looks at me with those eyes. She says that she sees me with those eyes, and I feel that warm, wide gaze that gathers me into itself as though I were a tiny insect and her gaze a drop of oozing warm honey.

Woman and space cannot be separated. When a woman dies, space collapses and dies like a plucked flower. The presence of a woman, even a dead woman, fills space with meaning and body. A day before my departure for Siberia something odd happened. Everything got jumbled, tense, and gave rise to an awkward situation. Lera was leaving the house to get cigarettes, and in the doorway she ran into a cop, who shouldered her out of the way and darted inside. As I learned later, there was no one in the house at all right then except the landlord's young son. The landlord and his family had been fighting for their home for twenty years, and the cop's visit meant that the fight was ongoing. Back when we were moving in, the landlord had strictly forbidden me to let cops or other municipal authorities into the house. Now the landlord was enraged; he screamed at me over the phone that we'd betrayed him. The following day, his wife insisted that we move, and on the day of my flight I was frantically searching for new housing. When I left, I knew that I would not return to the apartment on Mir Avenue again. That was how it curled up on itself, the space in which I'd lived for more than a year and where I had planned to live for a long time to come.

I did go back to that apartment one last time to pick up my books and other things. The place had been scrubbed until it shone and was awaiting new tenants, and my belongings were heaped under a table. Among books and socks I found a black-and-white photograph. In the photo, Mama sits on a camping mat in denim shorts and reaches for an enamel bucket. In the bucket, I assume, writhes a still-living fish; after my father caught a fish, Mama would clean and gut it in order to make ukha. Between her legs sits a little girl with a round head and long tousled hair gathered into a braid at the top of her head. I'm about five, I'm looking at the camera and smiling. In the photo, Mama and I are inseparable from each other, like a two-headed being. Our closeness is inexplicable, it's corporeal. As though the umbilical cord hasn't yet been snipped, as though I am her.

Mama had a crappy laptop that I bought for her in my second year at the Literature Institute. Mama, who'd worked at a factory her entire life, struggled with technology. TVs and push-button mobile phones were easy enough, but going online made her deeply anxious. Her computer, like the computers of many people her age, barely worked; it was virus-ridden and the modem kept breaking down. But she used it to go on Odnoklassniki, and, as I understood later, to check the weather. A year before her death I also made a profile on Odnoklassniki, to keep in touch with her in some way other than just the phone. Her phone calls irritated me, while messages that I could respond to at will suited me perfectly. Our correspondence was limited to brief formalities: she would ask me how I was doing, and I would respond that everything was fine. I often opened her profile and looked at her photos. Mama had uploaded many similar pictures from the seaside. There she was standing in water up to her knees, wearing a dark blue bathing suit with mother-of-pearl spots, there she was on the embankment, resting her arm on the railing. There were photos of her spending New Year's Eve with a friend, wearing a goofy red tinsel wig. There were photos in which she sat at a table at a bar. The Mama in these photos didn't resemble the Mama I knew. This was a middle-aged woman; I could see the wrinkles on her browned skin, she was dressed in cheap blouses and jeans. This image in no way accorded with the image of the mother I adored, feared, and hated. I adored a young and beautiful mother, cold and cruel. In the photos I saw a stranger prematurely aged by drinking and excruciatingly hard work. There were also collages made in special apps, about which I had mixed feelings. Mama had attached her face to the bodies of fantasy women: her face on the body of an elegant film noir heroine standing next to a bloated American car, and on the body of a woman who was also a flaming butterfly. I looked at these collages and the distance between me and my mother grew, filling with sadness and regret. My last message to Mama went unread. It was sent in the early days of January, when she wasn't getting up any longer.

I sat down in the kitchen and opened Odnoklassniki. It was important to me that Mama's funeral be attended by everyone who knew and remembered her. I went through the list of her friends on the website and sent the same message to everyone whose location was marked as Ust-Ilimsk: "Hello, my name is Oksana, I'm Angella Vasyakina's daughter. My mother will be buried on April 20. We're meeting at 2:00 p.m. on the Bratsk highway, by the central bus station. Please let me know whether you have a car: if you don’t have one, how many people are coming, if you do have one, how many spots you have. The wake will be held in New Town at the Burevestnik café. My phone number is 89689462600.”

Among Mama’s friends I found people whose faces I had forgotten, but whose names and surnames I still remembered. There were also people I didn’t know at all, and I decided they were most likely her co-workers from the factory. Some wrote right away that they would come, while other messages remain unread to this day. Much later I found out that many people on Mama’s friend list have been dead for a long time.

We planned the funeral for April 20 because it was a Saturday, when the largest number of people could make it. My aunt wrote to me that Mama’s spot at the cemetery had been confirmed, and the men in the family watched a YouTube video about burying an urn containing ashes. It turned out that an urn didn’t require a deep, two-meter hole, like a body did. A shallow niche in the earth would suffice. It was still winter in Ust-Ilimsk, and the men went to the cemetery to gouge the frozen ground with shovels and picks.

Having sent the last message, I shut the laptop, and it suddenly dawned on me that I would have to say goodbye to Mama’s ashes. We had lived together for about two months, and the urn had become part of my household and interior landscape. I often addressed it with looks and words. I talked to it. I stroked it, and sometimes I opened it, to be nearer to the capsule and to look at the dusting of ashes that covered it. At the bottom of the urn still laid a piece of paper with our surname and her initials, I couldn’t bring myself to throw it out. It was also covered in a thin sprinkling of ashes, it was part of this heavy object.

I packed for a long trip: several pairs of socks, underwear (a few of which I’d bought in Volzhsky after the farewell to Mama), jeans, T-shirts, and a pair of linen pants and a shirt. I had completely forgotten what April in Siberia is like. In Moscow the sun shone warmly and there hadn't been snow on the ground all winter; at night the snow-plows cleared it away and in the morning the migrant cleaners did. By April I was going around in a thin wool coat and light pants with no tights underneath. For some reason I assumed that Siberia would be similarly warm and free of snow. Into the carrot-colored bag, along-side my clothes, I put the box with Mama's urn. I got dressed, sat down as customary before the trip, and said: all right, Mama, we're going to Siberia. I felt like crying. I was traveling to bury my mother and bringing her with me. I felt like crying because of the uncertainty. Following some long, unpleasant conversations with the landlord's family I had found a new apartment through Facebook, and I knew that this was my last day of being here, in this lived-in, comfortable, familiar spot. My mother had died and I had become an orphan, and now I didn't even have a place of my own. There was nowhere for me to come back to.

In the subway, without taking off the backpack, I sat down on a bench and waited for the train. The corner of the urn case dug into my back, but I endured it. I was thinking that I needed the pain and discomfort, because I was on an important ritual journey, which is always marked by suffering.

I already knew that Aeroflot transported urns containing human ashes in the cargo hold, along with oversized cargo. At the airport I went to the check-in counter and handed over my passport. Without even looking at me, the woman began to search for my information in the database. I had to tell her about my luggage, and, clearing my throat, I said that I was traveling with ashes. The woman still didn't look at me. I repeated my statement and started opening my blue plastic folder with sweating hands. I told her I could show her all the necessary documents. She finally looked at me, said that she didn't need to see any documents, and handed me a tag for oversize luggage. She ordered me to put the bag in the hoist and to come back to her.

I went in horror to the iron hoist. I had to leave Mama unattended. In the hoist stood a covered bulky mountain bike and an enormous animal carrier. There was no movement in the carrier. I knew that animals get sedated for flights, so they'll sleep, and I felt unbearably sorry for this large invisible dog. It was sleeping and didn't know that it would travel in the cold cargo hold. What if it woke ahead of schedule? The noise, the cold, closeness, darkness—that's what the dog will see, I thought, and it'll bark in helplessness and desperation. But no one will hear. Will the dog survive the flight? Yet I was somewhat calmed by the thought that Mama wouldn't fly alone, but with a whole sleeping dog. I lowered the carrot-colored bag to the floor behind the carrier and whispered into the emptiness that everything would be fine and we would see each other again soon.

I was surprised by the airline worker's credulity. After my experience in Volgograd, where Mama and I, along with our documents, had been palpated and practically cross-examined, I expected that in Moscow I would be thoroughly interrogated. After all, I could have been carrying explosives, drugs, you name it. Though the certificate of non-inclusion from the Volgograd crematorium looked fake, it did have an official stamp and a signature. It confirmed that the urn contained no alien substances or objects. How strange, I thought, that drug dealers and terrorists haven't used this method to transport things. Though maybe they do use it, and I just don't know.

Annie Leibovitz photographs the sick, then dead, body of Susan Sontag, and then painstakingly captures the death of her own father. Ron Mueck makes a silicone sculpture of his father's dead body and adds hair that is neither artificial nor someone else's, but his own. Daphne Todd paints a portrait of her dead mother.

The picture of Sontag dead is repulsively confined; it's a narrow, horizontal photograph, its composition similar to Holbein's dead Christ. There's no room to breathe. It's dark and constricts the gaze on every side. It's insufficient, uncomfortable. This is also because the format forces us to look beyond the borders of the photo. Everything around serves to distract us from the terrible event: death. It's impossible to see a beloved body dead and preserve it in your memory. To connect with it. The world will always tremble and live on, distracting you from the most important thing—the dark rectangle of loss. Mueck creates an object, and in order to fix our attention on the fragility of the dead body, doesn't clothe the sculpture. His father lies naked and dead, reduced to two-thirds of his actual size. Mueck feared his father, who always seemed to him to be a severe and inflexible person; his death provided the possibility of taming him. Of making his father his, of no longer fearing him. But all that aside, working with a dead body always implies shifts in scale. We only need to adjust the size of an object to demonstrate the power we wield over it. We have the ability to control both body and memory, because we are living.

Todd's work, though extremely realistic, is painted in light shades. There's no place in it for the color black. Even her mother's dropped jaw bares not the black hole of unbeing, but a light brown space. The old woman's whitish eyes are open, and everyone can see the light, thin, sunken breast. This is death in old age and in prosperity. But here, too, we find a diminishment of scale: in a photo on the internet I can see Todd herself in front of her painting. The old woman's head is half the size of the living daughter's head. The dead hands are elongated by the perspective. Like dry branches they've fallen onto the white sheet. The depiction of Daphne Todd's mother's death is an emblem of ideal death. In deep, fortunate old age, when all control, including control over the image of your dead body, passes to your loved ones.

Why did they do this? Why am I doing this—steadily describing the dying and the dead body of my own mother? There's a lot of pain in this, along with an attempt to understand, to write out an experience. But there's also a note of vanity: to go on living is to retain control over your own body. And over the bodies of your departed loved ones. I'm finally taking for myself that which belonged to me, but wasn't available to me until after her death—her body. And I'm displaying it for everyone to see, like a trophy. Like a wound sustained in a long, difficult war. I have the right.

Leibovitz photographs her sleeping (or dead?) father. She photographs him as though she were looking at him very closely. Her father's face is calm. His head lies on a floral-patterned pillow. On his cheeks are the dark spots of old age; he's all dried up, like a sun-bleached branch, and very small, like all dead people. The photograph is open to viewers. It doesn't hurt me to look at it, and I don't feel constrained, though I know that death drowses there. Then I look at another photograph—in a large, well-lit room, its walls hung with photos and landscapes, stands a large hospital cot. It's like a heavy block of marble, glowing. The cot is empty. Behind it, in an armchair, someone sits covering their face with a hand, crying or just thinking about something. The photograph is called *My Parents' Living Room*. In a third photograph there's a rectangular hole framed with broad wooden boards. And next to the hole, a mound of damp earth and dry earth, mixed together.

These three photographs are part of the larger A Photographer's Life series. Leibovitz took pictures of her elderly parents, her sisters, and other people close to her. And also of death and its markers. They're very peaceful photographs. If you were to imagine a sound issuing from them, it would be a muted radio broadcast and the ringing of a small spoon against a plate, drowning in white noise. Life is happening there.

I flew knowing that somewhere in the cargo hold a dog was sleeping, and next to it lay the bag that held Mama's urn. Had the cargo workers been sufficiently careful with the bag? What if they'd tossed it into a pile of other luggage? What if Mama's urn had been dented? Or what if the change in pressure made the soldered tin lid with the cremation serial number pop off? The whole compartment would be covered in Mama's ashes. What was I supposed to do then? What would the people who work for Aeroflot do then?

Some things can be renewed or returned, but some things are unique. There's no other urn of Mama's ashes anywhere, and what's worse is there's no other Mama, and this urn is the final trace and remainder of her. What would happen if I lost even that? Half a year later, due to the carelessness of Aeroflot workers, some cats would perish in a cargo hold. They were simply crushed by the rest of the luggage. How did the owners of those animals feel?

I flew staring in front of me. I imagined the dog waking up because something was tickling its nose, and that something was Mama's ashes. The dog would sneeze. Instantaneously, all the other objects in the cargo hold—the mountain bike, the double bass, everything else—would be covered in fine gray-white dust, all that was left of the body of my mother. My jaw began to hurt, and I caught myself grinding my teeth. I was tense with fear.

The evening flight from Moscow to Novosibirsk ends in your landing, completely wrecked, at dawn. It was about five in the morning in Novosibirsk and getting light; my head hurt and I wanted to sleep. I got off the plane quickly and ran to the baggage carousel. One after the other, bags appeared on the carousel—a black sports bag, a huge fabric suitcase, a little suitcase with a pink pony and a rainbow, a checkered Chinese bag . . . I wasn't sure where the oversize luggage would be returned. I felt suffocated by panic, I frantically scanned the hall, I couldn't spot a single person who worked for the airport. Twenty minutes in, the gray animal carrier showed up, jostling now and then as it traveled around the carousel. The dog inside was still asleep. Or it was already dead, because its heart had burst after all that barking and panic. A man came up to the carousel, caught the carrier by its handle, and yanked it off the conveyor. He opened the carrier and took out a tiny bichon. For an instant I forgot about Mama. She hadn't been accompanied by a majestic beast with a huge body and steady breath, but by a quiet, nervous, cream-colored bichon. The little dog went on sleeping. The man passed it to the woman who was with him, quickly took the carrier apart, and taped its parts together.

Finally, the carrot-colored backpack appeared on the carousel. The bag had been overturned in transit; it was trailing the sleeve of my green linen shirt. This meant that it had been shaken, thrown, its zipper had popped open. I grabbed the bag and with shaking hands unzipped it the rest of the way. Everything inside was turned upside down—my underwear, socks, and jeans lay mixed up with toothpaste and books, and the box with Mama's ashes was open. I felt cold and pained. I reached out my hand and lifted open the lid of the box. The urn lay in its place; it had been saved by the fact that the box was large and I'd stuffed my clothes around the urn so it wouldn't roll around and knock against the wood. But I saw a small dent in its lid. I lifted it. Inside the urn lay a capsule wrapped in a small cotton sack; I had foreseen turbulence and careless handling, so I'd swaddled the capsule in a bag. Everything was in order. The capsule hadn't opened or cracked, it hadn't burst. It lay quietly inside the urn.

A farewell is always a slow and hollow procedure. When my father was buried, it was all very long and dreary. First everyone went into the reception hall at the morgue and wandered around the coffin. Then a lazy priest showed up, gray trousers with a metallic sheen showing beneath the hem of his cassock. The priest brought a stopwatch, which he used to time the prayers and the rhythm of the ritual. He approached my father's body and efficiently, with an audible crunch, bent the dead hands in order to insert a candle between them. As he prayed he kept looking at the stopwatch with one shifty eye, while I stared first at the priest and then at the old, scuffed sideboard in which folders of papers sat in stacks. By the sideboard, right on the floor, lay a large, eggplant-colored closed coffin. Interesting, I thought. I wonder whether there's a corpse in there. A woman who worked at the morgue said that we'd paid for double time, so we could spend an entire hour in the reception hall. So everyone milled around, saying farewell, chatting. They came and touched the shoulder and the arm of my grandmother, my father's mother. She howled and moaned. When the priest wrapped up, with another crunch he unbent my father's hands, took his work things out of the coffin—the crosses, the candles—and removed the cardboard icon from my father's hands and brought it to my grandmother. He said that she should keep it. The following morning she passed the icon on to me. It depicted the Mother of God with the baby Jesus. I later put it in my passport, and from there moved it to one of my books. By then it was tattered and bent, and once I had even washed it, because it had fallen out of my passport into the pocket of my jeans.

When our time ran out, the morgue worker asked us to hurry. Then the men rolled the bier toward the doors and carried out the coffin that held my father's body. They carried him out feet-first, so the mourners could see that my father's skull had been sloppily sutured shut, from ear to ear, with thick black thread. I had darned pantyhose with that kind of seam as a child, when Mama told me that I had to be an independent girl. I made large stitches, always using the same thick black thread, no matter the color of the hose—dark blue or pink. This rough thread was the only kind that fit the needle with the wide eye, so that's what I used. Everyone saw this horrible bloodless seam, and my grandmother's moans became even louder and more drawn out.

They sat me in the hearse, so that I, the daughter, could accompany my father's coffin. It was early fall, and unbearably stuffy in Astrakhan. The ride dragged on, and when we drove over the long bridge above the Volga, I felt someone's gaze on me. It was the gaze of the young mortician. He was eyeing me up while I sat there sickened by the car that had absorbed the smell of corpses and by the closeness of my father's dead body.

At the cemetery everyone wandered around the coffin again, wandered in circles, and it all seemed like it would never end. Then they brought me to the coffin and ordered me to kiss my father.

I kissed his forehead through the thin cigarette paper printed with the text of a prayer for eternal rest. He didn't smell like anything, but I knew that the seam on his head was very close to me. In the course of the kiss I must have fallen away somehow; I don't know how much time I spent standing like that, bent over my father's body with my lips upon him. I thought a second or two had passed, but suddenly I felt heavy, strong hands pulling me away from the body. It was my father's friend Uncle Sasha, he was saying, "Enough, enough." Then they closed the coffin and began to nail it shut. Shamshad Abdullaev has a long, beautiful poem called "On the Side of the Stones"; in it the speaker looks at a collection of stones and says that he does not try to shake them because the dull thud would remind him of his departed father. The thudding of earth against the lid of the coffin really does sound like stones rubbing and falling against each other in a small space. I threw down a handful of earth and heard it, then again and again. The men went to work with their shovels, including the unctuous young mortician. I squatted by the grave and pushed earth into it, and dry dust, and small stones.

Then they wanted to put me and my grandmother back into the same reeking hearse in which we had transported my father's body, but my grandmother refused, so they put us into a little 1999 Lada and drove us to the wake.

This extended farewell was meant to let the living have some sort of experience after which they could say with certainty that the person who was supposed to have died had died. But the entire ritual, from beginning to end, was hollow.

When we were saying goodbye to Mama, the farewell was shorter and even more absurd. The funeral home offered to rent me the room for fifteen or thirty minutes. What's fifteen minutes for a farewell? I chose the half-hour period between 4:00 and 4:30 p.m. We arrived fifteen minutes early, and Andrei stayed in the courtyard while I went to take care of the logistics. I walked into the gallery from which one enters the reception halls; by each entrance there was a plastic case on a stand, to hold a sign with the name of the deceased. All the signs were turned away from the main entrance, and at the far end of the gallery some guys from the funeral brigade were hanging out: they were tall, nearly two meters, and dressed in black livery and stiff woolen hats, like papakhas, with nonspecific red coats of arms. They were laughing uproariously. One told another to get fucked. Loudest of all was a large man wearing the longest frock coat. The buttons on his coat weren't steel, like everyone else's, but gold. Their laughter and rude jokes echoed around the gallery; they thought they were completely alone. I approached the men quietly and addressed the one in charge, saying that we had a farewell booked for Angella Vasyakina at 4:00 p.m. The man immediately grew serious, took off his hat and bowed to me, introducing himself as the head of the funeral brigade. I think his name was Eduard. Eduard was enormous. He asked me to follow him. By the second room he stopped and turned the sign to face out. Mama's name was on the sign. He went into the room first and switched on the light, and as the light came on the speakers began automatically issuing plasticky music, vaguely reminiscent of "The Lonely Shepherd," and I thought that I shouldn't have agreed to musical accompaniment. The music was empty and vulgar, as though produced by a cheap children's piano. I suddenly felt ashamed because of it.

Eduard led me to my mother’s coffin and said brightly that the sooner we started, the sooner we’d end. I nodded and joked that there was no reason to hurry now. He hemmed approvingly, and took off the coffin’s lid; I noticed that he was using special reusable latches, which functioned like jacks. He took them from the upper and the lower parts of the coffin and put them in the pocket of his uniform. Then he demonstratively loosened the bindings holding Mama’s arms and legs, complaining that relatives often didn’t trust the brigade. He leaned the lid of the coffin against the wall by the window. And he asked me to call him when we were done.

I called Andrei, Mama’s two friends, and Mikhail Sergeyvich. They came in and stood at a distance. The men took off their hats, and Andrei went down on his knees by Mama’s head and, cupping her cheek, touched his forehead to her and started to cry. I stood and waited. When everyone had said goodbye, I called Eduard, who came in and said that he and the brigade would now shut the coffin and carry it to the car, while we, the relatives, ought to follow them to accompany the deceased. He took the clinking latches from his pocket, deftly attached them to the lid, and summoned his colleagues. The men lifted the light-colored coffin easily and carried it to the exit, while we walked behind them. The hearse waited about five meters from the entrance. The men quickly put the coffin on the rails of the hearse and got in at the sides. Eduard got into the car last and said something to me. When I raised my head, I saw that he was holding a large, silvery insulated packet, shaking it as though he were showing off an impressive catch of fish or a fatty shashlik at a picnic. I looked at him questioningly. He said quietly, but clearly, that these were the organs, they were taking them too. I nodded at Eduard, and he got out of the passenger section and sat next to the driver. The men closed the doors and the car began to slowly ascend the hill toward the exit of the mortuary courtyard, then accelerated and disappeared.

That was the farewell. And it made for an empty feeling.

But I was most concerned about the organs. What would they do with them? Would they really dump them onto the snow-white coverlet? Or was the bag specifically for incineration, and would it be placed at her feet? All of this made me uneasy.

I told Andrei that he had done everything a partner could do—he had been by the side of the dying woman.

A dead, sick, helpless mother is not like a forceful, frightening, young mother. These two images wouldn't fit together in my mind for a long time. I'd buried a light, lifeless body—ravaged, old, dead. But within me my mother remained a frightening, difficult figure. In my dreams she appeared young. In the space of a dream she was so near, and I felt agitated. But her closeness was also torturous, because in my dreams she never looked at me, only somewhere above my shoulder, as if there, in that other place, there was something warm and significant. In dreams I often shouted at my mother, grabbed her by the shirtfront and shook her, and then fell down powerlessly and woke up in tears. My mother didn't hear me and wouldn't look at me. In one of my most recent dreams, her dark dead body came home. It was like the relics of a saint, dressed in rich, golden robes. It was for some reason very tall, several orders of magnitude taller than me. And also it was blind. I studied this dark body and knew that it was my mother's. The blind body sailed past me in its finery and disappeared through the window.

The image of the difficult mother won't let me rest. A difficult mother is the First Cause of the creative impulse and of writing. The mother is the cause and the body of language, as I understand her. A weak, dying mother is frightening because she's approaching death and living through her dying. A difficult, dead mother is even more difficult and more frightening. She takes up residence inside you as a dark spot and awaits your writing. Her death is impossible.

Cells—Spinners—Spiders

For Galina Rymbu

0

Writing about writing was always incomprehensible to me, impenetrable. I didn't know how to join one act to the other, and I didn't know how to put into practice what I wrote and what I read in the writing of others. It's difficult to find the "energy of connection" in the gap between these practices, to connect them or impose one over the other. But I believe that this energy does exist somewhere, just as there are metaphors and liminal genres that function precisely at the intersection of theory and practice. I think that we should look for this energy in places that aren't writing at all. We should look, for example, to art and myth.

1

I've long been fascinated by the similarities between a community of writers and a community of spinners, or weavers. Women who spin and weave work within an unhierarchical collective; they weave the fabric of text and of culture. And a variety of poetics is precisely that colorful, inimitable pattern in the fabric. We need only think of the ancient Romans, who called a text a textile, or the "word-weaving" of medieval Slavic literature. But who is the weaving woman and is she really not alone at her work? Here we encounter right away the myth of Arachne, the woman who competed with Athena, patron of the art of war and of crafts. The connection between war and craft is interesting in its own right, since these realms include not only the making of weapons but also such peaceful tasks as making pottery and, of course, weaving (master craftspeople decorated their creations with the depictions of the heroic war deeds of gods and men). Does this mean that every craft falls within Athena's purview, that they are all inseparable from war and violence? So it seems.

Penelope, with her cloistered waiting for Odysseus and her manipulation of the shroud woven over the course of a day. Philomela, who after losing her tongue reached her sister through depicting her story in a tapestry, and thus saved herself from imprisonment. And, of course, Arachne, the spinner from Hypaepa. Ovid writes that she came from a poor family, grew up without a mother, and used her craft to win over everyone around her; even nymphs flocked to see her flawless creations. Ovid notes that her craft was certainly the craft of a student of Athena. Proud of her professionalism, Arachne issues a challenge to the goddess, and Athena accepts the challenge, but loses. Here one finds not only the motif of the student becoming greater than the teacher, but also the attempt to destroy the existing hierarchy. Arachne, Philomela, and Penelope can be understood primarily as women who resist the order into which they've been placed.

Athena isn't just a patron of crafts, and she isn't exactly a woman. Athena is a symbol of the glory of war; she was born without a woman involved, springing from the head of Zeus, and she's also considered a virgin. So Athena assumes masculine positions because she essentially isn't a woman, but an emanation of the world of men. The contest between a woman and a masculine deity (even taking into account the former's objective victory) ends in the woman's defeat: Athena turns her opponent into a spider.

And it's a spider that became the symbol of the mother's house in the works of Louise Bourgeois. We need only consider her series of installations called Cells, and her countless giant spiders. The spider here merges with the image of the mother, and the house with the image of a cell. The image of the mother-spider didn't come to Bourgeois from nowhere. Her family ran a small tapestry restoration workshop, and her mother had a notably difficult personality. Bourgeois recalls her mother working at a loom, covered in textile dust and surrounded by gigantic rolls of tapestries: her terrifying mother reminds the artist of mythical Arachne. The spider spins her barely visible, sticky, suffocating thread; the spiderweb is a metaphor for close, noxious relationships, hypercontrol concealed behind custody and care, and also hatred.

In the art of Louise Bourgeois the mother is inseparable from the house-cell—a closed, impenetrable space. I think of her claustrophobic works that use dusty bobbins of scarlet thread, which seem to echo the outside of a cell as well as its interior space, with threads stretching from corner to corner. This multitudinous squeezing, this suffocating wrapping, proves reminiscent of a spiderweb. Heidegger says language is a house of being; Žižek talks about the poetic torture-house of language. Bourgeois says something else: a house is a cell.

In a series of works called Proto, the artist and poetess Anna Alchuk makes visual poems out of repeating letters. Repetition—is that not the first principle of spinning, knitting, or weaving a web? Looking closely at Alchuk's works, you can see fantastic pictures woven from the letters of the Cyrillic alphabet. In her diary, Alchuk notes, "The Russian language is my fundamental treasure, my only luxury, but it's also my golden cage."

Bourgeois's house is undoubtedly the house of mute, endless torment. The house grows into the body of the artist's memory: take, for example, the motif that repeats in her pictures and sculptures—a naked female body with a little house foisted upon it in place of a head.

A house is a closed, opaque space in which the weaver's work proceeds. Penelope weaves on the second floor of her house, in a special room, Philomela in a hut in the woods, and Arachne's house figures in Ovid's *Metamorphoses*. Is the house the source of all weaving? Even Virginia Woolf's "room of one's own" is a space of loneliness, a space for the solitary work of the writer-weaver, to this day. The weaver isn't watched over by a father, but by a mother or older woman who transmits the craft, building a mechanism for interpreting experience through myth, fairy tale, and depiction. She is the senior weaver, the iron spider who constructs the space of the home as airless, cobwebbed with silence and secrecy, arranging objects in whatever order she deems logical, casting her shadow over the house. The shadow of salvific darkness. The darkness conceals the work of the weavers, keeps them at home. The work of the weavers serves the house and lives within it.

Isn't this why Arachne is so famous and so unafraid of challenging Athena—because her mother is dead, and her craft comes not from an older woman but from a masculine deity in female guise?

2

This is a good place to pause, to catch one's breath. To ask some questions: how can spinners and weavers, blanketed by the shadow of the older spider, go out into the light, join their many tapestries into one and show this work to the world? If weaving contains the potential for resistance, how does this relate to the experience of ancient weavers; does it mean that a song of war or violence can metamorphose into something else? Into something that doesn't fit into the dichotomy of "strike/strike back"? Into something that can offer many permeable options?

These questions weave hope.

Hope warms and cheers the heart.

*

I lay in my dark room. On my stomach, wearing only pajama pants. Mama sat next to me. A yellowish ray of light from the hall bisected the wall and shone on the little delicate flowers there. The old wallpaper in my room was kitchen wallpaper for some reason. At least, that's what light wallpaper with little flowers and a delicate, sparse green pattern was usually called. I lay on my stomach and looked at the light. I felt Mama's presence next to me. I smelled the scent of wood, and my body felt the warmth exuded by her body. Mama traced her hand, the cool pads of her fingers, over my hot back, quietly saying:

Rails, rails, ties, ties.
On and on the late train flies.
And from the last car falls the grain.

First she ran her hand down my spine to show the rails; for the ties, she moved her hand from side to side. The train was a light pressure. And the grain became occasional touches of her fingernails. She continued:

Here come the hens, pecking — and she tapped her nails against my back.
Here come the geese, nipping — a light pinch.
Here's the cleaner, he sweeps up — she stroked my back.
Puts back the table, puts back the chair — light slaps.
And sets the typewriter over there — a final tap.

Then she began to move her fingers over my back as though she were typing on a typewriter:

I bought my wife and little girl. Period.
Stockings with a pretty swirl. Period.
The stockings I bought my daughter will wear. Period.
And my wife will praise me and hold me dear. Period.

At the final period her tap was more precise.

I asked her to do it again. Then she began anew: *rails, rails, ties, ties . . .*

With each repetition she was less and less focused. The tenderness left her movements, she performed them somehow absently. The third time she said, enough, time to sleep.

Leaving, she touched my face with her lips, and then wedged the door shut with a sock, so it would hold. Then the yellow strip of light beneath the door disappeared, and I lay there and wondered who this strange cleaner could be. And I imagined the cheap, colorful stockings that he bought for his wife and daughter. If only his daughter went on to wear them, like the story said, maybe the second pair was too big, or too small, for the cleaner's wife?

Sometimes I ask my wife to stroke my back. I lie down on my stomach, and she strokes me, quietly touching her lips to my back, and then she turns her own back to me to go to sleep, and holding her I touch my lips to her browned skin and hold them there for a long time, to feel the closeness of her body. She responds to me, squeezing my hand with her large, sturdy hand. The light from the street is cold, and I see the tree swaying in the wind outside the window. This is how, in the dark, we fall asleep. First her, then me.

Mama, like many of the women who surrounded her, loved houseplants. In Siberia the botanical options were limited, and plants grew so-so in the absence of sunlight, in the cold, poor soil that these home gardeners gathered at their dacha plots. The flowers, or rather the cuttings, were supposed to be stolen; it was generally believed that otherwise they wouldn't take. It also wasn't done to steal them from hospitals or schools, because these flowers would have bad energy and bring misfortune and suffering to the home.

On school windowsills stood stinky stubby geraniums and wilting pale spider plants. But Mama had an entire prayer plant in our apartment. Though it was faded, as though sun-bleached, and put forth leaves rarely. When a little tube formed, promising to grow into a new leaf, I'd hang around and wait for it to open. The leaves sometimes wouldn't open for several months, and in my haste I tried to unroll them. I liked the prayer plant, its brown spots and bent stems. It was only later that I learned that the prayer plant has a way of shifting its leaves: it responds to the light and lowers them in the morning, rising up at night. That's why the maranta is called the prayer plant. But our prayer plant didn't move at all. There was no light in our house, and probably no warmth.

All flowers had their particular powers. And the most powerful flower of all was the foul-smelling bindweed waxflower. My mother got it from my grandmother, who'd left the apartment to us. The waxflower trailed its stiff leaves from a spot near the ceiling. Mama called it the death flower. It bloomed independently of the season, it didn't matter whether it was spring or fall. The flowers were strange, vaguely resembling baby feet. When they bloomed, the smell in the apartment became stifling, and Mama said that it was corpselike.

Mama believed that the waxflower bloomed when misfortune was coming to the house, and she supported her theory with facts. She said that during arguments the flower emitted a stronger odor. It feeds on bad energy, she said. She kept the flower, but she was afraid of it. And when I was in eighth grade, she asked me to take it to school and leave it there. So I did. Now I wonder how plants like these, the prayer plant and the waxflower, wind up in Siberia. Somebody has to take them there. Somebody brought them from the tropics and from Asia, and they adapted.

After we buried Mama, my aunt brought me over to a lush croton plant in her apartment and said that my mother had given it to her when she moved to Volzhsky. My aunt took a small pair of scissors and snipped a cutting for me. I brought it to Moscow and much later planted it. For a long time, the cutting didn't put forth roots, and when it finally it did, it took a year for it to adjust to the new soil and climate. A year after Mama's death it finally produced two small, crooked, atypical leaves. And then it shot up. I take better care of it than any of my other plants, and it surprises me more than any of them. This brave little plant flew with me in an airplane and drove a thousand kilometers down a Siberian highway. Then it moved from apartment to apartment. There's nothing about it that could connect it to Mama. Mama gave my aunt a very tiny plant. But the thought that this croton was born from Mama's plant comforts me. At some point I went to the flower market and bought a young waxflower. The woman working there told me that when the waxflower blooms, it smells like honey. I asked her if it didn't actually smell like a corpse, like Mama's waxflower, and she was a bit disconcerted by my question and said that different waxflowers can smell differently, but she'd never in her life encountered a waxflower that smelled like a corpse. Mama used to say that a corpse smells like something sweet.

I think about the fact that Mama died slowly, and I want to believe that she died like a large, heavy tree. One by one, tumors destroyed and poisoned parts of her body. Her body was like a complex tree that was perishing. I've seen such trees in the forest—studded all over with burls, gray, enormous. When I see these trees, I think of Mama. About her and her quiet mute dying and her endurance. It thrills me and horrifies me all at once.

I became interested in the story of Julia Kristeva's patient, the one she calls Helen. Helen suffered from recurrent bouts of depression and melancholia. Her recoveries from these difficult states were accompanied by intense fits of nymphomania, after which she'd again go down to the bottom of her grave—that's what she called the darkness into which she sank in her depressive episodes. I read Helen's story and discovered a kinship with her. Kristeva writes about the lost mother figure, which causes depression in women, both during childhood and adulthood. Who knows—maybe this avoidance of one's own daughter is caused by postpartum depression, or by the inability to recognize oneself as a mother, or by poor quality of life, which forces a woman to consistently prioritize daily subsistence and survival, paying no mind to her own child. The reason could also be that the woman shifts her attention to an object of greater interest to her—a man, or other children. Or, possibly, it's internalized misogyny that prevents her from loving her own female child. Whatever the reason, I feel this stain upon myself, this shadow of abandonment by my own mother. Sure, she was functional, she fed me, took me to school, and cared for me when I was sick. But within this strict existence, filled with the usual procedures of everyday life, I felt an iciness and a blindness where I was concerned. Now I understand that I was a weed that had been pulled and tossed from the flowerbed. The weed refused to perish and sank its roots into the earth; it survived. But I remain marked by separation; death beckons to me, it fascinates me. The death I'm writing about now isn't physical death, it isn't a heart that stops, but the space of loss and my fascination with that space.

Love and warmth were the missing elements. This lack gave me the view of the world and of myself that I have now. In my consciousness, the figure of the mother was linked directly to enjoyment, pleasure, and shame. Our connection was formed in a such a way that these things didn't belong to me, but they belonged to her. Now I, a thirty-year-old woman, am trying to learn to enjoy things and to wrest back my pleasure from the powerful hands of my now-dead mother.

The figure of the mother was always closely tied to sex. My sex, not sex in general. My mother was often loose, and the debauchery was hidden behind a mask of decency. This was called "not airing your dirty laundry in public." At home I saw a lot of things no child should see—sex, humiliation, violence. My mother frequently put me in dangerous situations. When her drunk lover, chasing after her, climbed into our apartment via the balcony, she would run off to stay with a friend. Leaving me alone, one-on-one with that monster. Why wouldn't she take me with her? She assumed he wouldn't touch me, and also probably thought that my presence would keep him there. And it's true that he didn't touch me. But the constant sense of danger I experienced over the course of several years has made me unable to stand open windows or living on the ground floor, and when I hear a noise behind a door in an apartment building I break out in a sweat and start having a panic attack. If a delivery person skips the intercom, gets into the building, and rings my doorbell, I freeze and am unable to move; fear and panic rise to my head and shoulders, I feel cold. I feel that I'm in danger.

I lived in a dark endless night of depression. Sex never belonged to me. For me, sex was an awkward hassle of clitoral masturbation that brought on depressive episodes. I felt shame and guilt. For a long time, my vagina was numb. This tunnel, this route to my uterus, seemed to me a benumbed space of dumb insensitivity. Penetration didn't hurt me, but I didn't feel anything, either. Any object inserted inside me, whatever it was, caused no physical sensation. Inside I was dead, blind, dark. Sex belonged to my mother, and enjoyment belonged to her. During sex I often felt her gaze and thought of her white fleshy body.

After her death everything changed. My vagina began to gradually come alive. Initially I felt light shocks of excitement in my vulva around the opening. A bit later, mild responses inside, in the lower part. Now my entire vagina is a space of sensation. It's alive, in the same way as my stomach or tongue. The woman psychoanalyst with whom I spoke on the subject of female sexuality in psychoanalysis and maternal aggression toward the child, after hearing my story suggested that for a long interval my vagina had functioned as a navel. My body's connection to my mother ran through it. Then my mother died, and my vagina could breathe. After the distinct realization that her death was linked to the appearance of vaginal pleasure in my life, I got very sick. For no reason at all, I suddenly developed acute vulvitis. My entire vulva became hellish, swollen flesh. It looked like thousands of wasps had left their stingers in it. The gynecologist looked at my lab results, performed an examination, and took a swab. All my organs were fine and there were no signs of infection or injury, she said, holding up her hands. She didn't know how to explain my ailment.

But I thought I knew how to explain it, though my explanation was extremely esoteric. I linked the acute vulvitis with the realization that my bond with my mother's body had been broken. Obviously, I couldn't say this to the doctor. She prescribed a course of antibiotics, lotions, and salves, but at night I was still tormented by a searing pain in my left inner labia. Something was tearing its way out of me. Something very old and painful. My wife helped me through this time. At night she sang me to sleep and stroked my belly, applied salve, and carefully looked over my vulva in order to describe the symptoms to me.

I read online that vulvitis most frequently occurs in prepubescent girls. This fact filled out the picture. I was still a little girl in the darkness of my mother's blind shadow. I'm still looking at her with fear and adoration, and I can't acknowledge either myself or my body as separate from her body. I'm a little girl in the body of an attractive adult woman, and all my sicknesses are somehow the sicknesses of a child: colds, fevers, rashes on my thighs, vulvitis.

Manastabel, the warlike guide of the heroine Monique Wittig in the novel *Across the Acheron*, leads Monique into hell. She shows Monique the part of hell in which women survive. Manastabel is a woman, and she has another woman following her, and in each circle of hell they stop to consider the earthly torments of women in a man's world. In the hell I enter, I have no guide. It's my own, personal hell, in which I will have to battle myself and see my mother's face.

I'm traveling from Volzhsky to Ust-Ilimsk. From the city in the steppe to the town in the taiga. Through Moscow, the teeming metropolis, and Novosibirsk, the dusty flat industrial metropolis, to a little dead-end taiga town. In order to approach the source and to bury my mother's body in it, her body become ashes.

I also lack a guide because in this war I'm fighting my own people. Feminist rhetoric holds that women are always the victims of the patriarchy. Their own aggression is kept quiet, or it's understood as compensatory. Nobody will extend the right to subjectivity to a poor woman in trouble. A halo of victimization protects all women and harms those whom they've made suffer.

I walked out of the Tolmachevo Airport building and didn't recognize the places I had left behind ten years ago. The metal handle of the box containing the urn had turned cold. I put on my gloves. The early white Novosibirsk morning was everywhere. Dust mixed with snow rose toward the sky and mingled with it. The snowy steppe lay all around.

I called a taxi. A few men ran up to me to offer their services, but

I declined. One even tried to snatch the box from my grip, to put it in his trunk. But I jerked my arm away, and the man was somewhat taken aback by my aggressive gesture.

We drove through the forgotten, dreary city toward its outskirts. A feminist I didn't know personally and had found through the poetry community had offered me a place to stay. The car pulled up to an unprepossessing high-rise in the middle of an empty lot. I stood there and looked at the outskirts of Novosibirsk. It looked dreary in the April morning sunlight. My wool coat and the thin down jacket I'd worn underneath were failing to keep me warm. I stopped and lit a cigarette; I wanted to greet the city and to show Mama to it, but the city offered no response. A mean little dachshund popped out of the building entrance; after the dog came some glum guy in a ski jacket. The dachshund sniffed me and the man looked at me askance. I was dressed for spring, but in Siberia it was still harsh winter. My carrot-colored bag glowed brightly against the gray earth of the lawn. I didn't finish my cigarette, putting it out against the side of a can serving as the building ashtray, and called Masha. Masha came down to meet me with a little dog in her arms. She explained that while she walked Charlie, I could go on up to the seventh floor; the door was open.

I took off my shoes in a wide dark hallway and went to wash my hands. Upon her return, Masha remarked upon my summer clothes and offered to make tea.

We sat and chatted. She didn't pay any attention to the wooden box, though she knew what it contained, I had warned her in advance. Nobody wanted to talk about death. Death made everyone embarrassed and afraid.

Her girlfriend, Zoya, woke up. She and Masha looked somehow alike. Both of them large and friendly. Only Zoya had Buryat features, while Masha was a curly-haired blonde.

When Zoya left for class, I went to sleep. It was ten in the morning.

For a few days I wandered around the city. I hoped to recognize its features, but I didn't. Maybe this was because I'd never loved it, and upon leaving had instantly erased it from memory. I remembered only one thing: Novosibirsk is a city of dust and wind. In that sense nothing had changed. Broken, busted roads yielded up dust to the wind, and the gray vapor of the dust hung in the air. Through the vapor, the sun shone as a large whitish dot. I went to Studentechskaya to visit the coffee shop where I'd worked for a few years. But the coffee shop was closed; through the dirty windows I looked at the broken counter behind which I had once stood. The windows were covered with heavy-duty plastic, but I could make out chairs on the floor and construction garbage. The sign had changed, too, now it was a different color. In the café next door I ordered coffee and a sandwich. I liked the friendly server, and I asked him what had happened to Traveler's Coffee. He sighed and said that the company had gone bankrupt a few years back. I told him I had worked there once. It turned out that he had also worked in one of their coffee shops, but when they began closing, he left to work for the competition.

I left a tip and went out to wander the neighborhood. I walked in circles, peering into windows and people's faces. I was certain I'd run into someone I knew. But the faces appeared indifferent, and new shopping centers and fast-food shops had risen up to block out the market where I had once bought vegetables and dairy. And the secondhand shop where I used to get my clothes had also closed. The place was alive, but it was distant from me. Disappointed by my wanderings, I boarded a bus and rode into the city center.

Now I can barely remember what I did in Novosibirsk. I know that there were two evenings of readings. Two people showed up for one of them. The other one, at the library, brought in an audience of about thirty, but the local celebrity, a poetess whose name I've completely forgotten, was so drunk that she began shouting retorts from the audience, and then approached me with her arms held out, as though I were about to flee and she was going to catch me. A few men calmed her and took her away, suggesting a smoke. She was angry because I wrote free verse, and probably even angrier because of the clear strain of feminist pathos in my poems. She screamed at me that I was a murderer. I maintained an indifferent facial expression and suggested that if there was something she didn't like, she could leave. But she was even more outraged by the fact that I'd come from Moscow. On her way out, she shouted something about Muscovites. I shrugged and kept reading poems.

I remember going with Nadya, an artist, to Akademgorodok to see the ice on the Ob Sea and eat the local shawarma. We walked through the icy forest, and then over the train tracks downhill. It was a gray-blue space. Unbearably radiant. We sat on the snow by the shore, then walked along the water. The sun shone so brightly that everything around struck me with its spaciousness and color.

I remember drinking a few liters of beer with my friend Natasha. Then we argued with some young fascists who had latched onto us. All of these things happened, but I have the distinct feeling that inside me a different process was occurring, and it absorbed me completely. The process was bleary gray, tremendous, and long-lasting. I had expected happiness but felt only a great disappointment. On the morning of my departure, Natasha picked me up in her car and drove me to the airport. It was a cold, ugly morning.

Writing about your own body, your daily life, and your thoughts and feelings brings anxiety and shame. I'm ashamed that I'm writing this book. Hélène Cixous, in "The Laugh of the Medusa," writes: ". . . you've written a little, but in secret. And it wasn't good, because it was in secret, and because you punished yourself for writing, because you didn't go all the way; or because you wrote irresistibly, as when we would masturbate in secret, not to go further, but to attenuate the tension a bit, just enough to take the edge off. And then as soon as we come, we go and make ourselves feel guilty—so as to be forgiven; or to forget, to bury it until the next time . . ." Cixous links women's writing to their sexuality. For me writing has always been a way to discover bodily experience, to grant the body and its experiences meaning and visibility. Whenever I wrote I did so in spurts, like something unnecessary, vulgar, and pointless. I wrote in the subway, during the breaks between work and meals, while I ate. I put writing second, so that its insignificance wouldn't be so obvious. Wait, scroll through Facebook, eat, and at the same time write a poem. There were many important things that absolutely had to be done, but writing wasn't one of them. Writing is life, but a life I hide from everyone.

When writing burst out of me, I felt that I had done something wrong. After fits of writing I was left naked in a wide road in the steppe. I was as scared of sharing my work as I would have been if asked to publicly display my genitals, or to speak as an expert on a subject I knew nothing about, or to describe an experience of rape to a strange, hostile audience. I felt that the experiences I wrote about weren't really mine, and that I had no right to talk or write about them. And I was afraid of disconcerting other people, taking up too much space in their hearts or minds. I wanted to go unnoticed, but writing burst from me like something that couldn't be concealed. I can't conceal my own self, become invisible. And writing can't stand invisibility.

For half a year I've been writing my story. And everything in it seems unimportant, ragged, substandard. The narrative melts into the running streams of memory. The rhythm is off. Poems and essays have made their way into the book. The book falls to pieces, and it appears to be neither elegant nor comprehensible; it in no way resembles the books people are supposed to read and love. It doesn't have any actual constructed characters or complex plot lines. If you feel any tension, the tension doesn't come from feverish wondering about who the villain might be or where it's all going. You know everything already: my mother died and I took her ashes from Volzhsky to Ust-Ilimsk over the course of two long months. I lived in the same room as her remains and did a lot of thinking. And then I buried her in Siberia, in cold black earth beneath sparse pines. That's the whole story. And it is important. The tension you feel is caused by the text. It comes not from the efforts of a screenwriter but from the life of the body and the emotions, from the work of my attempt to tell you what I know. And also what I don't know, but am trying to understand.

I still don't feel entitled to write or to express myself. This may be connected to the fact that my writing is unconventional in form and criminal in content. Monique Wittig writes about lesbians as refugees from their own class; Cixous calls herself, as a writing woman, an escapee. I'm not escaping anything. Each time I sit down to write, I commit a crime. It's a sweet and onerous feeling, and I'd like to part with it. But what exists beyond the sweet and dreadful ache of writing? Is it nothingness or a Festival of Utopia? And what will writing be like if I overcome my feelings of shame and criminality?

It was cold in the Tolmachevo Airport. A comfortless hall, shady and forlorn. At seven in the morning the airport was unusually empty. Finally the sign for my flight lit up. The Utair website had said that I could bring the ashes with me as a carry-on. Beneath the sign with the number of my flight there was only a single open registration counter. Behind the counter sat a tired, underslept man with combed-back, greasy hair. Dark stripes had formed along the seams of his uniform vest. The vest was plainly dirty and worn. I approached and passed him my documents. He took my passport squeamishly and looked me in the face. I said hello, and told him I was carrying an urn containing human ashes and that according to airline rules I was allowed to bring it with me on the plane. Under no circumstances did I want to give him the box as cargo. After the Moscow-Novosibirsk flight my anxiety about the safety of the ashes had grown. The man asked me to put my box on a scale. By weight the box qualified as a carry-on. I offered to show him my documents concerning the ashes. He picked up his work phone and haltingly explained my situation, then listened briefly to the response, grimaced, and told me that it didn't matter to him one way or the other, and if I squared it with security I could fly with whatever I wanted. How odd, I thought, the airline has an official protocol for this, but here we are figuring it out on the spot. There's a crematorium in Novosibirsk, and I'd thought all people ever did was fly back and forth with ashes. But the expression on this man's face implied that it was the first time he'd come across such a carry-on. Seven in the morning and some crazy lady wants to take human ashes on a plane. I felt awkward, as though I were doing something deeply disruptive to his work.

When the box with the urn slid into the tunnel of the X-ray machine, the woman at the viewing screen glanced at me in surprise. She even blanched a little. I hurriedly began to explain and dug into my backpack for the blue folder with the documents. The woman gestured sharply to ask me to stop. Then she, too, started calling somewhere. She explained in short that I was transporting human remains. And then, nodding and pulling on a lock of black hair, she listened for a long time. I thought I could hear calm, measured speech coming from the telephone. The woman looked relieved, and she motioned for me to pass. I asked her if she wanted to see the documents. In a panic, she jumped and started shaking her hands, as though she were trying to ward off a disgusting rat or a foul odor. I shrugged and proceeded to my boarding gate.

The Novosibirsk–Irkutsk flight had a layover in Krasnoyarsk. A flight attendant explained to me that the plane would land in Krasnoyarsk for forty minutes, and people who were continuing on would have to deplane and go through security again. As the shuttle approached the plane, I noticed how tiny it was. There was a single propeller for each wing. The plane looked more like a vintage toy. The cabin was small, fitting perhaps seventy people. Its old gray-green seats were worn, and the walls reminded me of the interiors of coach buses and minivans. There were men and women boarding along with me, and I listened to them speaking. They talked loudly; many wore mink hats and sheepskin coats. The women guffawed, the men carried sports bags in their huge hands. From the general mood I understood that I was traveling with fly-in, fly-out workers. No one offered us any drinks; the plane flew loudly and made a strange rattling sound. I stood the box between my feet. On my right, a young woman perused the in-flight magazine and kept making affirmative noises at something or another. She had long, fake black fingernails with rhinestones on the thumb and pointer and wore a mink coat that she kept on for the duration of the flight. I kept drowsing, even though sometimes the turbulence was such that my butt flew up from the seat. Dull light shone through the window. Waking, I thought about death. This toy plane could fall at any moment. But as I drowsed, it was all the same to me whether I would die today or keep living. A kind of languid numbness overtook me. I was flying into the depths of Siberia, and warm goose bumps were running over my body in enormous waves. I wasn't afraid to die, I was afraid to be. I felt sad and tranquil about everything.

After landing, the noisy crowd rushed out of the airplane, ignored the shuttle, and started on foot toward the terminal. I boarded the shuttle, and it stood still for longer than it drove. My traveling companions were probably used to it and had known what to do.

At the airport entrance we were met by an airline worker who gave us boarding passes. I took mine and put it in the back pocket of my jeans. She explained to me how to go through the second round of security.

At security I put the box on the conveyer belt and walked calmly though the metal detector. A woman in a uniform vest asked me what I was transporting. I explained, and started pulling my documents out of my bag. In response, she said that she wouldn't allow me on the plane with such a carry-on. I told her that she was refusing to let me board the same plane on which I had just arrived. She replied that Novosibirsk was Novosibirsk, but here, in Krasnoyarsk, they had their own way of doing things. At this point I asked her to call management and added that I'd brought the urn on three fights from Volgograd, Moscow, and Novosibirsk, and I couldn't see why there should be an issue now, particularly since there were rules posted on the airline website about transporting ashes. The woman called management and they told her they didn't know what to do with me. There were fifteen minutes until departure. Past me, one after the next, went colossal men in sheepskin coats and puffy down jackets. I stood in a corner and awaited my fate, holding all my documents at the ready. They had told the woman they'd call her back, but the phone wasn't ringing. I was nervous. G. was supposed to meet me at the Irkutsk airport, and I was about to call her to say I'd be delayed because they'd taken me off the flight. After seven minutes of waiting, I asked the woman to hurry; my plane was about to take off while I stood here with my bag turned inside out, sweating, having just about had it. Then the phone rang. The woman picked up and listened to a question being asked of her. In response, she began to describe me and my luggage, then added that I was taking the ashes to Volgograd. Something was happening on the other end of the line. The woman listened for a long time. Then she nodded, hung up, and told me I could board. In my panic at security I had lost my boarding pass, but they let me on the plane anyway.

When I boarded, the plane was full. There was a new set of men and women sitting there, chatting with one another. These people somehow looked even bigger than the ones who'd flown to Krasnoyarsk. I had one ticket for both flights, so I sat in the same seat. There was no one next to me. I was flying alone. For the first twenty minutes or so the plane gained altitude, rattling and jerking like a heavy car being dragged from a swamp. Then everything was calm. I kept looking through the window: beneath us lay the endless, blue-black taiga. It rose up in low hills and went down in swamps. It stretched to the horizon, uninhabited, barren. It's difficult for me to imagine, now, a place where from every window you see the forest. When I was small, you could see the forest from our kitchen window, and I knew that it went on for a great distance, thousands of kilometers to the east, north, west, and even south. We lived in a taiga town, and the town was like a small island. We were alone in the forest and for some reason we weren't afraid that we would perish or be forgotten. We just lived our lives: shopped at the market, went to school, even had our own movie theater and cultural center. I had forgotten very quickly what Siberia is like. You forget a lot of things very quickly in Moscow. And how can a space as enormous as the taiga fit into your consciousness? It cannot be perceived. You can't see enough, and you can't feel enough, to fit it inside yourself. Nevertheless, the taiga is the place where I was born. G. later told me that it's impossible to be born in the taiga and not remember it with some complex inner organ. And it's impossible not to miss it. I recognized myself in those words. I believe that a person resembles the place where she was born and raised. Inside myself I am like a wild forest. Even Alina can see it.

Suddenly there was a jerk. And then another and another. And the plane started shaking like it was about to fall. I looked around me. Men and women were pressed against the seats in front of them. Through the crackling and noise I heard a quiet voice—to my right, across the aisle, a man pressed against his seat was praying. Gradually I felt we were listing to the left, and I looked through the window—the plane was turning so sharply that I was pressed against the cabin wall, and the box by my legs squeaked against the floor and fell heavily against my foot. The plane turned, bright light flowed through the window, and I saw the blinding surface of a giant cold river cutting through the body of the forest. It was the Angara. The Angara never freezes, even when it's forty below, because its current is so quick, and in the summer it doesn't warm up for the same reason. Every schoolchild in Ust-Ilimsk or Irkutsk knows this. I knew it by heart. And for some reason I couldn't feel afraid. The plane screeched like a piece of rusty metal whipped by the wind, women groaned and sighed, men prayed, and I sat staring at the cold metallic water and crying. The forest was black and the Angara was the color of steel. I wasn't afraid that we could all die, but afraid of the world that I had always seen from earth, thinking it was so simple and lived-in. Now I looked at the Angara and wept. On the inside I felt hot with awe.

Finally the plane righted itself and landed. Everyone clapped, someone yodeled. The man to my right crossed himself and put on his hat. I was the last to leave the airplane. I didn't see any reason to rush. I had brought Mama to our Siberia, and it was a festive moment. Also an awful one.

When I walked out onto the boarding ramp, the wind swept me up. The cold and mighty wind.

How long does dying last? Should I consider Mama's dying to have begun in the spring of 2016, when they found a tumor in her right breast, near the nipple? Or should my count begin on January 5, 2019, when she stopped getting up or eating, and practically stopped speaking? Or should the count begin on February 10, when we called a special medical transport service to take her to the Volgograd regional hospice? She was barely saying anything by then, could force out only a few words, and on the phone she told me, "I feel very bad." She no longer recognized anything and had only a vague idea of what was happening to her. I think that the pain she was feeling was unbearable. But for some reason she absolutely refused to take painkillers. I had to fight to call an ambulance; they would come, inject her with Tramadol, and leave. When I asked them how long we had to wait, they would throw up their hands, as though we weren't waiting for death but for a fever to break. They wouldn't look me in the eye. I was enraged by the idiotic medical ethics codes, remnants of Soviet-era injunctions against upsetting patients and their families. Everyone could see that death was very near, but nobody would say so. As though the silence could fix anything, as though it would give us some dumb, useless hope.

At the hospice they immediately put Mama in diapers that a nurse had instructed Andrei to buy. The nurse made a shopping list; in addition to diapers and disposable sheets, she'd included a three-plug power strip, wet wipes, and something else I no longer remember. When I asked Andrei why they needed a power strip he said that it was for the respirator machine. How strange, I thought, they have the machine but they don't have the power strip. At the hospice they dressed her in the diapers and a white half-transparent gown that didn't cover her single breast, and they put her on an IV of painkillers and a ventilator tube.

I had to use my own modest connections in the activist community to get Mama admitted to hospice: neither the doctor who treated her nor the district doctor nor the paramedics would send her there. Everything had to be done remotely from Moscow. When I finally learned that the hospice could take her, I found out that this required a visit from a special commission, which could come to her but couldn't take her anywhere, because the hospice didn't provide specially equipped transport. So I called a medical transport service. Some tall, brawny men showed up, laid Mama carefully on a stretcher, and carried her down four flights of narrow stinking stairs to drive her to a place where she would die insensate and without pain.

I wanted to be a witness to all this, but on February 9 I'd had to fly to Moscow; I dealt with all of these questions from there. I had tickets to go to Volzhsky on February 19, I was going to visit Mama at the hospice, but on the morning of February 18 she died, and I had to change my tickets and fly through the night of the 18th into the 19th in order to arrange the wake and the cremation.

Now I think constantly about her final days. Was it the right decision to send her to the hospice? I keep thinking about how closely connected she was to the space of home, and how wrong it was to decide for her, taking away the possibility of spending her last days there. What had she felt at the hospice when she opened her eyes and regained consciousness? Had she regained consciousness at all?

Andrei went to visit her two days before she died and said that she couldn't hear what he was saying to her. He tried to give her water in a teaspoon, but she didn't react either to the cold metal of the spoon or to the sound of his voice. He said that there was blood on her lips from a scratch: probably when they were intubating her, they nicked something on the inside and it bled. Andrei cried into the phone out of hopelessness and helplessness. I was silent, clenching my jaw. There was a can on the nightstand by her bed, the nurses used it for the flowers I sent to the hospice. Probably the flowers had a smell. Their presence altered the space. But can someone who is unconscious, pumped full of painkillers, and hasn't eaten for several weeks feel the nearness of the stiff shoots of chrysanthemums? Could she feel anything at all? Did Mama feel hurt and angry with me for arranging her dying in this way?

G. was angry with me for my actions and for giving my mother the option of cremation. She accused me of not loving my mother, and worse than that—of hating her, and feeling compelled to do something to her body that would utterly erase her from the face of the earth.

I had never hidden my coolness toward my mother. But I wasn't cruel, either. I did everything I was supposed to do. I had provided her with a peaceful, painless way to die. I held up my end of the agreement we'd made—I was taking her home, to our Siberia, to bury her in the ground where the bodies of her mother, grandmother, sister, friends, and other loved ones had been laid to rest. G. accused me of wanting to take my mother away from the man she loved. And I hadn't tried to hide that Volzhsky was a hideous, gray city where I would not want to bury my mother.

We argued for a long time in our DMs. Then she stopped replying. She was probably furious and terribly disappointed in me, because in her opinion I had acted inhumanely.

But later, in Irkutsk, we spoke late into the night. I tried to explain my reasons to her. For a while she condemned me for my poems and my fumbling, unmanageable, difficult memory. But I was able to explain to her how and why I write. And I think her understanding provided me with the greatest relief I've felt in my life.

G. was an important adult for me. Every summer, my mother sent me to spend summer vacation in Irkutsk, where G. ran a small sailing school for children. She lived extremely modestly. Early on, she rented part of a wooden barracks dating back to the early twentieth century, in the very center of Irkutsk; the other half of the building was occupied by a janitor and his family. Then she moved to a tiny room in a dormitory, where in the common spaces you couldn't leave anything on the floor or it would instantly become "lava" and be thrown away.

It was so dirty and dysfunctional there that you had to take your shoes off in the hall, and on the nightstand there was a wooden recorder that G. used to knock on the wall when the neighbors were raging. G. shared these minuscule spaces with her dog, Joyka. Joyka was a brindled boxer, a good-natured sweet tooth, not scary at all. She'd lived all her life alongside children and teens; she was a sweet and beloved dog. But strangers were, of course, scared of her. This often saved us. Thinking back to my time at the sailing school, I'm amazed at G.'s generosity and forthrightness. I'd come to Irkutsk and she'd take me to live with her in her tiny apartments and rented rooms. We'd spend three months together, during which she fed me and bought me clothes, and sometimes I got hand-me-downs from her or her friends. I had a pair of very cool mountaineering sunglasses that I didn't even take off on cloudy days, and a faded orange jacket I wore out, wore until the sleeves got too short for me.

We survived on very little money, since Mama's factory salary was constantly deferred, but she saved enough for my tickets to Irkutsk and sent me there on planes, trains, buses. From the age of seven I traveled alone, and G. would meet me at the station. Mama didn't give me money to bring along; it's possible that she sent some to G., but I assume it wasn't enough to support a growing child over the course of several months. Caring for me, feeding me, and watching over my hygiene and upbringing all fell to G. I was often left to my own devices and grew into a fairly independent child. After G. broke her spine in a car accident, I helped with her recovery—in the evenings I gave her massages, cooked, took Joyka for walks. When she traveled to adult regattas on Lake Baikal, I was left alone to run things. As the situation at home drastically worsened, G. offered to take me from Ust-Ilimsk to Irkutsk, so I could finish school and enter university there. Mama did not let me go.

G. truly loved my mother. They had grown up together and gone camping together. They were those young Soviet tourists who hiked up mountains and sang songs by the fire. They went their separate ways after my parents divorced and Mama's young lover Yermolaev appeared on the scene. Mama fell into drinking and the drama of her love life. At that point G. had already been living in Irkutsk for several years. She really disliked Yermolaev.

I feel that there's a lot in me that came from G., and to simplify things in conversation I often refer to her as my godmother. I don't know how else to succinctly explain her role, to get across the measure of our closeness. What should I call her? My mother's very close friend who played a large part in my upbringing? It sounds clunky.

G. had something within her that enchanted and astonished me. Her love of open, unconquered spaces and bonfires. She still likes wandering through the woods with her dog, and every week she builds a bonfire in the birch grove behind her house. When I was a teenager, I was amazed by the fact that as an adult she had managed to hang on to a sense of wonder and belief in miracles. Once she led me to some large white boulders by the foot of the cliffs and told me that stones could hear. She said that I could speak with the stones and the trees if I wanted. It was hard for me to believe her then, but now I'm beginning to understand what she was trying to tell me twenty years ago. Trees really can hear. And communicating with living nature is absolutely necessary for me. This doesn't happen in a human language but it in a language of shared presence. I didn't understand this then, and thought that G. was just a little odd. And she was odd. I was amazed by the fact that she could simply be herself, could look and speak the way she thought was right. Whereas I was always a weathervane. I was always changing myself to fit, and I didn't fully believe in anything. If it weren't for G. I probably wouldn't have started writing. I wrote letters to her. The letters were heartrending. It was awful for me at home without her, in Ust-Ilimsk, in the midst of constant chaos and violence. She responded to my messages with heartfelt calls and letters. I think it was then that I understood how powerful an instrument writing can be. Writing titillates, flusters, stings. It was probably precisely then that I decided to become a poetess.

I walked out of the Irkutsk airport terminal and came to the iron fence by the road. It was plastered with powdery gray snow. I shrugged the backpack from my shoulders and placed the box down by my feet. My phone was silent, G. wasn't there; I sent her a text and lit a cigarette. Then G. called out to me. She was walking out of the airport, and when she reached me, she explained that she'd wanted to get a cup of coffee at the airport café, but the plane had landed before its scheduled arrival time, so we hadn't crossed paths in the lobby. A little gray hatchback pulled up just then, driven by a plump woman G. called Sveta. Sveta drove us home. She was the mother of a friend and classmate of G.'s older son. That's how the two of them became friends, in a parents' group chat. Sveta came into the apartment with us, petted the dogs, and exchanged a few words with G. We warmed up the teapot and poured the tea, drinking it silently with slices of berry pie.

When I was a child, I saw G.'s world as dynamic and brimming with people and events. Now G. had slowed down, and the world around her had become very tranquil. Maybe I had this sense because I was coming from my neurotic, bustling Moscow life. I washed for a long time, spent a long time unpacking the books I'd brought as gifts, and then for a long time paged leisurely through the books with G. and her younger daughter.

That night we built a bonfire in the birch grove and talked. A few friends from Mama's youth came along, bringing a large, crimson velvet photo album and looking through the photographs with G. The photos in the album were faded, gray-white, some of them partly blown-out by clumsy hobbyist photographers, some stained with oily yellow smears. Everyone spoke fondly of Mama; they discussed cancer and reminisced about climbing mountains together. Occasionally one of the women would see a photograph and burst out laughing, telling the story of someone falling through the ice, drinking themselves silly, or getting lost in the woods, and she’d show everyone the evidence—the picture. The other women passed the photographs around in a circle and laughed with her. That had been a different, very capacious, world of their youth. I had no access to their experiences. I could only look at them and feel saddened by their joy. At times I felt particularly awkward, because I didn’t know the people they had named. Their memories were of a time before I was born, when they were all around seventeen. They were individual, separate people, and their separateness both surprised and charmed me.

I had never known these women, but I’d heard their surnames from Mama and G. When it grew dark, the wine ran out, and the pictures became impossible to see, we went inside. There we drank tea and talked about the bonfire. About the fact that the bonfire was in Mama’s honor. G. and the other women declined to look at the urn. G. promised to say her farewell at the funeral; she had already bought tickets to Ust-Ilimsk. The rest were afraid to be near death and its harvest. The box with Mama’s urn stood on the floor in the room by my bed. At night I went to it, clicked open the lock, and checked to make sure everything was all right in there.

The next day we left the house early, and when we reached the city center we boarded a minibus to Lake Baikal. A trip to the lake was obligatory whenever I visited Irkutsk. The minibus drove through the city and I recognized places from my childhood. There was the Lisikha neighborhood, green and crowded with five-story buildings, G. and I had lived there when I was about thirteen. From Lisikha you could take a bus straight to the Solnechny neighborhood, to the city yacht club that's still there now, where G. used to work. At that club I sailed a little dinghy with a spritsail, Optimist class. When we had no money, as was often the case, I walked to Solnechny. The walk took a couple of hours; I carried a backpack loaded with boating equipment, ropes, and runners. Sometimes I carried nothing, or brought Joyka on a leash. You had to walk straight down broad Baikal Street, past stores, churches, and the abandoned Jewish cemetery, and after a large fork make a slight left turn and follow the same road to Solnechny. Past Solnechny was the Istok yacht club, not a city club, where we'd live in tents and sail in the bay. I was afraid of the forest surrounding the Istok club; I had gotten lost in that forest when I was seven.

Mama, packing my things for sailing camp, somehow without giving it a second thought bought me a shirt with a still from *Titanic*, and G. lamented Mama's short-sightedness for a long time. Who would do such a thing, she said, send a child to go sailing in a *Titanic* shirt? It must be said that G. disliked Leonardo DiCaprio, but loved Brad Pitt and loves him still. For G., he was and remains the masculine ideal. But Mama didn't buy me the stupid shirt because I liked DiCaprio or *Titanic*. I had seen the movie, but I didn't have any particular feelings about it. Now I think this didn't have to do with any opposition to mainstream culture but the fact that I was, in general, a pretty callous child, indifferent to sentimental movies. I didn't agonize over Leonardo DiCaprio and Kate Winslet's romance; I was more amazed by the fact that such a huge machine still lay somewhere at the bottom of the ocean. I was astounded by the fact that it existed and took up space in the world. But I had no way of expressing this. The *Titanic* shirt was big on me and looked like a full-size T-shirt; it had been the last one left and had a pull on its sleeve, which is why the woman at the market gave us a discount. I'd assented to the purchase of the shirt because all the other girls had shirts like it, and I didn't want to be left out.

I was afraid of the forest around Istok. Giant poison hemlock bushes grew there, and the spruce grove was grooved with long furrows. When we ran around the woods playing Indians I thought the furrows were actually trenches left over from the Great Patriotic War. But what Great Patriotic War had happened in Siberia? The furrows had been dug by rangers to prevent forest fires. At night, beneath the spruce trees, spots of fungus flickered like little stars in the earth. A long ways off, the older kids said to scare me, there's a woman who lives in the forest. She sits at old graves by the ravine and cries. They'd seen her. I feared the forest: it was frightening, deep blue, alien. One day Joyka ran off into it, and I chased after her. I ran along the grass, past the spruce trees and the ruined fence topped with barbed wire, desperately calling her back. And then, out of breath from running, I stopped and realized that I was deep inside the forest. And the forest was alive. I felt it looking at me with all its being. Its gaze was wild, unpleasant, and somehow lifeless. I was lost. I wandered toward a light, since I knew that light meant the shore of the bay, and walking along the shore I could get back to camp. But the light turned out to be a little clearing studded with low deciduous trees and nettles. I started breathing heavily, I was afraid, but I refused to show the forest my fear. I called very loudly for Joyka again and listened. There was a forest silence everywhere, and I had no idea where to go. I knew that our camp was there somewhere, with its large canvas-covered field kitchen and the rusty boathouse where yachting equipment was stored. But all of that was very far away, and I had fallen into some kind of parallel world, devoid of people or dogs. I called once more and in response heard an answering cry: someone was looking for me. I walked to meet them, and they brought me out of the woods. Joyka came back in the evening.

Joyka died of old age when I was about eighteen. They didn't want to tell me about her death for a long time. When they finally did, I was standing by a grocery store in Novosibirsk, about to buy some kefir. When I heard that Joyka had died I could say nothing in response. I only listened to the rustling on the line, and inside me it was like a large grayish cold bubble of sorrow was rising. And I started to cry.

Everybody knows where the Angara comes from.

Angara was the beloved and only daughter of old man Baikal. Then she fell in love with Yenisei and ran away from her father to be with him. Baikal was livid, furious, but he couldn't catch up with Angara, so in his rage he threw a stone at his daughter's back. This stone now lies at the border between the lake and the river. They say it's shamanic. Everyone knows this story; there's even a cartoon based on the legend of Baikal and Angara. In the cartoon Baikal is a very lively old man, and Angara is a tempestuous beauty.

When you look at Lake Baikal from the shore it bears no resemblance to the character the animators created. Baikal is a large, steady body of water, rather than a nervy, splashing lake. If it rages, it kills. In Siberia, everything is very large. It's hard to write about Siberia without resorting to the propagandistic clichés dating back to the construction boom of the sixties, the discourse of taming wild nature and the heroic accomplishments of Soviet man. But when you come face-to-face with these places, they really do provoke ambivalence. They're gigantic and in a class of their own. And the tropes of Soviet propaganda become the language for expressing your relationship to them.

I looked out of the windows of the ninth-floor apartment, from which the white, plaster-cast-colored curve of the bay was visible, framed on all sides by the rough, wolfish taiga. I tried to see these places as a stranger, a visitor, or as the opposite, a local, made of the meat and sinews of this place. And I still couldn't understand it. I just felt a hollow kind of fear.

The day after the funeral, we went to burn a bonfire by the Angara, beneath the cliffs called the Three Sisters. When she was young, Mama learned to rock climb on these cliffs. We walked along a forest path trodden into immense, prickly white snow: past firs and pines, past stumps protruding from the snow, covered in moss and lichen. Everything around was very bright. There was so much light that I squinted, but the light cut still more stubbornly and painfully into my eyes. It was the light of the large bluish sky, in which briefly but intensely the near-spring Siberian sun was shining. The forest murmured and crackled. By the cliffs we lit the memorial fire and fed the dogs baked chicken and bread. I kept looking down the slope at the wide white ice, the paths of wintertime fishermen and skiers sketched on it in blue-gray lines. The ice, like a great white screen, reflected the light, and the light went on endlessly, blindingly, so much so that it seemed this light had its own sound and breath. Everything around was alive and shifting gently in the wind and cold.

People kept talking and talking but I wasn't listening. I sat on a fallen tree, drinking beer, and feeling empty from the expansiveness of space.

At Listvyanka we left behind the cramped minibus and approached the black scaly shore of Lake Baikal. Not far from the road, in a deep ditch, we found a little white restaurant shaped like a yurt. It was hot and smelled like a woodstove inside; to the right of the door, behind a partition, hung an aluminum sink. We ordered soup and a couple servings of buuz, and the server called to us to pick up a red plastic tray holding disposable plates: yellow soup with glistening spots of fat and buuz giving off a salty urine scent. We ate silently at a table covered with flowery oilcloth, then drank green tea with milk. The food made me feel hot and dizzy.

We wandered on along the lakeshore. On a hill, we sat down in the dry grass and started to smoke. Grass stems and burls stuck all over my black wool coat. We sat by the side of the footpath at the very top of the hill and looked into the clear air before us. There, on the lake's other shore, we could make out the blue, white-tipped Khamar-Daban mountain range. A deep interior rumbling sounded. G. thought it was an avalanche coming down from the mountains, but it soon became evident that the sound came from low-flying passenger planes, passing over us one after the next, and the mountains and the water, reflecting it, created this long-lasting echo like the sound of an approaching avalanche. We sat silently and looked out before us.

And then I told G. about how Mama died. Talking about her death on the shore of Lake Baikal felt wrong to me. And her death seemed absurd and miserable. Everything here, in Siberia, suggested a solemn, ceremonial register for events. There was no place for pain or weakness. I felt powerless, as though I myself didn't really believe in her death or in my own experience.

Closer to evening a storm began. The snow came down wet and hideous. It clung to my hat, my coat, my pant legs were soaked. In the city we bought a braided berry pie to have with tea.

Since childhood I have felt a stable connection between experience and writing. For me, articulating and thinking through an experience never meant sharing it in conversation. The addressee of my message didn't matter. It could be G., and before her my pain would be reduced, depreciated. It could be strangers, and then my experience would become a neat tragic toy. I could marvel at it through a stranger's eyes. But in order for experience to gain a body, I have to write; it's writing that helps me gain true distance. And to deal with it. I feel that my tale, slowly, circuitously, is moving toward its end. But I also feel that something isn't right here. The text is lacking. There are dark places that I haven't been able to make out or trace.

In order to describe writing I use the metaphor of the flashlight. I live in the dark, in a thicket of shady, obscure things, but I always keep a flashlight in my pocket, and by shining it at these things I make them visible and meaningful. They begin to exist on the same level as things that have been articulated and named by other writers, men and women. A flashlight is a small instrument. It glows dimly in the dark, fighting for the stuff of life. It's not the bright, piercing, cold ray of the iPhone. It's an old, analog device. Its light is dim, but soft and living. A flashlight is also good because it's mobile. The things I light with it begin to cast their own shadows and create more darkness. Then I rotate the flashlight, shining it at the newly created shadow, and illuminate the places that had been condemned to die in blindness and oblivion.

G. asked me several times to write a funny book. But I keep writing and writing a long, unfunny one.

I feel that my story is still missing one particular place. Without it, the story is incomplete. Thinking about this space, I searched with my dim light in the world of dark things and found nothing—until I caught a certain scent. People don't describe smells as large, but I'm going to write that it is, in fact, a large smell. It's terrifying and causes suffering. It's like a mixture of the smells of a fetid rag, damp rotting wood, and waterlogged oil paint on worn flooring. It's like tossed-out, meager, yellowish food.

It's the smell of my great-grandma's old house. Smelling it, I suddenly see the shadowed nook behind the stove. The floor is tin-tile in the small village-style kitchen. And the damp that rises from the cellar glistens on the wooden boards around the tin square. The curtain is dull orange, filthy where dirty hands have pulled. And there's Great-Grandma Olga's mean stare.

She had to be kissed each time they took me, as a child, to her green wooden house. Her cheeks were covered in pink patches of eczema, and the skin on her hands was flaking. Unsightly mousy tendrils of hair stuck out at her nape from beneath a scarf printed with large flowers. Her eyes were cold and blue. I was brought over to kiss her, and I would hold my breath. When I was small, I thought the smell of the house was harmful. I thought that if you breathed in that house and Great-Grandma Olga for too long, you yourself could become an ugly, damp creature. And she really was mean; she despised my mother and had little love for her older daughter, my grandmother Valentina. I learned about this lack of love later, but as a child I only felt the cold.

When I was nine years old, Great-Grandma Olga died after a long period spent bedridden following a stroke. All of her serious skin diseases were inherited by her grandson Alexander; my mother only got the psoriasis, which played up after acute angina. I also knew that Great-Grandma Olga had been a home-front worker during the war, and that she'd come to Ust-Ilimsk from a village affectionately called Winter Station. The Soviet poet Yevgeny Yevtushenko was born there, but our family wasn't proud of the connection. I didn't like him when I got older, either, I was drawn to the darker side of Soviet poetry. Underground Soviet poetry was dearer and more comprehensible to me than Yevtushenko's performative ardor. Whenever I asked Mama about where we came from, she only shrugged, referring dismissively to Winter Station. Grandma Valentina flinched visibly when I asked her that. She'd wave me off, saying she had no way of knowing. Great-Grandma Olga was already dead.

The feeling of being deprived of history—not even a great history, what great history are you going to find deep in Siberia—but a minor, personal history, frightened me. Could it really be true, I wondered, that we're people from nowhere, from a cold white desert? Even if we were from a cold white desert, we still had to appear in that desert sometime. My mother's and grandmother's deliberate silence and detachment surprised me. And I, too, started thinking of myself as something that had just appeared there, in the taiga. Just surfaced in the snow-swept forest and began to live. Like an orphan, like a stray mutt.

On the long, twelve-hour night journey from Irkutsk to Ust-Ilimsk I carried on a quiet conversation with my aunt, who was named after that very same great-grandmother. That's when I found out that that Great-Grandma Olga had hated Stalin. I had heard of Stalin when I was a child, but I had no opinion of him. I loved Grandpa Lenin, whose portrait hung above our coffee table until I was ten. Of my actual grandfathers I had known only one, Great-Grandpa Sergei Sokolov, my father's grandfather. But he lived very far away in Astrakhan. Whereas Grandpa Lenin was close by, and it was as though he fulfilled all grandfatherly functions, standing in for all my grandfathers at once. I experienced Grandpa Lenin as a warm stuffed animal old man. In my childhood consciousness he wasn't a politician. He was a fisherman, a carpenter, a factory worker, he was anything you liked. I didn't know about and had no sense of Stalin. This was possibly because people were still afraid to speak ill of him or hate him openly.

According to my aunt, Great-Grandma Olga, who lived on Kamchatka back then, had a lover in the 1930s who got her pregnant. Everything indicated she was madly in love with him, though nobody in the family ever managed to learn his name. In 1937 he was charged under Article 58, accused of counterrevolutionary activity, and immediately shot. Great-Grandma gave birth but couldn't keep the baby fed, there was a terrible famine, and her child died within the year. Then she met Great-Grandpa Ivan, married him, and bore him six children. Ivan was a drinking man and beat Olga, and no one knows what became of him after they divorced. How Great-Grandma Olga and her husband, Ivan, got to Winter Station, no one can say. Why did they leave Kamchatka? Was it because of the war? Or maybe they were looking for a better life, like so many others who found their way to these parts?

Great-Grandma Olga's heavy face appeared before my eyes. She wasn't just strict, she was a mean old woman. And I finally understood everything, all at once. She was mean because of her misfortune and because her love and the fruits of that love had perished, and instead she had wound up with unbearably punishing work on the home front, a mean, drinking, cheating husband, and children who after the war were born one after the other. All of them had to be fed. When you have nothing to feed your children, loving them is hard, too. This pain, building up inside her over years of repressions and war, manifested as coldness toward Grandma Valentina, and she, in turn, having never been taught love or warmth, took it out on my mother. Pain and anger rolled on into subsequent generations, the way rings appear around a pebble tossed into the water, one after the next. Why did my great-grandmother hate Stalin, and why, for the younger women of my family, was our history a murky, difficult subject? Our silence had become automatic, it formed the background of our lives. It was like we had all been wounded and now endured our unbearable existence. We came into being because Stalin killed Great-Grandmother's love, and on some level, since childhood, I had felt a heavy lump of guilt for my own being. Sometimes I can still find it inside myself. The lump isn't as large or heavy as it used to be. It's a little clump of guilt, like payment for the fact that I exist. And all the time around me there's a nearly muted but still somewhat audible hum. As if there were another stream, an underground river, that keeps washing away the ground soil, causing perpetual weakness.

———

Grandma Valentina, Mama's mother, also died of breast cancer. I remember the giant lace cups of her bra, sturdy like sails. The way the semitranslucent band of the bra cut into the tender white skin of her back, beneath the shoulder blades. The glorious heavy folds on her sides were sprinkled with little brown birthmarks; some of them protruded, others were orangish and flat. Grandma Valentina was an enormous woman. Not tall, but broad and curvy. She sat in her colorful robe in an armchair across from the TV, knitted, scratched something in ballpoint pen on the TV guide, and emitted loud, echoing burps. She had many pairs of glasses that I would try on, and my eyes hurt from the farsighted lenses; I teared up. She didn't like me. I was a cold, difficult girl, closed-off and incomprehensible to her. She liked my cousin Valentina, who'd been named after her. She made moonshine and went to the market. There's a photograph: ten-year-old me, in a very festive velvet dress with several satin flounce skirts in a tender pink, and a pink bow on my messy ponytail. I'm standing and leaning on her shoulder. It's her jubilee, she's fifty, and this brown-eyed, faded woman in a crimson blouse with a triangular collar looks into the camera and smiles. We're both smiling, but I'm standing next to her while also trying to keep my distance. I'm afraid to bring my body near hers; I look tense. Her birthday was May 9, Victory Day, and after the celebration we always went to watch the parade and stroll on Mir Avenue. It was a cold, stony day. I was supposed to kiss my grandmother and congratulate her, and also to recite war poems I'd learned for the school holidays. Everything ran together on that day: victory, and jubilation, and numbness because of the nearness of her body.

Her breasts were as big as the rest of her, E cup, and as she grew older she gained more and more weight. The causes were likely her eating habits and the ever-present fear of starvation. The surgeon who operated on her asked which she'd prefer: that he remove the tumor and sew up her breast or remove the breast completely. Grandma waved her hand, telling him to cut it off at the root. I often think about her large breast, weighing as much as a newborn child. They neatly removed all of it. A large piece of heavy, sickened, stricken flesh. And then what? Did they burn it? Yes, they probably did burn it, in a special crematorium for biological waste.

I never saw Grandma Valentina without her breast, and it troubles me to this day. How did she get by without it? Did her back hurt? The remaining breast put pressure on only one side of her spine. Did she suffer from neuralgia or shame because she was missing a breast and had to wear an unconvincing prosthesis? She drank concoctions made from special Siberian herbs to treat her cancer. And also, I think, she cast spells on her first diseased, then sliced-off breast. When I was little, women came to see her, and she whispered something quietly to their reddened legs; this was called "putting a spell on the plaque." In exchange, the women gave her meat, sugar, and milk. In our family it was said that you weren't allowed to put a spell on yourself; instead of helping, this would make the illness worse. But I think that mortal illness teaches you to have a different relationship with magic, and I'm sure that Grandma Valentina whispered spells to her cancer late at night.

You can learn to cast spells by participating in treatment and watching an older woman do it. When Grandma Valentina wanted to teach Mama how to put a spell on the plaque, Mama declined. Just as she had declined Grandma Anna's offer to teach her to tell fortunes with beans. Ever since I was a child, I had been enchanted by women's abilities to affect the bodies of others with their words and with some other thing, which, I felt, was present in them during treatment. I dreamed of learning to heal through the laying on of hands, of feeling another person's pain and managing it. Even now, I believe that the power of a woman's attention and her words can cure anything. Sometimes at night, when Alina is worried or very tired, I give her a simple massage. I imagine that there's a great deal of power concentrated in my hands, power to feel her pain and her exhaustion. And I feel that I can heal her. After I touch her she falls asleep immediately and sleeps deeply through the night.

I like to imagine that pain spreads like rings in water. I want to use this metaphor to describe the structure of my book. The trajectory of a pebble cast into water is my trajectory, the process set off by the death of my mother. I fall and glide and sink down to the very bottom of myself and I travel far and deep into Siberia, into the wide-open dark. This trajectory of a heavy hard object troubles the space through which it falls. "Troubles" in both senses—it creates waves and anxiety. My trajectory makes me anxious; it disturbs my memory and gives rise to rings of little stories, which quietly, one after the other, separate, grow larger, and encircle my story; they're the background of my movements. I power the movements, make them visible. A dull thud against an earthen bottom is the thud of a metal, mother-of-pearl urn with a little black beaded flower landing on snow-white waffle towels pulled taut. A glide through time, through water, is a complicated, slow glide. Because the water resists and has its own density. Water distorts, and the ripples raised by the wind of large time throw blips of light against the bottom. The water shifts, splashes, and the small black pebble glides fearlessly through it. The rings radiate farther and farther from the axis of movement, they grow thinner and disappear. Pain, like rings in water, becomes unnoticeable, transparent. It dissolves.

I know that no one is looking at me as I walk to the store carrying my bright pink vinyl bag, as I wander along the footpath in Timiryazevsky Park or descend into the Pushkinskaya subway stop. I'm an ordinary woman in the crowd, a dot. But I can't rid myself of the stubborn feeling that someone is constantly watching me. The entire world is a gaze directed at me. Psychiatrists have told me that this indicates a narcissistic aspect to my borderline personality disorder.

As a child, I thought I was the main character of some show, and searched for hidden cameras in the walls and the furniture. I felt that even when I was left alone, I couldn't slouch, couldn't pick my nose; when I was a teenager, I couldn't masturbate in the bathroom. Any opening presented an opportunity to spy on me—the hole in the door left by a missing handle was one such opening. I plugged it with a sock so that no one could look at me through it. But sometimes, doing my homework at the table, I heard a quiet rustling behind the door, and turning, would discover my mother's lover spying on me. I saw his glistening eye through the small opening, and I thought that the eye was mocking me. It was dangerous. If as a child I had liked the thought of a show that was all about me, when I was a teenager the thought began to scare me, because it was now somewhat real. When I learned to masturbate, I did it several times every night, until I was so weak I couldn't breathe. I masturbated in the bathroom, and as I lay on my back I stared at the ventilation opening between the bathroom and the small separate room that held the toilet. The opening was technically impossible to reach, but I was convinced that there, in the dark, someone was watching me. This person was evil and wanted to do me harm.

Then came the rented apartments, full of other people's things, saturated with other people's smells. Hallucinations, which made me believe that there was someone next to me: the apartment's dark soul, a dead old lady, the evil spirit of the house. These shadowy beings watched as I cooked vegetables and rice, ate, slept, showered, watched movies, and talked on the phone.

In 2017, when I was chased by cops in Krasnodarsk Krai, my background persecution mania intensified. If before that the presence of watchful beings didn't trouble me, because they were mythical, otherworldly, meaning that they couldn't hurt me, I was now being pursued by very real massive meatheads in black jackets. Any minute now they'd knock on the door, break the windows, and get into the apartment. They'd get me while I was sleeping or taking a shower. When they weren't chasing me they were standing beneath my windows and watching, waiting for the moment when I could be punished.

As the mania intensified, I began having terrible panic attacks. Sometimes I'd fall into a stupor, incapable of doing anything for hours, because I felt almost physically that I was being observed. I didn't understand that what was happening to me had a source not based in reality but in my illness. It's an illness that splits me and my world into several parts. I was certain that everyone around me wanted to hurt me; I felt that my friends hated me, and my acquaintances, and saleswomen at the store, even my colleagues, but in reality they were all just me multiplied, hating myself, relentless and cruel. I was convinced that what went on in my head was equivalent to reality. I lived in a dark cloud of enemies, but things weren't really like that at all: no one was thinking about me, everyone was going about their own business and had no intention of wasting time and energy on causing me harm. There were no evil spirits and no aggressive men beneath my windows, there was only my mind and my illness. I'd felt the evil stare since childhood, so I didn't know that things could be different. This was the world I lived in. I was used to never being alone and always being in danger.

A doctor prescribed me one combination of drugs, then another, then a third, and so on, until it became clear that the pills exacerbated my suicidal thoughts, caused by apathy. On medication I would go into the garden by my house with a folding fishing stool, drape a blanket over myself, and sit staring at a point in space. The ever-present enemies had been replaced by a deserted landscape. The pills did away with the spirits, the meatheads, the nasty saleswomen. But I didn't know how to live without them, or honestly, why I should. After half a year of suffering and alternating between medications, I decided to stop taking them. I just threw the pills away, and that was that. Then the illness returned.

It came back in Yuzhno-Sakhalinsk, when after my flight there landed I went to walk in the woods and look on the mountain for buildings left over from the period when Sakhalin was Japanese territory. There was a small concrete house, all covered in graffiti; it stank of shit, someone had used it as a latrine. I went around it and kept going up the path, past ferns and some gray trees that looked like giant mountain-ash. It was quiet in the woods, and occasionally the wind carried over the smell of that house, a sharp scent of oxidized excrement. I walked and walked up the path. It was a dark and foggy morning.

And then I encountered the snake. Upon seeing me, the giant snake attacked, biting me again and again. The snake brought me crashing to the ground and kept smacking me with its dull snout. It didn't hurt, but I had frozen in fear and was unable to defend myself; I broke into a sweat and couldn't breathe.

There really are vipers on Sakhalin, fairly big ones. But snakes don't just attack. For a snake to attack rather than flee, you have to make it really mad. In the woods where I was walking there weren't any snakes at all, since nearby, at the foot of the mountain, major construction was happening, workers building a memorial alley. The noise could be heard even here, a few kilometers away. No snake was going to crawl around a place where there was so much noise and so many people. This was most definitely a hallucination, and when it ended I experienced an extremely powerful panic attack. I fell down on the path again, suffocating. Then I was running through the woods, tripping and falling, until I found myself on the noisy construction site.

From there I descended to my hotel, and in my clothes and shoes collapsed onto the bed. I was woken by a phone call. A rotary phone was ringing in my suite. On the other end of the line, a concerned young woman was asking if I was all right. She said that my colleagues and friends had lost track of me and couldn't get through. It was late evening, and my iPhone showed more than ten missed calls.

After worsening, the illness eased up. I returned to Moscow from the Sakhalin work trip, where I'd been selling books at a film festival. Then the store where I had been working closed, and I was laid off. The day that I found out about the layoff, my friend Dasha called and invited me to work with her at a gallery. I agreed, since I had no other options and no strength to look for something else. Then Mama died and I was thrown out of my apartment on Mir Avenue. I had to move into the apartment of an acquaintance, which was very far from the subway. But this apartment was on the eleventh floor, and nobody else lived on the landing but me. I couldn't hear my neighbors, no men could look through my windows, and inside the apartment there was nothing but a sofa and some cooking utensils. Seemingly there were no living creatures in the apartment except myself and the cat. For the first time in life, I had the feeling that I was alone and that there was no insistent, malicious gaze. By that time I had been working with a new therapist for six months, and the therapy was slowly but surely helping.

Only once was I woken by the sound of my own screaming: above me hung a thick black cloud, with tendrils that were shifting slowly, as though submerged in water. It wanted to swallow me up. I had been screaming so loudly that the neighbors above me pounded on the radiator until I woke. This was the last shard of the illness tearing its way out of my subconscious. My mind spat it out like a final lump of phlegm after bronchitis. And then there was silence. Silence in my mind and an astounding sense of calm. I was still working on the Ode to Death cycle and beginning my relationship with Alina, and soon I would move into a new apartment and start a new life. That life had no illness or danger in it, everything in that life was peaceful.

All those years the world had been looking at me through my mother's resolutely unseeing eyes, the cold eyes of Grandma Valentina, and the hateful gaze of my stepfather. The world kept its eyes trained on me as I walked, slept, ate, had sex. Grandma died in 2016; in 2018 my stepfather rotted to death due to medical neglect; in 2019 Mama died. They shut their eyes—first my aunt Sveta, from acute tuberculosis, then my father from AIDS, then my grandmother, then Yermolaev in a puddle of his own shit, and then my mother's heart stopped. I'm flying like a rocket, and the boosters fall from me one after the next, lightening my path and my flight.

Today I woke up and saw my wife's eyes. She was smiling and swept me up with her hand, like a delicate little body. She looks at me for such a long time and with such love that the world around me trembles and transforms. It looks at me with her eyes.

I'm afraid of finishing this book. One night about half a year ago I opened my laptop and wrote the first chapter. I thought I was writing ordinary nonfiction about taking my mother's ashes to Siberia in order to bury them there. Then something inside me went off course, and the narrative scattered. First I spent a long time remembering the way Mama ate fish, or how we would go to the market together. Then I tried to understand how my writing works, and how memory is connected to it. Other people appeared, at first glance totally irrelevant to the book—my girlfriends and acquaintances, my grandmothers on both sides. Then the book began to draw in women writers and artists, their ideas, my poems, my essays. And everything I wrote and the way I thought about these things had to do with Mama. I thought I'd write the book in two months, but it's already October, and I still can't get a handle on myself, finish writing a few chapters about how I went to Ust-Ilimsk, buried Mama, and returned home to Moscow. It's as though I'm deliberately putting off the moment when I can say that I've completed the book. I'm afraid of this because I have an unambiguous feeling: once I finish the book, the wound will close. The wound that for a long time I didn't want to treat, the wound that for a long time was part of my consciousness, my practice as a writer.

I thought that bidding farewell to the wound meant denying myself, losing part of me. I'm procrastinating even now; instead of explaining myself here I could've been writing a chapter about how I spent fourteen hours on a night bus driving along the blindingly blue Siberian highway beneath a dauntingly dark sky, listening to Monetochka and Auction. Not because I didn't have other music; I thought that the sorrow and nostalgia of the songs would help me feel through something very important. But I'm not writing that chapter, though I run the memory through my mind every day, the forest moving past the windows and the poles flickering in the nighttime fields. Light from streetlights and headlights, reflected by the snow, sometimes bounced back into the bus full of sleepers. It was dark, and a few passengers snored loudly, while the television up front played and replayed the same cheap melodrama about a fading love affair in a dacha near Moscow. My aunt was sleeping next to me. We had talked until it grew dark. Then she threw her head back against the seat and fell asleep in her light purple down jacket, while I sat there staring at the road that all my childhood I had taken from Irkutsk to Ust-Ilimsk and back again: fall, winter, spring, and summer. I knew this road; I knew that it took four hours to get from Bratsk to Ust-Ilimsk, I knew that after Bratsk the highway breaks up into two concrete lanes on either side of a median. Halfway along the route is the village of Tulun, where you can use a public toilet and buy something to eat in a dinky café with plastic plates and pink, butterfly-patterned curtains. I knew this road, a long road through the taiga beneath a big black sky sown with the white pinpricks of stars. It was bordered by white snowdrifts, and the trees along it were wreathed in delicate spiderwebs of frost. Snowdrifts, minute powdery snow danced in the yellow beams of the headlights along the gray asphalt. I knew this road. It was like a dead body and quiet gray ashes in a steel urn that had been standing by my feet all this time. Everything around was dead and didn't know me, and this was a great disappointment. The world's indifference surprised me, but the most frightening thing was that I myself felt nothing.

A few days later my sister, Katya, picked me in her car and drove me to the Old Town. A river runs through Ust-Ilimsk. Construction of the city began on the left bank, which is why that part is known as the Old Town. To this day, some two-story wooden houses with three entrances still stand in that neighborhood. They're weather-beaten, red and green, like monuments; there used to be more of them, but they were built quickly and perished quickly in the frost, wind, and heat. Later came the Khrushchev-era apartment blocks and high-rise dormitories. Some of the high-rises are still called bolgarkas, because the Bulgarians who built the city and the Ust-Ilimsk Hydroelectric Power Station lived in them. Near the Bratsk highway, on Yuzhniy Lane, stands the apartment block where I grew up. I still don't understand the logic used to name this place. A lane is called a lane because it connects two large streets, but in this area there are only four five-story buildings, unconnected, like domino tiles, standing parallel to one another. I've often looked at the place on Google Maps and felt a suffocating sorrow. Google won't let you into the courtyard, but you can stand by the side of the building and peer into it, at a lifeless green photograph. Still, it's strange that Yuzhka—that's what people call the place—is classified as a lane. Yuzhka doesn't connect anything; the buildings stand between a large vacant lot, beneath which there's an abandoned bomb shelter, and a barren hill, topped by a kindergarten, a school, and a hospital. Yuzhniy Lane connects nothing to nothing, instead it bisects a curve in the landscape. It tears apart the place where a valley becomes a hill.

Katya drove me into the courtyard of my building. Everything around was gray, and there were no people in the street, only a skinny dog circling the courtyard looking for scraps. For a while we sat in the car studying this empty, generic building. Above the third entrance, on the second floor, I had spent seventeen years of my life. It was a heavy, suffocating place. Now the apartment belonged to someone else. Mama had sold it a few years ago and bought the other one, in Volzhsky. But I still remembered the five-digit phone number, 7-27-83; it had seemed so clear to me, so laconic and appropriate. After all, by reversing the two final digits, you'd get the number of the apartment where I lived. And 38 was also the number of our region. The elegant universe of my childhood and adolescence fit into these five simple digits. Now I was sitting in Katya's car and looking through the window. It was early Siberian spring, in no way distinguishable from winter. Really it was winter, and there was nothing other than that.

I've been afraid to write about the road to Ust-Ilimsk and about sitting in the courtyard of my old house. Because writing about it meant that all of these things had happened to me. That I had experienced them. I sat in my own courtyard two days after Mama's funeral, but somewhere inside me I was still carrying her in a little gray vessel. Nothing had happened, it's only that every time I lose sight of her, I lose her forever. Today I dreamed a long, torturous dream that resembled all the dreams I've had over the last six months, while I've been writing this book. The two of us, Mama and I, are on a long journey somewhere, and then, as often happens in dreams, something important occurs, and I realize that Mama is dead. That was the case today. We were speeding on a river rocket; sunlight assailed the windows; I was looking at the blackish deep water. We were going somewhere very far away, and throughout the trip we'd been slowly discussing something. Then I had to use the restroom. When I returned, I found out that Mama was already dead, and someone was handing me papers from the funeral home, a list of purchases and a bill for sixty-eight thousand, four hundred rubles and seventy-six kopeks. The papers were yellowed, old. I ran to find Mama. Why, I wonder, in dreams that could provide me with fantastic metaphors of forgiveness and farewell, does some functionary's hand present me with a bill from an institution? Why is that every time I lose Mama in dreams I'm obsessed with how I'm going to bury her? Why is it that every time I worry about her dead body, I don't feel anything a person who has lost her mother should feel? Why am I obsessed with the logistics of funerals and money? Why can't I see her face and look into her eyes? Maybe that's when the tender quiet click would sound, and I would see her slowly moving off, away from me. Slowly, as though floating down a river, sailing away and looking at me. While I just watch her as she goes, and say farewell, and forgive. Then the wound will begin to close on its own, and I'll hear the crackling of flesh coming together.

On the second day after Mama's funeral Katya took me to the Old Town so we could walk on the dam and I could visit my courtyard and my old school. She sat me in the passenger seat, and the dog, a shepherd-laika mix, went in the back. On the way there Lana, the dog, kept trying to get to us, but Katya would look at her sternly, and the dog, whining in embarrassment, would retreat. At the entrance to the reservoir, which everyone calls the sea, we left the car and wandered along the dam. People haven't been able to drive onto the dam in a long time, said Katya, that's why they leave their cars at the parking lot and walk along the road. We were walking toward the observation deck on Lysaya Mountain, in the direction of the power station. The sky was low and white, pressing down on us as though cutting off our air; my head was spinning a little. The spinning was because of hunger and cigarettes. We hadn't had time for a proper breakfast, and I hadn't had coffee because Katya only drank instant, while I'm used to drinking two strong cups brewed in a moka pot every morning, so I felt totally dazed. We passed by crumbling, broken ice. Spring had come, and only the most daring fishermen were still going out on the ice. Here and there on its flat surface ran dark paths filling with meltwater, and dark ice holes were visible, while in the distance a few fishermen sat at the edge of the harbor, tiny moths on a white sheet at the horizon of merging ice and sky.

Somewhere below us, beneath the fishermen, lay the underwater world of the village of Old Nevon. In order to build the city and everything in it, it had been necessary to flood an inhabited, low-lying area. Beneath the surface there's a village and a church—an underwater monument to Soviet colonization of living nature and old settlements. In his *Farewell to Matyora*, Valentin Rasputin wrote about the construction of the Bratsk hydroelectric station, which is four hundred kilometers away from our station in Ust-Ilimsk. The little island was swallowed up by the great waters, and all living things trembled in fear before the new world. When I was a child I looked out at the reservoir and knew that we lived in a surface kingdom, while beneath us there was another city in which underwater people and creatures lived. People told tales about underwater currents washing away the village cemetery and coffins floating up to the surface. But these were probably make-believe, legends reflecting people's fear of a dark, nearby, submerged place, where roads no longer led and which held ruin at its heart. There were also stories about how people boating in the years immediately after the flood could see, as though through glass, the small dead village, and how in dry weather the dome of the church rose above the waters. Along with the village, a large section of forest had also been flooded. The underwater forest died and began to rot; the water bloomed from the decay, and in summer you can see that here, in the Ust-Ilimsk Reservoir, the cold clear Angara water turns a murky orange-green. Like the green fog of time, it conceals a tragedy. A world built on the ruins of other worlds is not a kind one. But we live in it, and it is constantly renewed, consuming itself, forgetting itself.

Most of all I felt sorry for the Losyata. The Losyata were three little islands. Before the flooding they were actually large hills, the Angara running between them. They'd been given this sweet name, meaning "moose calves," but when the water rose, the calves perished. There are still black-and-white photographs of the islands, in which they're already doomed but haven't yet gone under. Either because I know that they'll soon be gone, or because with their hulking bodies they themselves foresaw their impending death, the photograph is painful to look at. It fascinates with its awesome sense of impending doom. And I think I can hear the Losyata crying.

We reached the observation deck and looked out over the hydroelectric station. There, below, beneath the mountain, boomed the wide restless Angara; above it stood the spillway, and on the other side of the wall there were deep, enormous waters. Ever since I was very young I'd been obsessed by the question of what would happen if the dam broke; would the water reach Yuzhka? Maybe Yuzhka alone would remain above the flooded city, since it's high up on the hill. We stood looking at the wide river, and Katya asked about my plans to start a family. She asked if I was going to get married, and I told her that I was a lesbian, that everything was a little different for me, not the way it is for most of our folks. She nodded, called the dog, and didn't ask any more questions. I also didn't know how or why we had to talk about these things.

I'm tormented by the fact that I constantly have to justify myself. I have to justify being a lesbian, justify writing such indecipherable and hideous poems. Here, in this text, I'm constantly trying to find a justification for the way I write. I look for support in the writing practices of other women writers. I'm afraid that my book is somehow clumsy, wrong, skewed. It doesn't fit within the accepted concept of literature. And I'm afraid to speak about what I really am.

But I don't know how to make up stories. The world around me is structured in the way I write it. And I'm structured the way I write myself. I don't have a different self and I don't have a different understanding of the world or of writing. Even the phrase "I don't have a different self and I don't have a different understanding of the world or of writing" sounds like a justification. I'm tired of justifying the fact that I am who I am. I'm tired of searching for grounds to call the literature I write literature.

At night I lay in the dark and again, time after time, ran through the contents of this text in my mind. I was thinking about whether this story could fit into a different, more conventional form. Could it exist without all of these complicated, unpleasant details? Could I write a sterile book? No, I can't, I can't and I don't want to. Because my flashlight shines through the green gloom of darkness and wins my own self back from the dark.

I found a poem by Gennady Aygi, written sixty-two years ago. He wrote it before my mother even existed. The lifetime of the poem is longer than my mother's lifetime. If I'd read the poem to Mama, what would she have said? She would've said that the poem is very complicated and hard to understand, or that the poem is very beautiful, but she didn't really get it. She wouldn't have understood and wouldn't have accepted my own poems. Aygi, who was born and spent his youth in southern Chuvashia, saw white fields and the endless winter. Once I visited Cheboksary in wintertime. It was a cold, bleak, gray-white city. In an alley of pagan idols stands a modest wooden post dedicated to the poet. By this post we read poems. There's a recording of the event on YouTube: me reading poems in the gray Cheboksary forest. I remember how my feet froze in the snow; I wasn't dressed for the weather: I wore thin cheap imitation leather boots with cardboard soles, a thin denim coat, and a faded pink hoodie. I felt freezing in the forest immediately, because I hadn't slept and was terribly hungover. I'm embarrassed by this recording; I'm just a seed of myself in it, it isn't yet me but someone who's just beginning to understand herself as a poetess. Alina loves to rewatch this video and tease me about it.

Aygi saw endless fields of white, bordered by gray woods. He knew something about space and death that feels intelligible to me, raised in the sad eternal Siberian winter. But I'm probably mistaken. I understand nothing about Aygi's poems, or death, or the wide-open endless white expanse he called the exhalation of God the Creator. But I think he understood the connection between places, people, and life, all of which intertwine in some particularly complex way in his texts. Both life and nature are imagined in these texts as independent processes, not controlled by people. As if through dying a person enables life to exist. The world is thrown open when you release it and let it live. And a person isn't anything important, because the white wide-open field blinds you and presents you with the possibility of living through infinity.

HERE

like forest thickets we have chosen
the essence of secret places
that keep people safe

and life ran into itself like a road into the woods
and beginning to seem like its glyph
was the word *here*

and it means both earth and sky
and what lies in shadow
and what we see plainly
and what I cannot share in a poem
and the riddle of immortality
is no greater than the riddle
of a hedge lit by a winter night—

white branches above snow
black shadows along snow

here everything speaks to everything
in high primordial language
answering in the same way—high and free always—
as life's supernumerary free part
to an adjacent indestructible part
an adjacent and indestructible part
here
at the tips of wind-broken branches
in the quieted garden
we do not search for hideous congealings of sap
resembling mourning figures—

embracing the crucified one
on the woeful night

and we don't know the word or sign
which would be above one another
here we live and we are beautiful here

and here growing silent we trouble reality
but if bidding it farewell is cruel
life participates even in that—

as self-delivered
news inaudible to us

and moving off from us
like the reflection of a hedge in water
it remains beside us to take up—
after they've served us—
our places

so that spaces of people are replaced
only by spaces of life
in all times

Two years later Aygi would write another poem, and in this one death wouldn't be so abstract; the poem addresses the death of his mother. Aygi admits that he's crying out of pity, though not pity for his helpless dead mother, but rather for "the pathetic sight of her homespun dress." After this line his gaze returns to the wide white fields and snowbanks. Aygi employs the images of pagan burial mounds and a demon's wing, and he designates the snowflakes falling from the sky the hieroglyphs of God. The trajectory of his gaze begins with the scarf on the head of his dead mother, which for some reason I see as black, and which she never did remove, as though through this gesture demonstrating her refusal to die. After all, you can only cross over with your head uncovered. The gaze travels from the dead head, through the syncretic enumeration of all available divine forces, to the sky, from which slowly, in the windless expanse, large mute snowflakes are falling. This is the trajectory of a gaze marked by loss. And the scarf falls from the dead head like writing, like a message.

DEATH

Without taking the scarf from her head,
Mama dies,
and once only
I cry at the pathetic sight
of her homespun dress.

O, how silent the snows,
as though brushed flat
by the wings of yesterday's demon,

o, how rich the snowbanks,
as though beneath them lie
the mounds of pagan

sacrifices.

While snowflakes
keep carrying and carrying to earth

the hieroglyphs of God . . .

The snowbanks that conceal pagan sacrifices within them, like pregnant bellies, here testify to the fact that a mother's death has symbolic meaning. In "The School of the Dead," Hélène Cixous writes that in her imaginary school of literature the first step is an encounter with death, a requirement to locate the departed woman or man. Then she admits that she wrote her first book on her father's grave. I wrote my first book on my father's grave, too. His death gave me the intimacy of writing. A shrieking writing, writing-as-crying, writing-as-war. Cixous insists that a father's death is very different from a mother's death, and here she pays her dues to psychoanalysis and writes that the death of the father is equivalent to the destruction of the load-bearing walls of the world. She writes nothing about the death of the mother, just mentions that losing the bosom of the family is not the same as losing the world. I'll venture a guess that at the time of writing, 1990, Cixous's mother was still alive, and her experience of losing the bosom of the family lay in the realm of fantasy, expected rather than experienced.

Find the departed man or woman, Cixous writes. To which I'll add—look at them intently, and also look at yourself, and inside yourself, and "ascend the staircase down," in order to hear, in the darkness of your despair, horror, and confusion, how the mute snowflakes whirl and carry writing within themselves—the hieroglyphs of God.

The death of the mother is not the same as the death of the father. A father's death destroys the world, but a mother's death destroys the sanctuary of the world. A father's death gives birth to a writing-cry, a mother's death gives birth to something lengthy, exhausting—like a pair of attentive, half-blind eyes—a writing-gaze. Writing-as-experiencing-mastering-constructing-space. To look and to see, by which I mean to learn.

One long cold childhood winter, I climbed a wild unplowed hill and rolled down. And having rolled, found myself chest-deep in a deep, dense snowbank. It was a long way to the cleared road, and as I walked, I used my own body to blaze a deep, ragged path. That's what this writing is like. It is writing-as-body. It is the body.

A bird that symbolizes poetry, be it a swallow, a nightingale, or Philomela, is always disabled. We need only think of Mandelstam's blind swallow. The swallow of Gennady Gor flies into his eyes and goes on to beat "in our heart," which actually isn't too far off from the hall of shadows. Gor's "we," having welcomed Mandelstam's blind swallow into our own eyes, both give the swallow sight and also become the bird. It's a kind of primitive exchange, sympathetic magic. Maurice Blanchot writes that "art is experience because it is experimental: because it is a search—an investigation which is not undetermined but is, rather, determined by its indeterminacy, and involves the whole of life, even if it seems to know nothing of life." And the swallow that once flew into your heart will transform your life into the endless experience of a wounded bird's fluttering inside of you. It'll turn you into Philomela.

Elena Shvartz, in her poem "Tower, Cages in It" describes a poem as cages of birds stacked one atop the other. From stanza to stanza the subject gradually transforms from the *observing-I* and the *cage-opening-I* to an *I-surviving-the-splitting-of-the-body* and then into a collective subject, a *singing-we*:

> But I'll unlatch the doors of cages—
> And they'll scream like idolaters,
> Aloud in tongueless tongues.
> Jostling, they'll swarm out,
> And chirp, and twitter,
> And chirrup, and titter.
> And swell their throats,
> And drop pink feathers,
> Spray snow-white ordure,
> And trilling, peck each other.

They have sated themselves on my blood,
They have opened my veins deftly,
And by my own hand (what a shame, really),
My mind was scattered among the tiny heads.
Shards of my eyes I fit into their eyes . . .

If Gor's collective "I" turns into a swallow, then Shvarts's body transforms into a flock of raving birds. All it takes is shutting the book for the noise of poetry to grow quiet, and for the body to be calmed:

And we sing,
Since God taught us to sing, we screech, we roar,
Throw a cloth over—we'll sound no more.

About a year and a half ago I wrote an essay about Philomela, and at first glance it contradicts everything I've written in this part of the book. But that isn't really the case. The part about the swallow and the essay "Philomela's Tongue" form a diptych.

Philomela's Tongue

Recently I became interested in the Greek myth about the origins of the swallow, the nightingale, and the hoopoe. This is the myth of Philomela, whom King Tereus deceitfully hid away in a cabin in the woods. There, he raped her. Philomela resisted, and Tereus cut out her tongue to prevent her from telling anyone about his crime. But Philomela found a method of conveying her story to her sister—she wove an epic tapestry and used embroidery to depict what had happened to her. Procne received the message. During the festival of Dionysus she went into the woods with the other women. She freed Philomela. And back at the palace she killed the son she shared with Tereus and cooked her husband a meal of his flesh. When Tereus was shown the child's head, and the liberated Philomela emerged from behind a curtain, he understood what he had consumed and wanted to take revenge on the women. But as he chased them, all three grew wings, and their bodies became feathered. That's how Procne and Philomela became a nightingale and a swallow, and Tereus a hoopoe. Since then, the hoopoe's comb has been a symbol of Tereus's kingly armor, and the red spots on the bird's head and chest symbolize drops of a child's blood. The swallow and the nightingale have lost their connection to their earlier incarnations, and in later sources Philomela is sometimes a swallow, sometimes a nightingale.

In poetry, Philomela, just as much as the swallow and the nightingale, serves as a symbol of the poet's voice. Many poets, from Batyushkov through Brodsky, have used this image. Why is it that in men's poetry the symbol of the poetic spirit is a woman who was raped and deprived of the organ of speech in order to preserve the reputation of a powerful male rapist? Responding to this question could lead us into the discourse of condemnation of men's art and their ideas about the nature of poetry. But that conversation would direct everyone's focus to the figure of the male poet, and once again the woman would function as an instrument of his elevation.

I prefer to write about Philomela. What happened to her? She was locked up in a cabin in the woods. Many feminist theorists and theorists of women's writing have written about the significance of the territorial and symbolic placement of women. We can look to Luce Irigaray and use the spatial metaphor she uses to locate the place of the subject within discourse. Philomela has not only been removed from public space—from the city into the woods, where she's imprisoned in a cabin, guarded by Tereus's soldiers, and doesn't have a chance of getting back into the city. She has actually been subjected to a double exclusion, and after she's raped, to a third one. She threatens Tereus, saying that she'll speak out in the city about what he did, and he cuts out her tongue so that she can't tell anyone. It's interesting that in Ovid's *Metamorphoses* Philomela swears that she'll be heard not only by people, but by the stones, the trees, and the gods. The power of her revolt is so great that her speech can be understood by nonhuman creatures and objects.

Irigaray says a woman must reject androcentric language in order to arrive at her own means of expression. Philomela doesn't have the option of denial; her tongue has been forcibly removed. But what happens to that tongue? Ovid writes:

> Its stump throbs in her mouth, while the tongue itself,
> falls to the black earth trembling and murmuring,
> and twitching as it flings itself about,
> just as a serpent's severed tail will do;
> and with what little life is left, seeks
> its mistress's feet . . .

Philomela's severed tongue hisses on the ground. Its fury is so great that even as it dies it continues to speak the truth. Not for nothing does Ovid compare the tongue to a hissing snake: a woman's speech here is understood as chthonic, prehistoric, which also means that it pertains to the creation of the world and remains connected to all of its creatures and objects.

Philomela leaves her forest prison. She has found a language for expression—an imagistic one. The language of applied arts has always been considered lowly and anonymous, remaining in the shadow of great art and politics. But Philomela arrives at this language out of necessity. This is why Shakespeare's Lavinia has her hands chopped off—the rapists remember Philomela's lesson.

It seems like there's nothing more to wish for—Philomela is free.

Procne believes her, and after all, the worst thing for Philomela wasn't that she was raped, but the fact that her rapist was her own sister's husband. This situation made Philomela Procne's rival. And Procne acts within the framework of classical ethics, but her actions can also be understood from the viewpoint of sisterly feminism. She exacts brutal revenge on Tereus for her sister and for his infidelity.

Still, Philomela's severed tongue is already dead. It's decaying on the earthen floor of the forest cabin. It hasn't been brought into the light, but it remembers, and it waits. And the swallow or nightingale has to return for the tongue, to free it from captivity and regain it, in order for the song to sound and wake the women, the stones, and the forest.

*

I have a small piece of her flesh. No, I didn't keep a handful of ashes for myself, and I didn't cut off a lock of her hair. She left a fragment of herself inside me. I didn't know about it for a very long time, until someone told me that when you're showering you need to clean your navel so that it doesn't smell. My navel had never smelled, but it was deep and dark, like a hole in ice. When I found out that you're supposed to wash it every time you bathe, I bent over to look inside and slid a finger in. The finger went half a joint deep and hit something dry and hard. I felt a jolt in my belly. It wasn't painful, but it was very unpleasant, and somehow the sensation made me feel heavy and sad. I moved the finger inside myself and discovered that there, inside my navel, was a little piece of something hard. This thing was a bit like flexible plastic. I was surprised by the presence of this small object inside me, and I put in a second finger to try to take it out. The thing inside me didn't have any sensitivity; it was like nails or hair, not like flesh. I tugged, and the inside of my navel began to ache dully, but the thing didn't want to come out. Initially I thought that my carelessness had led to some foreign object becoming lodged in my belly button. I'd seen my father withdraw little blue balls of fuzz left by his clothes from inside his own navel, where they'd become tangled in hair. Maybe this thing inside me is also fuzz, I thought. But it was sharpish and dry and didn't resemble a clump of dust or hair. I pulled again, and my navel stung again. Then I picked up an old compact from a shelf by the bathroom mirror and used it to peer inside my dark navel. There really was something in there. But it wasn't blue or pink, like my father's fuzz. It was white. And I understood what it was: a little speck of umbilical cord. After they had cut me away from my mother and tied off the cord, it hadn't fallen off or dried up; it had remained part of my body. It was inside me. This little piece of cord that had connected my body with Mama's.

Tenderly, I call it a crouton and say that I have a little crouton in my belly button. Alina sometimes turns on the flashlight on her phone and looks to make sure it hasn't gone anywhere. She's touched it several times to make sure I wasn't just imagining that it can't be removed. Once she understood that it was part of my body, she smelled my navel and realized that it didn't smell like other people's.

Something isn't right about my body. It keeps foreign tissue inside itself. A fragment of the old corporeal connection and a symbol of my lack of detachment from my mother. The impossibility of detachment. As though I had returned from a distant country that I would never again visit, bringing back a twig from a local tree, or a small stone. My body kept this relic in the memory of the time when I was part of that large cold body, which first ejected and then rejected me. Without ever having let me go—or, rather, I had been unable to separate myself.

Today she spoke with me from beneath the earth. It sounds like a ballad: dead mother speaks with living daughter from underground. I heard her voice. I knew that she was there, underground, speaking with me from inside the small gray urn. This is the recurring plotline of my dreams: I'm driving past the Ust-Ilimsk cemetery and I can't stop the car to visit my mother's grave. I keep driving and driving past the cemetery, along the Bratsk highway, and I see dark graves swept with white snow; I see pink, light green, and orange plastic wreaths, and black, beige, and white marble memorials. I'm unable to stop the car, and in these dreams sadness overtakes me.

Today I made it off the highway and turned right. I walked past winter, past summer hills riddled with pits, past the gray boxes of institutions, and found myself by a fence with three graves. I recognized the place by the identical, rough concrete gravestones with colorful aluminum plaques depicting the faces of Sveta, Grandma Valentina, and Mama. They're the cheapest stones the funeral home offers, the plainest and least conspicuous. But I recognized the three crooked concrete slabs and leaned my cheek against the dry whitish earth beneath Mama's. And she spoke to me. Her voice sounded as clear and loud as if the two of us were together in a large empty space. She kept speaking, speaking, speaking. Her voice was ordinary and cold. I stopped her and said I was writing a book about her. She grew silent, and I felt her slowly drifting away to start chatting with someone else. I heard the din of voices beneath the earth. I screamed into the hollow earth about the reason I was writing my book. I was trying to scream loudly enough to reach her. I ate the earth, touched it with my hands as though it were an impenetrable wall, while Mama kept blithely chatting and chatting in the underworld with strangers. Her voice was friendly and warm.

I shouted to her, I begged for an answer, and she replied that this was my method. The reply sounded like an accusation. All the noise disappeared. I found myself in an unfamiliar cemetery, and for a long time looked for a path leading out. But as in any other dream, the path confused and misled me. I felt disappointed by our encounter; I walked back along blue and violet hills, emerging one after another. I found an exit, and on the way Alina joined me. Together we walked out onto Naymushin Street, heading toward the bleak reservoir. The storm clouds above it were dark blue and black.

It was a clear beautiful day; in the morning there had been a blizzard, and everything around was white and then turned blue, like glass. I carried the box with Mama's ashes out into the street, got into the car, and we drove to bury her.

On the way out of the city, on the wide shoulder of the Bratsk highway, there was already a gathering of people in winter coats and hats. A large, half-empty Ikarus bus was parked by the shoulder; factory management had provided it for Mama's funeral. A lot of people had come. They all approached me, introduced themselves, and told me how they'd known Mama. I shook hands and accepted their condolences. Some women had brought little piles of photos in thin cellophane bags, to give to me. I had seen all those photographs before—mountain bonfires, other people's weddings and children. Everywhere in these blurry photographs I saw a smiling Mama. I finally understood that it was an important ritual, returning photographs of someone to her children after her death. Grandma Anna did this after my father died. People did this because my generation has a different relationship to photographs, and different ways of remembering. They wanted to pass their way of remembering on to me. Some carried flowers, red roses. Mama had loved red roses. In the cold the flowers wilted a little and lost their scent.

Then we got into our cars and in a slow caravan crawled along the Bratsk highway toward the cemetery, the one I keep dreaming and dreaming about now. In the blinding snow, to the right of Grandma's gravestone, a small black hole had been dug. A tiny grave for Mama's ashes. The blindingly white sunlight beat against my face and eyes. People in black and beige clothes squinted and shielded their faces with their hands.

When I placed the gray urn, sparkling in the sun, on the newly made stand, everyone formed a long line, as though on command. No one had to explain; everyone knew that the first to say goodbye were the closest relatives, then distant relatives, then friends, colleagues, and acquaintances. The line moved very slowly, and everyone dealt differently with Mama's ashes. Some humbly placed a hand on the metal urn, warmed by the sun, others touched it with their lips and whispered something tenderly to the lifeless ashes. When the line ended, the men picked up the waffle towels and carefully lowered the urn into the earth. Then the others, in the same order, began to toss in handfuls of hard soil. Mine was first.

Then we had to drink vodka. There was no vodka, but there was some diluted alcohol that everyone drank out of little flimsy plastic cups and chased with pickles from cloudy jars. The remainder of the alcohol went to a special cemetery worker, who was also given a hundred rubles and asked to take care of the grave. The man said thank you and respectfully took the money, food, and alcohol.

The banquet hall at Bagulnik was festive in a provincial way. Tulle curtains and golden drapes of heavy artificial silk. The chairs were upholstered in fake burgundy leather. When people began arriving, the employees brought a few spattered stools from the kitchen. There aren't any others, they explained; there was a quiet wake going on in the next room, and they also didn't have enough chairs, so when one of our guests left, these women would snatch the chair and carry it to the hall next door. I looked into it—it was on the side of the building that didn't get light, the drapes weren't gold but dark red, and this made everything seem more mournful than in our hall, where people were laughing a little, remembering their tourist youth and their work at the factory. Everyone took turns standing and saying a few kind words about me, about my having done a very important thing: I had brought them their beloved Angella. All of them—the hikers, the factory women, the relatives—had a lot of affection for her. As though she had opened herself up to each man and woman and given them a piece of her heart. They looked lovingly at the portrait of young Mama that stood at the head of the table, and whenever the sanctuary lamp flickered out, they lit another candle.

Later my aunt gave me that photograph. I wanted to take it home without the frame, but she looked at me in shock. As though I'd decided to take a kilo of potatoes, but without a sack. She grabbed the photograph out of my hands and slid Mama's Photoshop-enlarged face back into the dark blue, golden-braid picture frame. I brought the photo to Moscow. Mama is smiling in it. Thin tangled gold chains glow around her neck, and her eyes are sparkling. The photo was taken on the day of my third cousin's christening; Mama was her godmother. It had been a group shot with my exhausted postpartum aunt and a pink tender infant Mama clutched to herself. My aunt had asked the women at the funeral home to edit it to show only Mama, and they cut out her head and turned the background into a light blue blur—it had been shelves piled with baby clothes and videotapes. In the photo Mama is happy and enigmatic, like a Hollywood star; she's half-turned away and looking into the camera. Her tanned dark gold skin glistens, and the dark brown birthmark on her neck gives her a kind of seductive flair. I have a birthmark on my neck too. In the same exact spot as Mama's. An oval dot of darkened, raised skin, making for charming asymmetry. Mama looks out from the photograph, and behind her is an endless light blue space. As though she's floating in it. With the light blue haze the funeral home editors create an impression of eternity and a light that streams out of it toward us, into the world of the living.

This photograph is in my kitchen, on the microwave. I don't know why I didn't put in my room, on my desk or the windowsill. Moving into a new rented apartment, the first thing I did was stand Mama's portrait on the microwave oven. The blue backdrop goes well with the kitchen décor, which is in the style of the late nineties or the early aughts: marble-print wallpaper, a heavy brown banquette dining set. Mama liked this kind of kitchen; she bought a banquette set for her own kitchen and put up light wallpaper that looked like marble. This kitchen, in which I now spend so much time as I work, write, and eat, all resembles Mama. Sometimes I feel that if I turn around, I'll see her profile. She'll be standing there in the chick-yellow bathrobe with the little zipper, with manicured hands pink from the water, and hair dyed an eggplant color and held back with a brush clip. Sometimes I can even smell our kitchen. Mama is still here.

We brought only alcohol and pickles to Bagulnik, everything else was provided by the banquet hall. They served Caesar salad in little square bowls, with large croutons and creamy dressing. Then there was clear, fatty noodle soup, and the main course, a pinkish chicken drumstick and mashed potatoes. It was all a little pro forma and cold, but I ate all three courses, one after the other, because I'd been taught that at a wake you had to eat everything down to the last crumb.

After the first two rounds of drinks the men and some of the women went outside to smoke. I went with them. Many people asked what I did for work. I couldn't properly explain my job. I didn't mention poetry. I just said that I had an administrative position at a gallery. When they asked what exactly that meant, I hemmed and hawed and began telling them about dealing with artists and planning and curating exhibitions. My work seemed stupid and pointless to me here, and I felt separate from everything. Incorporeal and alien.

The light was white and large, as though it were my limitless pain and loss. But I didn't feel anything. Our great voyage, mine and Mama's, from Volzhsky to Ust-Ilimsk was essentially over. But it keeps unfolding inside of me. Like a long road in the night.

V

And what I wanted from you, Mother,
was this:
that in giving me life, you still remain
alive.

—LUCE IRIGARAY, "And the One Doesn't Stir Without the Other"

You taught me to speak. You taught me to read. You taught me to write. You gave me language. The language I use today to write about you. The language in which I name the things of this world. I name the earth and the tree, the glass, the flower, and the truth. I make judgments—this is good and this is bad. I do all this in your language.

Your language is a very tough language, it's clumsy and cramped. It struggles to accept new words and concepts. I get angry the way you got angry, I feel and I hate the same way that you did.

I feel through your language. And I describe you in it. I describe your life and your dying, your gaze and your pain.

And never before this have I addressed you. I spoke about you and wrote you and about you: she, Mama, mother, her. But I didn't write to you: *you*. Not once did I address you. I didn't look you in the face. And because of this I was drowning in you, as in long dark water, because you, without being named in the second person, had become a quagmire. You became a dark quagmire without oxygen or the possibility of movement. You, without being called *you*, had become my grave.

Without my using it to address you, your language became a dead, constrained language. Because you didn't speak it with me, but you spoke me through it. And I, in turn, did as you did and began speaking you. Making you a thing by doing so. A dead thing, dead even before your death. And I was a thing in your eyes, in your understanding, in your language.

Remembering you, your face, I see you half-turned, or with your head tilted up. I remember your ear and the solid rectangle of your Tatar jaw. I see you looking somewhere past me, your gaze taking in only the curve of my cheek. I see you standing with your back to me by the sink in the corner. Against the marbled wallpaper your pink hands move quickly; you're washing dishes or peeling carrots. But I don't remember your direct gaze and I don't remember speech addressed to me. Just as I don't remember my own speech addressed to you. Not everyday speech: Mama, pass me a spoon. But wide-open speech. Speech open to you, addressed to you. Was it because I was afraid you'd freeze me with a passing glance if I opened myself up to you? Because you could petrify not just the outside but the inside of me? But you were inside me already, because I'm your daughter.

I was inside you and later I fed on you. Did I really make you tough from the inside? And if that is true, if I was the reason for your pain, then the pain is also mine, it's your stone inside me, an unburnt piece of your flesh or the fragment of the umbilical cord in my navel—isn't that the stone that we both created inside you? Separately, could we have turned this stone into our shared, difficult experience? Each one of us alone?

Is it really possible to be the source of each other's objectification and at the same time to resolve the conflict of our shared interior stone? Didn't you want to look at me and say *you* to me? To open up to me? Didn't I want to open up to you, to say *you* to you? Didn't we want to open up to each other? Didn't I want to open up to you? To open up to each other?

To open in order to acknowledge and make visible our shared

stone. Not yours and not mine. Not your stone and your pain, not my stone and my pain. But ours, our shared pain.

Don't I want to rid myself of it? To be free of it, so that it will no longer determine my feelings and my understanding of the world? Don't I want to create my own separate language, a rich language, a wide-open language? A language that isn't separate from yours, but is yours, a language that includes and refers to your language. Speaking with your accent, but still mine.

In order to do this, I have to say *you* to you and address you as an equal elder. And you can look at me, too. Look at me. I'll say in my own language: *I love you, Mama*. In your language this was impossible to say. But my language is different, it isn't harder or simpler. It isn't better or worse. In it you can say: *Mama, I love you*. You know my language, because it is derived from your own language. And *you* will hear me and understand.

OKSANA VASYAKINA is a Russian poet and curator. Her debut poetry collection, *Women's Prose*, was short-listed for the Andrei Bely Prize in 2016, and the original Russian-language edition of *Wound* won the NOS Prize in 2021.

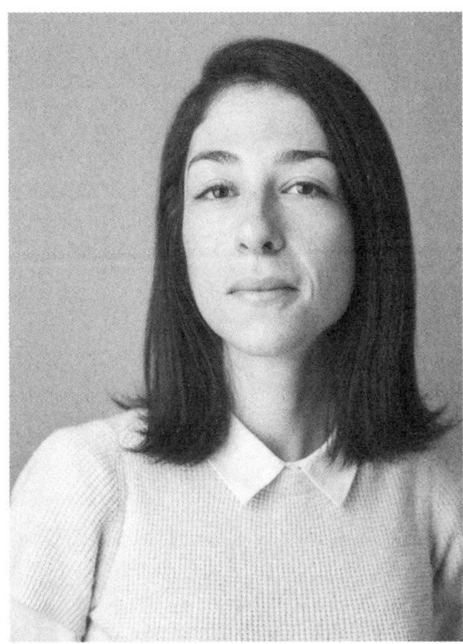

ELINA ALTER is a writer and translator. Her work appears in the *Los Angeles Review of Books*, *BOMB*, *The Paris Review*, *New England Review*, and elsewhere.